LINE
OF
DUTY

LINE
OF
DUTY

HARRISON TAYLOR

DEDICATION

For Chris - for the game nights,
old consoles, and better days.

BLACK FRIDAY 2004

"Damn, this is amazing!" Mer laughed, his mouth full, bits of sausage biscuit crumbling onto his tray. He squirted grape jelly onto what was left of his sandwich and devoured it.

"It's the bomb!" Gwen said, stabbing her plastic fork into a Styrofoam container of macaroni and cheese. Gwen glanced at Rick, hunched across from them at the heavy wooden bench table, his arms folded tight against his body. His face was pale, his skin slick with sweat from a fever, but his expression was stone. "Hey!" Gwen snapped her fingers at him. "What's the name of this place?"

"Timeout," Rick muttered flatly. His voice raspy. He picked up a napkin and blew thick green mucous into it. No longer stuffed up, the greasy aroma of fried chicken and biscuits flooded his nostrils. The small Chapel Hill diner was packed, with a line of people stretching out the door. Through the fogged-up windows, the first hints of dawn painted the horizon in soft pink hues, streetlights still buzzing under the early-morning sky. Rick tucked himself closer to the window, trying to fight the shivers rattling through his flu-ridden body. His eyes drifted downward, catching the glimpse of the handgun nestled beneath Mer's half-open dress shirt.

How the hell did I get into this? Rick thought bitterly. *I should be home, studying for my exam. A plate of turkey, some cranberry sauce...* He sighed. *All for some video game console.* Rick closed his eyes and shook his head. *Because of a stupid electronic toy that'll be obsolete in four years... I'm here, stuck with them. Up, up, down, down, left, right, left, right. Up, up, down, down, left, right, left, right.* Rick chanted this to himself whenever he felt stressed. A coping mechanism from his eighties' childhood.

When he opened his eyes, Mer was watching him, one eyebrow raised as he spoke. "You're not planning any funny business, are you?" he asked, his voice casual.

Rick scoffed and shook his head.

"You sure?" Mer pressed.

Rick closed his bagged eyes and nodded.

"Good." Mer leaned back, stretching an arm over the back of the booth. "Because I'd hate to have to... well, you know."

STAGE 0

THE APARTMENT GODS must have been smiling on Rick the day he signed his lease. His one-bedroom was perched on the twentieth floor and boasted a bay window with a perfect view of the Durham skyline. Rick sat at his desk staring out the window. He took a deep breath, rubbing his tired eyes. The weight of sleepless nights pressed against his fingertips as he massaged his temples.

"Fucking hate sunrises," he muttered, glancing at the stack of textbooks on the floor. His gaze returned to the open book in front of him: *Ace the Series: Chapter 7.* The page, marked with a multiple-choice section, mocked him. A pile of freshly sharpened No. 2 pencils lay beside wooden shavings near a dark-green pencil sharpener, their perfect tips aimed at his textbook like tiny arrows.

Rick reached for an Oreo, bit into it, and chased it with a sip of cold coffee. "All right, moment of truth…" He grabbed the plastic answer key propped against a stack of CD-Rs atop his bulky CD burner. Sliding the key over his mock exam, he winced. Ten answers wrong. His shoulders sagged as he shoved the rest of the Oreo into his mouth and crammed in two more, as if trying to suffocate the disappointment.

"Shit," he whispered, slumping back in his chair.

Shaking his head, Rick powered on his IBM desktop. The light-gray tower whirred to life with a hum that filled the silence. "Great job, Rick," he muttered, rising from the desk. "Don't ever wonder why Penn State told you to take a hike."

While the computer booted, he clicked on the radio icon and cranked up the desktop speakers. The crisp sound of a newscaster's voice filled the room as Rick shuffled to the bathroom, a cramped space barely bigger than a phone booth. He splashed cold water on his face and leaned closer to the mirror.

There it was: a single white hair dangling from his left nostril.

"Dammit," he groaned, plucking the offending strand. His face twitched at the sting. He held the hair up for inspection, a tiny thread glowing in the fluorescent light. "Not even thirty yet," he whispered, dropping it into the sink. He closed his eyes. "This is all a bad dream. The practice tests. The white hair." Clapping his hands together, he declared, "Sleep time!"

Back in the bedroom, Rick yanked the dark curtains shut and stood by his desk, catching snippets of the news.

"Good morning, good afternoon, and good evening wherever you may be," the announcer chirped. "The market has yet again found itself in the forest and not on the farm. It's lions, tigers, and bears, oh my, as we trudge through another consecutive bear week. Yesterday, the Dow dropped another hundred points.

"But there's a silver lining. The video game market is expecting a boom after Vision Software CEO Jo Gabe announced the company's new console, *The Link*, slated for release this Thanksgiving. Despite its late entry into the console wars, previews have the gaming community in a frenzy. Lines are already forming at retailers—not hours, but *days* before the launch. Stores warn that stock is limited, so if you want one, you'll have to camp out and skip the turkey. That's right, folks, Black Friday just got darker."

Rick rolled his eyes as he crawled into his narrow bed. "Yeah, just what the world needs, another gadget for nerds." Rick's stomach started to growl. He wanted to grab a bite but sleep was calling. He yawned; his body was getting heavy. All Rick could do was let the thought of food lull him to sleep. "Waffle House. Covered, chunked, peppered…" The words drifted into silence as he dozed off, mouth slightly open, his breathing steady. Ten minutes later, his cell phone rang.

"Son of a bitch." He snatched the phone before it slid off the edge. The lime-green screen glowed with a 984 area code. He groaned, slumping back into the bed. Pressing the Accept button, he held the phone to his ear. "What is it, Candace?"

"You've been summoned," she said.

"What?" Rick's eyelids drooped so heavily that his face twitched trying to keep them open.

"I think you heard me."

Rick rubbed his eyes, groaning. "Candace…I just—"

"You think he cares? Go ahead. Ask me."

"I took this week off for my Series 7. You know that. *He* knows that."

"I keep repeating this for you, Rick," she said sharply, "because of our past. But I hate it. You're an intern for one of the richest men in North America. He doesn't care about your study schedule."

"Candace—"

"What do you think happens if you don't show up?"

"He fires me."

"That's right! You're as replaceable as—?"

"—a member of Destiny's Child! Thank you, Candace!" Rick threw his phone across the room, the clatter of it hitting the floor drowning out her laughter.

He screamed into his hands and stumbled toward the closet to throw on some clothes.

STAGE 1

"TIME?" MER ASKED. He sat in the bucket driver's seat of a black two-door Mustang with a white racing spoiler welded to the back. Water dripped from the hood exit exhaust. Mer looked over at Gwen leaning back in her seat with her hands resting on her stomach and her feet propped on the dash. Her sleeves were rolled up. Her pale skin was the perfect canvas to show off her brand-new set of purple track marks covering her forearms. Her long, dirty-blond hair was wrapped in a single braided ponytail that rested on her shoulder. Mer snapped his fingers. "Hey!"

Gwen stared at him, wincing. "What?" she asked. Mer held up his watch and started to tap at the glass.

"Don't you hear me talking to you?" Mer asked.

"Don't you have a watch?" Mer sighed and twisted in his seat, glancing over his shoulder at the two young men cramped in the back seat. Both wore unicorn masks, one with a black horn, the other with a gold horn. As planned, everyone in the car wore black tracksuits and white sneakers. The two unicorns in the back seat however were a bit off-script. Mer stared at them shaking his head. Frustrated, he ran his hands through his short, dirty-blond hair and asked, "Why?" The two unicorns looked at each other.

"Why what?" the gold-horned unicorn asked as Mer turned around, gripped the steering wheel, and slammed his forehead against it. "You talking about the masks?"

"Yes," Mer said.

"Oh," the black-horned unicorn said. "We just thought we needed to be discreet about our identity." He rolled up his right sleeve and started rubbing three branded Greek letters on his forearm. The wound was still pink and raw. "Shit, this itches," he mumbled to himself.

"Good thinking," Mer said, looking at the two in his rearview mirror. Gwen chuckled.

"Yeah," Gwen said. "Nothing says discretion like wearing a big unicorn mask to an armed robbery." Gwen looked at the two unicorns in the rearview mirror and asked, "Why are you wearing it now?"

"To keep our identities." the gold-horned unicorn said.

Gwen twisted her face and said, "But he already knows what you look like."

"Yeah, but you don't," black-horned unicorn said.

The gold-horned unicorn scoffed and said, "Yeah and by the size of those track marks you have there, you'd sell us out in a New York minute if it meant a fix." Gwen took her feet off the dash and sat up. She quickly pulled down her sleeves and held up her right palm.

"You can talk to the hand," she said.

"Can we please focus?" Mer asked. He looked around at the parking lot. It was almost empty. Only a few cars were parked in front of a stone-washed brick building that resembled a chapel. "Gwen, you sure kids are gonna be in there?"

"It's a college library!" Gwen said. "Look I went here, OK? Students are here like twenty-four-seven."

The gold-horned unicorn gently raised his hand and asked, "May I say something?"

"No, you may not," Gwen said. The gold-horned unicorn lowered his hand shrugged his shoulders.

"Listen," Gwen said, "Best part is these are all rich eggheads who carry cash and wear Rolexes. It's a win-win."

"Ok," Mer said, pulling out the sawed-off shotgun from under his seat. He took out a black stocking and pulled it over his face.

"Oh, shit," the gold-horned unicorn said. "This 'bout to be like that movie *Heat*!"

"What?" Mer and Gwen said. Mer grimaced under his sock.

"The fuck did I just say?!" Mer asked.

"What?" the gold-horned unicorn asked, his tone whiny.

"What did I just say?" Mer asked.

"Umm… no one gets shot?" the gold-horned unicorn asked.

"Exactly," Mer said. It took everything in him to keep his composure. "Did you see the last hour of that movie?" Gwen sat in the front seat, laughing uncontrollably.

"Of course," the gold-horned unicorn said.

"Then why in the actual fuck would you use that to describe the next hour of our lives? Huh? *Heat* is the exact opposite of what we want to happen! Got it?!"

"OK," the gold-horned unicorn said, holding up his hands. "Sorry. I get it." By this time, Gwen's face was bright red. She wiped her eyes.

"Great find in these two, Mer," Gwen said.

"Shut u—" Mer stopped and stared at Gwen for a moment. "You on something right now?"

Gwen wiped her nose with the back of her hand and said, "Just a little bump."

Mer shook his head and said, "You fucking *shanda*."

"You're a *shanda*," Gwen said, putting a black stocking on her face.

"Unicorns," Mer said. "You frat boys got the bags?" The black-horned unicorn held up a roll of brown plastic bags. "Goodie gumdrops. Just as planned. You wave your gun in the air. No one gets shot. You understand me?" Everyone in the car nodded. The four stepped out of the Mustang, each carrying a sawed-off. Mer cocked his weapon and said, "Let's go to work." The four of them started walking up the cracked cement steps toward two giant, faded red double doors.

To no one's surprise, the doors were unlocked. They creaked open, revealing a dull gray hallway. The four of them moved in pairs. Gwen and Mer were in front with the two unicorns behind them. The group traveled down the hallway until they reached a thick tan door. Mer looked at Gwen.

She nodded and said, "I got it." Mer returned the nod as Gwen handed him her shotgun. He took a step back and stood next to the unicorns.

"That's a pretty thick door," the gold-horned unicorn whispered.

"She's got it," Mer said.

Gwen took a deep breath, her nostrils flaring. She stepped forward with her right foot and rammed the door with her left leg. The wooden door split in two. Mer flashed a smile.

"Told ya." He said. Mer tossed the shotgun back to Gwen

and the four of them marched into the room. Inside were three elderly women, their gray hair tied up with pencils. They shrieked and threw up their hands.

"Shut the fuck up!" Mer shouted; shotgun raised.

The women fell silent, their hands trembling in the air.

"Ladies," Gwen said, acknowledging them with a nod. The two unicorns stood side by side. Their hands trembled as they held tightly onto their shotguns.

One of the women, adjusting her thin-rimmed glasses, stared at them and whispered, "Are they OK?"

Mer's snarl cut through the room. He pressed the cold double barrel of his shotgun against her forehead. "That's none of your business now, is it?"

She shook her head, eyes wide with terror.

"Good. Now, listen carefully. I'm sorry, Mrs….?" Mer's voice softened, almost polite.

The librarian flinched, her lips quivering. "W-what?"

Mer sighed and lowered his shotgun slightly. "Your name."

"Rita," she whispered."

"Shalom, Miss Rita." Mer nodded, a faint smirk on his lips. "We're not here for you. We're here for the students."

Rita blinked. "S-students?"

"That's right." His voice dropped to a low growl. "Is there anyone else back here? Think carefully. Lies kill."

Rita's gaze fell to the floor. She frowned, hesitating before shaking her head.

"Good." Mer's eyes glinted. "Now, here's what's going to happen. When I open this door, the three of you are going to walk in a single-file line to the library. You'll calm everyone there down while we scare the hell out of them."

"But—" Rita began, her voice faltering. Mer pressed the

shotgun to her forehead again. Her eyes crossed, focusing on the cold steel.

"We were doing so well, Rita," Mer said. "Let's not ruin it. You're going to tell them to stay seated, to hand over their wallets and phones, and drop them in these brown plastic bags. You do that, and this will be over soon. Got it?"

Rita's lips trembled. She nodded, unable to speak.

"Good."

The three librarians moved as ordered, forming a line. The four robbers followed, weapons raised. They approached the red double doors at the end of the hallway. Rita and the two other women grasped the handles, pushing the doors open.

Sunlight poured in through tall arched windows, casting long beams across the dark wooden floor. The library was silent, its five long tables eerily empty.

Suddenly, the librarians collapsed to their knees, hands covering their heads.

"Get on the ground!" the robbers shouted, their voices echoing off the brick walls.

The deafening blasts of buckshot followed, shattering the silence. Mer's eyes widened as he scanned the room.

"It's empty," Mer's voice echoed, hollow and tense. He glared at Gwen and the two unicorns. Even through the black stocking they could see the disbelief etched on Mer's face.

"Where…?" Mer marched up to Rita, tapping his temple with the butt of his sawed off. "Rita? This library is empty."

Rita's eyes flicked toward Mer, lips curling into a nervous fragile smile. "W-why y-yes, it is."

Mer's eyes narrowed. "Where are the students?"

Rita's knees buckled, her face flushing deep red. "I… I… "

Mer raised his shotgun again, pressing it to her forehead. "Again! Rita! Where are they?!"

Eyes tightly shut, tears streamed down Rita's face. A high-pitched groan escaped her lips as a dark stain spread down her pants. Urine pooled at her feet.

Between sobs, she whispered, "Students… don't… come to the library… during Thanksgiving holiday."

Mer looked at and said, "Gwen! What the fuck?"

"What?" Gwen asked.

"You didn't know it was Thanksgiving break, Gwen? For fuck's sake! What is wrong with you?!"

"Hey, jackass," Gwen said. "You want to stop using my name? Besides, how I was supposed to know that?"

"Because you went to school here!"

"Yeah," Gwen said, shaking her head, "like five years ago!"

"Guys," the gold-horned unicorn said, "that's what I was trying to tell you two in the car."

"Then why didn't you speak up?" Mer blurted.

"I tried, but you told me to…"

"Shut the fuck up!" Mer said.

Gwen walked past Mer and said, "Seriously, I can't speak to you when you're like this." Unfazed, Gwen stepped toward Rita, placing a steadying arm around her. "OK, ladies," she said, guiding the librarians to the a nearby table. "Thanks for your help. We've got to tie you up now, but don't worry, the heat is on. Feels very cozy in here."

"Fuck," Mer whispered. A sudden scraping sound rang out behind him. It was the unicorns taking a few backward steps before darting for the doors. They scrambled through the red double doors to the hallway; the doors slammed against the walls and swung wildly on their hinges.

"Hey!" Mer shouted.

"There they go—saw that coming," Gwen said while tying up the librarians. Mer stared at Gwen biting his bottom lip.

"You knew they were going to run?" Mer asked.

"Yup."

STAGE 2

"Mer!" Gwen's voice rang out, cutting through the din on the crowded street.

Merlin glanced back at her, then down at his watch: 12:05. He winced, pressing a hand gently to the rising shiner around his left eye. Two wads of tissue stuffed in his nostrils barely stemmed the blood dripping onto his black silk tie. Loosening it, he undid the top button of his shirt.

"Merlin!" Gwen called again. She caught up, her black mock-neck dress clinging to her, her hair and sunglasses doing little to hide her bruised eye. She sucked on her split lip, wiping sweat from her forehead. "He's going to kill us!"

Merlin scoffed as he lit a cigarette. "Maybe," he said, blowing smoke into the humid air.

"Maybe?" Gwen grimaced. "What do you mean, maybe?"

"Possible. Probable. You know, maybe." He shrugged, continuing down the cracked sidewalk lined with parked cars. The bass from a nearby makeshift club thumped through the ground.

Gwen shook her head. "I don't understand."

Merlin smirked. "Don't you need an IQ of one-forty to be a doctor?"

"Where are you going?" she demanded, jogging to keep up.

"Home."

They crossed the street toward an old brick hotel with green windows.

Gwen frowned. "You're not serious."

Merlin exhaled another cloud of smoke. "Dead serious. Go home, Gwen." He turned around, only to bump into a six-foot-three giant dressed in a stonewashed denim suit and tan Timberlands.

"The fuck? My Tims!" the giant barked, shoving Merlin back.

"Sorry," Merlin said, apathetic.

"Sorry?" The giant took a step forward, glaring down. "You scuffed my suede, white boy."

Merlin glanced at the man's feet, a faint mark on the left boot. He sighed. "My apologies. And I'm not a white boy—just a fellow child of Abraham."

The giant pulled out a knife. "Give me one good reason not to drag your ass out back and pop a trunk."

Merlin chuckled, wiping sweat from his brow. "Because rock beats scissors." He opened his jacket, revealing a black nine-millimeter.

The giant's hands shot up and the crowd scattered. Merlin pulled out two hundred-dollar bills and handed them over to him. "Again, my apologies."

Gwen stared at the giant as they walked away. "Do you have your Nokia phone on you?" she asked, wide-eyed. "I need his number."

"Gwen!" Merlin snapped.

She grinned and said, "Chocolate City indeed."

"Shut up, Gwen."

"What? He was cute."

Merlin rolled his eyes. "Weren't you just ranting about how Braff's going to kill us? I'd rather stick to that conversation."

Gwen stopped in front of a RadioShack. "Stop walking, Merlin!"

Mer sighed, turning back as she gestured to a window display of plasma screen TVs behind a chain-link fence. Gwen's eyes were wide, fear etched across her face. "Humor me," she said. "Rewind four hours. Play it in your mind like a movie."

Merlin blinked, his expression unreadable.

✧

Four hours ago

"Hurry up!" Merlin said, stepping out of the car. Gwen's body shook at the sound of him slamming the door shut. He was about to cross the street when he stopped. Turning back, he saw Gwen frozen in the passenger seat, her gaze fixed straight ahead. Merlin sighed, brushing dandruff from his black dress suit.

He walked to the blue Honda Prelude and bent down in front of the window. Sweat streamed from Gwen's forehead, smearing her mascara into dark streaks. Merlin tapped on the glass. Gwen slowly turned her head toward him. He gestured for her to roll down the window. She shook her head.

"You know," Merlin shouted through the glass, "it may not be as bad as you think."

Gwen raised a dark-brown eyebrow and mouthed, "*Oh, yeah?*"

"Seriously! OK, he might get mad. No, he *will* get mad. But he's not gonna kill us!" Merlin let out an uncomfortable chuckle. "Right?"

Still staring at Merlin, Gwen leaned forward, looking like she might pass out.

Merlin bit his bottom lip and banged his palm against the window. "Are you coming with me or not?"

Gwen shook her head.

"You know what? You're really something! I didn't want to do this stupid job, but you suckered me in!"

Merlin turned away and slammed his back against the window, grunting. He pulled a pack of cigarettes from his pocket, teasing one out with his teeth. ""Let's rob the library,' she said," he muttered, lighting the cigarette. The tip glowed orange as he inhaled deeply, then blew the smoke into the crisp November air. "'Quick score,' she said. Probably high when you…" He whipped his head around. "Were you high or just stupid when you came up with this pla—"

Merlin sidestepped just in time to avoid being hit in the face by the car door. Gwen's black high heels tapped against the sidewalk as she stood up. Her intense light-brown eyes locked onto Merlin, nostrils flaring.

Merlin stumbled back, raising his hands defensively, bracing for the slap he could feel brewing in Gwen's jittering palms.

"Don't joke about my sobriety!" Gwen shouted.

Merlin dragged his hands through his hair. "Sobriety?" he asked, grimacing. "When?"

"What do you mean, *when?*"

Merlin looked up at the night sky and sighed. "Just five hours ago, you were ranting about feeling the needle in your veins!"

"I decided to go sober three hours ago," she snapped.

"Three hours ago?" Merlin laughed. "Just like that, huh?"

"Damn skippy!"

Merlin shook his head, exhaling smoke. "Great. Just great." He scoffed and said, "Yiddish and Ebonics? Had no idea you were trilingual."

"The plan was perfect."

"Junkies also think sticking hepatitis-infected needles in their veins is a stellar idea, so…"

"Half of those kids are trust-fund babies! They carry thousands on them at a time!"

"What kids?" Merlin asked. "It was an empty fucking library!"

"Well…" Gwen said, shaking her head, "it normally isn't… during the school year."

"Which brings me back to my original question," Merlin said, walking past her. "Were you high or just stupid?" Merlin glanced both ways before crossing the road.

Gwen whipped her head in Merlin's direction, watching him as he crossed the street. She slammed her fist into her palm before adjusting her dress. She trailed behind Merlin, head down, her sneakers squeaking against the ground, fists balled up and white-knuckled. She looked up at Merlin's back, clenched her teeth, and shouted, "If he kills us, it's on you!"

"Shut up!" Merlin shouted. He took the last puff on his cigarette and flicked it over his shoulder.

The two headed toward the three-story brick colonial in front of them, following the long driveway and passing the roundabout planted with red and yellow roses. In the center was a bronze statue of a monk meditating, the bright lights shining on its stoic face. They walked up a short brick staircase to a giant open front door. At the entrance were two men dressed in black suits, each of them wearing side holsters.

"Merlin! Gwen!" one of them shouted.

"Fellas," Merlin said.

"Hey," the other guard said, "I got a great score for you guys. Preschoolers! We steal their bikes!"

Merlin and Gwen walked into the foyer. The dim glow of the crystal chandelier cast soft shadows over the black stairwell. They passed it without a word, heading toward the kitchen, where caterers bustled over a white marble island. Industrial fixtures bathed the space in ambient light, the air rich with the scent of roasted meats and freshly baked bread.

Merlin stopped, swiping a hot latke from a platter. He stuffed it into his mouth, only to regret it instantly as it scalded his tongue. He coughed, fanning his mouth, then yanked a paper towel from the roll by the farmhouse sink.

Gwen barely spared him a glance, moving past him toward the back living room. The shift in atmosphere was immediate. Whereas the kitchen had been full of warmth and movement, the living room was quiet.

An eighty-four-inch plasma screen sat dark, the air still. Dim lighting reflected off navy-blue leather furniture. Along the brick wall beside the television hung a collection of photographs. In one, an older man stood with a pair of red-handled scissors, cutting through a ribbon. In another, the same man wore a construction hat, shovel in hand, breaking ground. Below each picture, polished plaques gleamed in the low light. To the left, a set of janitor keys dangled from a hook. Beyond the row of French doors, a large swimming pool sat undisturbed. And in front of the doors, seated alone in a leather armchair, was their father.

The silver-haired man wore a crisp black suit, white shirt, and black tie. He leaned back slightly, the posture of someone at ease, yet his sharp gaze—framed behind wire-rimmed glasses—missed nothing. A white yarmulke rested atop his head.

He looked up as Gwen entered, his expression unreadable. A few minutes later Merlin walked in with his hands resting on his hips.

Merlin and Gwen greeted him with stiff smiles. Their father lifted a single finger, pointing at his yarmulke.

Merlin muttered a curse under his breath, patting his pockets until he found his own black yarmulke. He placed it on his head with a forced smile.

Their father leaned back in his chair, rubbing at the white stubble on his chin while gesturing to the chairs in front of him. Gwen and Merlin brushed off their clothes before sitting down. Silence stretched. Their father, his lips tight and head tilted slightly, scrutinized them. Gwen and Merlin exchanged quick glances.

The older man crossed his legs, his expression still unreadable. Slowly, he sighed and clasped his hands in his lap, his gaze never leaving them.

Gwen inhaled sharply, forcing a smile. Too wide, too forced, too rehearsed. "Hi, Daddy."

His lips curled into a small, knowing smile. "Hi, *bubbeleh*."

Gwen started blinking rapidly, the right side of her face twitching. "H-how have you been?"

"I'm sitting shiva, Guinevere How do you think?"

"How's Mom?" Merlin asked.

The man smiled faintly. "Your mom just lost her brother, Merlin." His smile faded. "How do you think she is?"

Merlin and Gwen stood up, both mumbling, "Maybe we should go check on her."

"Sit. Down." The two slowly took their seats. "I should say I *was* sitting shiva, mourning the death of my dear brother-in-law. But I can't say that now. Because now I'm sitting with the likes of you two. You two *schlemiels*. And now, I am no longer feeling grief. Just anger and curiosity."

Merlin looked away and said, "Pop, I…"

"No 'Pop' today, Merlin," the man said. "Today, it's Mr. Braff."

Merlin and Gwen each sank into their chairs. Braff picked up a glass of dark liquor from a side table and took a sip. He swirled the drink, the ice tapping against the glass. Taking a sharp inhale, he said, "I don't even know where to begin."

Gwen and Merlin could hear footsteps and the door to the living room closing behind them. They turned to face two well-built guards dressed in dark suits. Braff snapped his fingers, and Gwen and Merlin whipped their heads back to him.

"So? Whose bright idea was this?" Braff asked.

Merlin raised his arm and pointed at Gwen. She folded her arms, glaring at him. Braff looked at Merlin and laughed. "Pray to God you never go to jail," he said to his son.

Braff then turned to Gwen. "This was your idea?"

Gwen stared at the floor and nodded.

Braff winced. "You decided to rob an Ivy League school?"

"No, Dad…. I mean, Mr. Braff," Gwen stammered, smacking her forehead. "Just the library. And, OK, it's prestigious, but it's not Ivy League."

Braff bit the inside of his bottom lip, glaring.

"She's right," Merlin chimed in. "In North Carolina, sure. Nationwide? Not so much."

"Thank you for the geography lesson, Mr. College Dropout." Braff uncrossed his legs, leaning forward. His gaze settled on Gwen. "Were you high?"

Gwen folded her arms and groaned, tilting her head back to stare at the ceiling. "Why does everyone keep asking me that?!"

Braff scoffed, his voice sharp. "Let's look at the facts, shall we, my dope-fiend daughter? You tried to rob the most prestigious university library in North Carolina—during the Thanksgiving holiday."

"I thought it was finals!" Gwen interrupted, rolling her eyes.

"Shut up!" Braff snapped, pointing a rigid finger at her. "When no one worth robbing was even on campus! Gwen—" He paused, rubbing his temple. "You went to med school there. You didn't figure out how connected those kids were while you were studying?"

Gwen muttered under her breath, "Didn't even want to go to that dookie school. I wanted Chapel Hill."

A vein pulsed visibly on Braff's temple. He straightened, his voice a quiet storm. "What?"

"Nothing," Gwen said quickly, shaking her head.

"And to make matters worse, you used my organization," Braff continued, his tone icy. "My guns. My car. My resources. Hell, half your crew had the common sense to go running!" He folded his arms, shaking his head in disbelief. "You know why your mother and I named you two Guinevere and Merlin? Because when we saw you both for the first time, we thought you were magic. Now look at you." He let out a bitter laugh. "Just a hot jigsaw mess. I've got a good-for-nothing bum of a son and a brilliant junkie."

Gwen sniffled but managed a tight, sarcastic smile. She held up a hand. "Don't forget MD."

Braff laughed coldly. "How could I?" He shook his head. "Funny how curses are a form of magic too."

A thick silence blanketed the room. Merlin glanced at Gwen, noticing the way she wiped her nose with trembling fingers. He looked down at the polished wooden floor. Merlin could hear footsteps. It was Braff's guards walking into the living room. Braff turned away, walking toward the row of French doors. He picked up his drink and pulled open the blinds. Outside, the pool lights cast soft white and purple hues across the still water. The amber liquid of Braff's old fashioned caught the light as he swirled it in the glass and took a measured sip.

Braff raised his hand, gesturing upward with a single finger. One of the guards stepped around the chairs, his heavy boots thudding against the floor as he positioned himself in front of Merlin and Gwen. His face was tight, betraying a flicker of hesitation.

The guard glanced at Merlin, voice low. "You sure about this, chief?"

Braff didn't turn, his eyes locked on the pool outside. "Not really," he admitted, the faintest edge of weariness in his tone. "But they didn't leave me much choice, did they?"

The guard exhaled sharply. "No, chief.… Guess they didn't."

Braff lifted his glass to his lips. "Make it quick."

The hesitation vanished from the guard's face. He clenched his fist, turned toward Merlin—and swung.

The punch landed hard, a sickening crack against Merlin's cheekbone. His head snapped sideways as he staggered backward, colliding with the massive plasma TV. His arm flailed, grasping for anything, knocking Braff's janitor keys from the wall.

Braff barely spared him a glance. "Watch the wall, guys!" he barked. "That's ten years of hard work. Legitimate property ownership."

"Merlin!" Gwen shrieked, lunging forward, only for another guard to seize her by the arm, yanking her back.

The first guard delivered a vicious kick to Merlin's ribs. A strangled gasp escaped his lips as he crumpled to the floor. His hands weakly shielded his head, but the next blow crashed into his forearm, then another into his side.

"Daddy, make them stop!" Gwen cried, her voice breaking. She turned to Braff, her expression pleading. "Please!"

Braff sighed, swirling the amber liquid in his glass. The dull thuds of fists against flesh filled the room.

Gwen turned, desperate, toward the second guard, who was restraining her. "You don't have to do this. Please, just—"

The guard glanced toward Braff, visibly uncomfortable.

Through the reflection in the French doors, Braff caught his hesitation. Slowly, he turned, his cold gaze locking onto the man.

"I wouldn't dawdle if I were you," Braff said softly, clicking his teeth.

The guard swallowed. "Chief, I—"

Before he could finish, Gwen arched her back and threw a kick over her shoulder. Her left foot rocketed toward his jaw, landing flush against his face, sending him sprawling. A sickening pop echoed as his jaw dislocated.

Braff clicked his teeth. "I warned you," he said, almost amused. "She is not as she seems."

The fallen guard barely had time to groan before the others rushed in.

Two fists slammed into Gwen's face, her head snapping back. She crumpled to the floor, blood pooling at the corner of her mouth. A tooth clattered onto the polished hardwood, spinning in a slow circle and coming to rest near Braff's feet.

The assault continued, the guards' boots landing blow after blow on the siblings. Each kick sent sharp bursts of pain through their bodies, leaving them gasping and writhing on the floor. Gwen coughed violently, blood spattering the polished hardwood as she curled into herself. Merlin groaned, clutching his ribs. The guards stopped. Each grabbed one of the siblings by the ankles, dragging their limp bodies across the room. The dull scrape of their bloodied forms against the floor mixed with their ragged breaths and faint whimpers.

"Pop!" Merlin croaked, reaching out to grab the edge of the couch.

"Daddy!" Gwen sobbed, her fingers clawing at the leather upholstery. "Please!"

The guards yanked their hands free, one of them pulling a hunting knife from his belt. The blade glinted in the dim light as he crouched beside Merlin, gripping his trembling hand.

Merlin's voice cracked as he shouted, "Pop! I'll fix this! I swear—I'll make it right! Please, give me a chance!"

The guard's grip tightened. He positioned the blade above Merlin's index finger. Just as he raised the knife, Braff's voice cut through the air like a whip.

"Stop!"

The guards froze, stepping back immediately. One slipped the knife back into his belt; the other wiped his bloodied hands on his pants. They exchanged uneasy glances but kept their eyes averted from Braff.

"This is wrong," Braff muttered, shaking his head. He rubbed his temple and placed his drink down on a nearby table. "Completely *farkakteh*."

Battered and bleeding, Merlin and Gwen crawled toward him. Blood dripped from their faces onto the polished floor. Gwen coughed violently. Tears streaked her cheeks. Merlin dragged himself forward with shaking hands, his breath labored.

Braff sank into his chair, his gaze cold and distant as he watched them inch closer. The faintest twitch of something—guilt, regret, or perhaps frustration—crossed his face. He didn't move to help them. He simply sat there, silent, his children bleeding at his feet.

"Exodus 34:6: The Lord, The Lord God, merciful and gracious, long-suffering." Braff's voice was calm, deliberate, but laced with disappointment. He shook his head slowly, his gaze heavy as it landed on Merlin and Gwen. "You two don't even read your Torah anymore, do you? Where the hell did I go wrong?"

He picked up his drink and finished it, setting the empty glass down on the table beside him with a soft clink. "I promised myself that this week I would properly mourn. That I would be a good Jew. And I'll be damned if I let the likes of you two schmucks ruin that."

Standing slowly, Braff adjusted his suit jacket and sat back down, crossing his legs. His voice dropped to a low growl. "With that being said, my darling children, you owe me damages. The weapons and my car. Going rate is thirty thousand dollars."

The words hit like a hammer, and he let the weight of them settle before continuing. "Right now, your best friend—and your worst enemy—is time. While I sit shiva, the jungle is quiet, and the lion sleeps." He leaned forward, his sharp gaze piercing through the dim light. "But if you don't have my money in twenty-four hours, the lion awakens. And when he does, he feeds." His tone turned even more venomous. "Do you understand me?"

Merlin and Gwen nodded weakly, their battered bodies trembling as they sat on the floor. Braff's eyes lingered on them for a moment longer before he stood, turned his back, and walked toward the French doors. The rhythmic click of his polished shoes on the hardwood was the only sound as the guards hauled the siblings to their feet.

Merlin stood motionless outside the RadioShack, his bruised face bathed in the soft glow of the televisions in the display window. The rows of screens played the same commercial in perfect synchronization, their vibrant colors cutting through the night. On the largest screen, he watched as a family of four dressed in off-white linen sat on a couch, their faces glowing with joy. Each held a sleek black controller with multicolored buttons, their bodies swaying in time with the action on the screen. A knight in green armor wielded a glowing sword and shield, slicing through enemies in a dazzling 3D world.

Merlin's mouth hung open slightly, his eyes wide and glassy. "Oh… my… God."

"Merlin!" Gwen's voice cut through the air like a whip, raw and edged with frustration. She limped toward him, her face streaked with dried blood and tears. "What are you doing? Merlin, what the hell are we going to—"

Her words were drowned out by the booming voice of the commercial's spokesman from the TVs in the storefront window, which were at full volume.

"The Link: a whopping four gigabytes of storage capacity with 512 MB of shared RAM. What does that mean? Who knows? But has family night ever been this jiggy?"

Merlin squinted at the screen. His split lip curled into a slow grin.

"Do you see that?" he said, his voice tinged with something between awe and calculation.

Gwen groaned, throwing up her hands. "See what?"

"That." He pointed at the commercial.

"What?"

"I haven't played video games since I was twelve, but…" he said, his eyes locked onto the screen like he was seeing the future unfold in front of him. "This is a fucking game changer."

"That's great, Merlin! Dad's going to kill us in twenty-four hours, and you want to reminisce? What's next, huh? You want to talk about your bar mitzvah?"

Merlin turned to her, his devilish grin now fully formed. He wiped the blood from his nose with his sleeve, leaving a dark smear across his cheek. "You don't get it, do you?"

"Get what?!"

"This Link thing," he said, jabbing a finger at the TV. "It's Black Friday. Limited stock. Crazy demand. People will do anything to get one." He let that sink in, then turned back to her with a smirk. "That means, Gwen, it's not just a game changer for them." He tapped his temple, then pulled out his flip phone and started dialing.

Gwen watched as her brother paced, his eyes sharp, his expression darkening.

"I'm surprised you picked up," he sighed, pressing the phone to his ear. His other hand dove into his pocket, pulling out a set of janitor keys that he'd swiped from Braff's wall.

Gwen's stomach twisted. "Mer…"

"Don't apologize," he muttered into the receiver. "I don't want your fucking excuses. You and the other unicorn fucked me." His voice was low, threatening, but eerily calm. He listened for a moment, his lips pulling into a cold smirk. Then he winced. "J… J… are you crying?" He let out a breath. "Stop it. I'm not going to do that, all right?"

Gwen felt the hairs on her arms rise.

Merlin's grip on the keys tightened. His voice was casual, almost playful. "But you two owe me. And I'm cashing in." His gaze moved to Gwen as he spoke his final words into the phone. "Stay by your phone. Understood?"

STAGE 3

RICK PULLED INTO the parking lot of the Branson and Lloyd Securities building, a standalone brick complex nestled among a row of manicured trees. He cut the ignition of his white Toyota Corolla and leaned back in his seat for a moment, staring at the blue-and-gold sign gleaming in the morning light.

The corner of his mouth twisted into a sneer. He opened the car door, hopped out, and walked around to the passenger side. Tugging open the glove compartment, he pulled out a thin black tie and slipped it around his neck. As he straightened it, his gaze flicked back to the sign. Without hesitation, he let out a sharp cough, spat directly on the tie, and wiped his mouth with the back of his hand.

"Still got it," he muttered under his breath, brushing invisible lint from his wrinkled shirt as he headed toward the entrance.

Inside, an older man with silver hair and matching eyebrows looked up from the security desk. The guard's frown deepened as Rick strolled past, patting his pockets.

"You're not supposed to be here," the guard said, his gravelly voice carrying a note of warning.

Rick stopped mid-stride, raising both hands in mock surrender. "I know."

"Rick," the guard said, his tone softening slightly. "You gotta develop some—"

"Boundaries?" Rick smiled wryly. "Yeah, I know. Believe me, Leo, I've heard it before." He walked to the elevator, jabbed the button, and smirked at the guard as the doors slid open.

Stepping inside, the elevator operator, Patty, greeted him, her blue-and-gold bellhop uniform as neat and pressed as ever. She tilted her head, her wide eyes scanning him with equal parts surprise and exasperation.

"What in the name of Dru Hill are you doing here?" she asked, hands on her hips.

"I know. I know. I already got the sermon from Leo. Can we just ride this elevator in peace?"

Patty raised an eyebrow but then broke into a smile. "Fine, Rick," she said, pressing the button for the upper floors.

"Thank you," Rick muttered, leaning back against the elevator's brass interior of the elevator.

The ride was silent for a moment, the hum of the machinery filling the space. Patty smoothed her uniform hat in the elevator door's reflection, then cleared her throat. "The thing is, Rick—"

"Oh, my God," he said with a sigh, pinching the bridge of his nose.

"We're all rooting for you, you know?"

"I know, Patty," Rick said, staring at the floor. "I know."

She glanced at him, her voice softening. "I remember when you started in the mailroom. You were just a kid back then, still going to Jordan High. We all watched you grow, finish college."

Rick's jaw tightened as he crossed his arms. He shifted his weight, glancing at the floor indicator as it ticked upward.

"It's like that McDonald's commercial," Patty continued, her tone wistful. "You know, the one about the kid who gets a job and makes good?" She tapped her chin thoughtfully. "What was his name again? Calvin?"

Rick groaned, his head dropping back against the elevator wall. "Calvin," he muttered. "It was Calvin."

Patty nodded, smiling. "That's it. Calvin. You reminded me of him back in the day."

Rick's lips twitched into a faint, reluctant smile. "Yeah, well," he said, straightening as the elevator dinged, "Calvin probably didn't have a boss like mine."

Rick exhaled in relief as the elevator doors opened. Patty placed her wrinkled hand on Rick's shoulder and smiled. "Whatever bullshit they've got you doing today, just remember—you got this."

"Thanks, Patty," Rick muttered, stepping out of the elevator.

The entire fourth floor gleamed with modernity. Clear glass walls revealed every inch of the four-thousand-square-foot space, save for one exception: Lloyd's office. The frosted glass cube that jutted out in the center was a fortress of power, isolated from the buzzing hive of cubicles and desks. The office hummed with activity: muffled voices, humming computers, and the mechanical rhythm of fax machines and copiers. Cutting through it all was Lloyd's voice, shouting in rapid-fire Spanish.

Rick groaned, shoving his hands deep into his pockets as he navigated the maze of desks. His pace slowed as he neared the sleek glass desk stationed outside Lloyd's office. Candace Jeong was etched on the name plate.

A young woman with sharp, delicate features sat with her toned legs crossed, one tan high heel tapping an absent rhythm against the chair's leg. The soft clatter of her long, French-manicured nails against the keyboard filled the quiet space. Her jet-black hair was pulled into a sleek ponytail, though a stray strand had slipped free, brushing the rim of her black-framed glasses as she typed effortlessly. Rick stopped in front of her desk and waited, but she didn't look up. Her fingers continued to fly across the keyboard. He cleared his throat.

Without pausing her typing, she glanced at him with a faint smile, then returned her focus to her screen.

Rick folded his arms, waiting. Finally, Candace pushed her glasses up the bridge of her nose and said, "Morning, Rick. Didn't see you there."

Rick licked his teeth and shook his head. "Uh-huh."

Candace pushed up the sleeves of her navy-blue sweater. "Didn't see you at the Carolina–Duke game last night."

"That's because I was studying, Candace," Rick muttered, leaning against her desk.

"Probably wouldn't have seen you anyway," she teased, her tone light. "You being a member of the enemy and all. Damn Chapel Hill."

Rick groaned and rubbed his eyes. "Candace, not this morning. Please. I just want to do whatever bullshit assignment Lloyd has for me so I can go home and—"

"What I don't understand—" Candace interjected, her fingers pausing mid-keystroke.

Rick threw up his hands. "Here we go…"

"—is why you even stick around." She leaned back in her chair, tilting her head. "I mean, you're obviously miserable."

Rick was caught off guard by the bluntness of the question. He opened his mouth, then closed it.

Candace smirked, turning back to her screen. "See? You don't even have an answer."

Rick sighed and rubbed the back of his neck. "Maybe because quitting means I lose more than a paycheck."

Candace glanced at him over the rim of her glasses. "Fair enough," she said, typing again. "Well, good luck in there. Lloyd's been on a warpath all morning. Something about 'fixing numbers.'"

Rick straightened his tie. "Fantastic. Just what I needed."

"You know," Candace said, "I always wondered how you became such an inhospitable Southerner."

"Because I grew up in Durham," Rick shot back. "Now, what does he want?" He leaned in, his patience thinning.

Candace chuckled. "I keep forgetting you're a Durhamite."

Rick's face twisted in mock disgust. "Don't call me that."

"Anthracite, termite, Durhamite, Sodomite—funny how all the words that suit you end in *-ite*."

Rick's jaw tightened. He stepped forward, planting his hands firmly on Candace's desk. "What. Does. He. Want?"

"He'll tell you. Hope you packed a sleeping bag."

"What?" Rick's brow furrowed.

She glanced up at him briefly. "Go on. He's waiting."

Rick turned his head toward Lloyd's frosted-glass office, where the man's muffled shouting reverberated through the floor. The words were indistinct, but the aggression was clear.

"How the hell did this guy get his name on the front door?" Rick muttered.

Candace didn't even look up. "Easy," she said dryly. "His daddy's name was Dean Lloyd Senior."

Rick shook his head in frustration and was about to head in when he paused. "By the way—"

"What?" Candace asked, still focused on her keyboard.

"Did you sign the papers?"

She stopped typing and rubbed her thumbs over her perfectly manicured nails, then shot him a sharp glare before resuming her work. "I'll sign them when I sign them."

Rick smirked. "Take your time. No rush, right?"

Candace tilted her head, her voice laced with venom. "By the way, your taste in music still sucks."

Rick grinned as he started toward Lloyd's office. "Yeah? Well, your breath smelled like crap on our wedding day."

Candace froze, her eyes narrowing. "No, it didn't."

"Really?" Rick tossed over his shoulder. "Then why did your dad shove a Mentos in your mouth at the altar?"

Candace's jaw dropped. She quickly checked her breath. Rick chuckled to himself as he pushed open the door to Lloyd's office, stepping into the gilded chaos.

The door hissed shut behind him, muffling the noise from the outer office. Rick glanced around the gaudy space. To his right, ESPN highlights blared from an eighty-two-inch screen, a swath of black among the gold-plated columns, massive golden desk, and matching conference table that dominated the space. Even the chairs had a metallic sheen.

Lloyd stood by the floor-to-ceiling window, barking into his Nokia like a drill sergeant on caffeine. On the desk behind him, a Motorola and a BlackBerry buzzed relentlessly, nearly drowning out the hum of the PC displaying a stock market ticker. His thick fingers gripped the phone tight, spit flying as he shouted, his entire frame seeming to pulse with barely contained fury.

Gel and sweat mingled in his graying blond spikes, dripping onto the collar of his Italian-cut, double-breasted black suit. He turned abruptly, his sharp, predatory gaze locking onto Rick. For a brief second, the tirade paused—just long enough for an unspoken message to pass between them.

Then, without missing a beat, Lloyd snapped back to yelling, his free hand slicing the air in agitation. He jerked his chin toward the chair in front of his desk. A silent command.

"Just do it!" Lloyd shouted, flipping his cell phone shut, and hurling it over his shoulder. Rick ducked just as the phone whizzed past his ear and crashed against the wall. Lloyd sighed dramatically, leaning back in his chair. "You were supposed to catch that."

Rick glanced at the shattered remains of the phone on the floor, his jaw tightening. Slowly, he stood up and placed his hands in his pockets. "You called for me, sir?"

"Yes," Lloyd replied, ruffling his frosted tips like a man posing for a *GQ* cover. He snapped his fingers and pointed toward the coffee machine in the far corner of the office. "Light sugar, light cream."

Rick clenched his teeth but nodded, walking over to the machine. He crouched down, retrieving a coffee cup from the cabinet below. Behind him, Lloyd twirled his chair back and forth like a child bored in a classroom.

"I know you're studying for your Series 7," Lloyd called out, his tone patronizing. "How's that going, by the way?"

Rick gripped the counter as he fought the urge to scream. *Great,* he thought. *It'd go even better if you'd leave me the hell alone.*

"OK, I guess," Rick said, forcing a neutral tone.

"That's good." Lloyd knocked on his gold-plated desk to get Rick's attention, smirking as Rick turned. "You need to do well on that if you want a spot here, you know. Especially coming from a program like UNC."

Rick's eyebrow twitched, but he managed to keep his face neutral. He coughed lightly, hiding his irritation. "Chapel Hill?"

"Chapel Hill may be a lot of things, sport, but let's not kid ourselves—it's no Wharton."

Rick stirred cream into the coffee with slightly more vigor than necessary. *You must be so proud,* he thought bitterly. *Daddy buys a wing at an Ivy League school, and suddenly you're a genius.*

"That's light cream, right?" Lloyd called.

"Yes, sir," Rick replied, turning off the machine. He walked the coffee over to Lloyd, gripping the cup tightly. He hesitated for a moment before putting the drink on the desk, imagining the scalding liquid splashing across Lloyd's smug face. He could almost hear the scream, see the skin blistering. The fantasy was so vivid, it made him smile.

"Rick!" Lloyd snapped.

Rick blinked, jolted back to reality. Lloyd was glaring at him, his clean-shaven face scrunched in irritation. "Sorry, sir," Rick muttered, setting the coffee down.

Lloyd shook his head, taking a sip of the coffee. He leaned back, tapping his temple with one finger. "What do you know about video games, Rick?"

Rick frowned, his hands still hovering awkwardly near the desk. "Video games?"

"Yes, video games," Lloyd repeated, waving a hand dismissively. "The little boxes with the blinking lights that nerds and teenagers are obsessed with. What do you know about them?"

Rick straightened, blinking a few times as he tried to process the question. "Uh… not much. Why?"

Lloyd smirked, leaning forward with a glint in his eye. "Because we're about to make a lot of money off them."

Rick grimaced. "Sir?"

"Video games, Rick," Lloyd said, waving his coffee cup for emphasis. "You know, the little games you play on a TV with a funstick."

Rick blinked. "You mean a joystick, sir?"

"Great!" Lloyd exclaimed, slapping the desk with both palms. "We're on the same page. You ever play one of those things? Would you call yourself a 'gamer'?" He punctuated the word with exaggerated air quotes.

Rick hesitated, choosing his words carefully. "My brother and I had a Nintendo growing up, but I can't say I've played much since then."

Lloyd snapped his fingers like he'd solved a riddle. "Exactly. I don't get it. Billion-dollar industry filled with grown-ass men playing make-believe in front of a television screen." He leaned back in his oversized leather chair, scowling. "Has got to be the laziest, most ego-stroking experience a fat fucking lame-o could ever have."

Rick studied Lloyd's face. His boss's eyes were bloodshot and his cheeks were flushed. The man radiated a manic energy, fueled by too much caffeine or too little sleep—probably both.

Lloyd grabbed his coffee, reclined in his chair, and placed his feet onto the desk, his black loafers with gold buckles clanging against the polished surface. "I've got a mission for you," he said, his voice suddenly low and conspiratorial.

Rick straightened in his seat. Any trace of drowsiness or irritation vanished in an instant. A mission? His heart pounded like a drumroll. His mind raced.

Some people wait years—decades—to hear those words, he thought. *And here I am, barely a year in, and Lloyd's already trusting me with an assignment.*

Rick tried to keep his voice steady as he leaned forward. "What do you have in mind, boss?" He rubbed his hands together, careful not to show just how badly they were shaking.

"A doozie, sport. You up for the task?"

Rick nodded quickly, licking his lips. *This is it. The break I've been waiting for. Today, the assignment. Tomorrow, the job offer. By next year? Youngest partner in the firm.*

His chest swelled as adrenaline coursed through him. Blue Lamborghini. Not yellow. Too cliché. Blue's classy. Where will I live? Definitely not here in Durham. Cary, maybe. Somewhere with space for a pool.

"Get me a Link."

Rick squinted. "I'm sorry. What?"

"A Link," Lloyd repeated, leaning forward. "You know, the new video game console. Snag one for me—and I need it before the Sight Beyond Sight Summit this Friday."

Rick blinked, trying to process. "You… want me to play video games?"

Lloyd laughed sharply, taking his feet off the desk. "Me? Playing one of those? God, no! It's for Zelda, my daughter. The kid's been whining about it nonstop."

"For your kid?"

"Zelda would be tickled," Lloyd said with a wide, empty grin.

Rick opened his mouth to protest, but Lloyd raised a hand.

"Hold that thought." He rose from his seat, strolling around the desk until he loomed over Rick. His hands, soft and manicured, settled heavily on Rick's shoulders. The air seemed to thicken.

"I'm sorry," Lloyd said, his smile fading to something sharper. His eyes, cold and soulless, bored into Rick. "What exactly do you think I should be considering here?"

Rick swallowed hard, his voice faltering. "Well…"

"Well," Lloyd repeated, his smile widening into a predator's grin, "is not a statement, Rick. I sincerely hope this next sentence *is* a statement."

Every muscle in Rick's body coiled tight. He closed his eyes, murmuring, "I'll do my best."

"I'm sorry?" Lloyd leaned in, his breath warm against Rick's ear.

Rick straightened, his voice louder. "I'll do my best, *sir*."

Lloyd clapped his hands, the sound echoing off the gilded office walls. "That's the spirit!" he said, slapping Rick's back with enough force to sting.

Rick winced, gritting his teeth.

"Only one thing," Lloyd added, strolling back to his desk. "Here at Branson and Lloyd, we don't 'do our best.' We *get the job done. Comprende, compadre?*"

Rick exhaled through his nose, the effort to keep his temper in check almost visible. "Understood."

Lloyd smirked, savoring the submission. He took a sip of his coffee, only to grimace. "Terrible," he muttered, tapping the call panel on his desk.

"Yes, Mr. Lloyd?" Candace's voice chirped from the speaker.

"Can you call in a proper cup of coffee for me? This is undrinkable."

"Of course, Mr. Lloyd. The usual?"

"Of course," Lloyd smiled, his white teeth gleaming. "And Candace?"

"Yes, sir?"

"It's *Adam,* OK?" Lloyd leaned closer to the intercom, feigning warmth.

A brief pause crackled through the speaker. "Of course.... Adam."

Lloyd chuckled, turning off the intercom. "That's my girl." He turned to Rick, his smile shifting to something smug. "Man, she's something, isn't she? But you knew that already, right?"

Rick licked his teeth, fighting the urge to wrap his hands around Lloyd's neck. "Yup."

"I'm glad you're here, Rick." Lloyd leaned forward, his voice again dropping to a conspiratorial whisper. "I know you and Candace have a past, but that's just that, right? *Past?*"

Rick bit his lip, his jaw tightening. "Yes, sir."

"Good!" Lloyd clapped his hands, sitting back. "Because I don't want things to get weird after this next move I'm about to make."

Rick frowned. "Next move, sir?"

Lloyd's eyebrows shot up in mock surprise. "You didn't know? All secretaries on my desk get slayed." He leaned forward, his Cheshire cat grin widening. "Skee skee, you know what I'm saying?"

Rick stared blankly as Lloyd erupted into laughter, nearly spilling his coffee.

"All secretaries, huh?" Rick said, forcing a tight smile.

"That's right," Lloyd wheezed, wiping his eyes.

"So, Gary got *skeed* too?"

"Hey!" Lloyd shot up in mock offense. "Gary was a *temp,* not a secretary!"

"My apologies, sir." Rick shrugged. "What was his title again?"

"Office *coordinator,*" Lloyd said curtly. "And you should have more respect for the dead."

"Of course, sir."

"You know what?" Lloyd said as he stood. "Get out of my office. Go do your job."

Rick rose, nodding stiffly.

Lloyd smirked. He rubbed his hands together and said, "'Bout to be *on* tonight!"

Rick froze, his stomach churning. He clenched his fists, willing himself to leave.

As Rick closed the office door behind him, Lloyd's Black-Berry buzzed. He straightened, pressing the speaker button. His face lit up. "Hey, kiddo!"

A raspy, high-pitched voice crackled through the speaker. "Adam, fire Buckley."

Lloyd blinked. "Buckley? Our butler? Why, Zelda?"

"I wanted Reeth'th and Thprite Remith'th for breakfatht, and he wouldn't give it to me."

Lloyd rubbed his temple, chuckling nervously. "Uh, buddy? Maybe you could call me Dad, just once? And why didn't you just grab it from the pantry yourself?"

"Why do you think, Adam? Becauth we don't have any. And even if we did, that'th not my fucking job, now ith it?"

Lloyd closed his eyes, massaging his temple. "Kiddo, Buck-ley has been a member of this family for more than twenty years. We can't just—"

"You know what?" The gremlin-like voice on the other end laughed, shrill and mocking. "You're right. You can't…"

Lloyd exhaled, somewhat relieved. "That's the—"

"But I can! Jutht like you can't."

Lloyd pulled the phone away from his ear, mouthing, *Shit*, then placed it back against his head. "OK, OK. He's gone. I'll fire Buckley"

"Good. Now, onto more pressing matterth. Did you get my Link?"

"Not yet, Zelda, but I've got my best guy on the job."

"You'd better, 'causth if I don't have my new Link by Thanksthgiving Day, it'sth gonna be a Red Friday thith year. You get me, Dad?"

Lloyd swallowed hard, his tone low. "Message received loud and clear."

"I mean it, Adam. Sthhape up, or I'm sthhipping you out!"

The call ended with a loud beep, leaving Lloyd holding the silent BlackBerry in his hand. He slowly slipped it into his pants pocket, shaking his head. "Shit."

STAGE 4

"GET YOUR GAME up, Malin!" the young gamer shouted, his voice cracking as he sneered.

Malin turned his thick, cherry-colored neck and glared down at the fifteen-year-old mocking him. The kid's boy-band haircut swayed as he tossed his head, his freckled smile half-hidden beneath the floppy bangs. Shiny braces gleamed as he grinned, his words carrying a faint lisp.

"Do you even know how to play *Madden*?" the kid snorted, his laughter spilling out like soda fizz.

Malin stayed quiet, gripping the controller with sweaty fingers. The two of them sat on fold-out chairs in front of a thick, black thirty-five-inch screen. Malin's frustration mounted as he mashed the buttons, hoping to gain a first down. Instead, the ball carrier fumbled.

"Who told you to use Dallas?" the kid jeered, his voice dripping with mockery. "They fucking SUUUUCK!"

On the screen, a defensive lineman picked up the ball and barreled downfield for another touchdown.

Malin stared at the scoreboard:

SAN DIEGO 52

DALLAS 0

The kid doubled over, laughing. "Look at that score!" He turned to the crowd gathered around them. "Are we playing *Madden* or *NBA Live*?"

As the clock ticked down to zero, the room erupted in laughter. Sweat poured down Malin's face, pooling under the tips of his lopsided glasses. One side slid off his ear, dangling awkwardly.

"Get that controller outta your hand!" the kid shouted, slapping the joystick from Malin's chubby middle-aged fingers.

The crowd roared louder. Malin stared through his crooked glasses as the kid danced around him, pointing and shouting, "Bang! Bang!" like a victorious cowboy.

For a moment, Malin chuckled. He adjusted his glasses, pressing them firmly against the bridge of his nose. Then, without a word, he stood up. Calmly, he folded his chair.

The room quieted slightly.

Then Malin raised the chair over his head and slammed it down on the console. The crack of plastic and metal echoed through the room. Gasps replaced laughter. Malin's eyes burned with rage as he brought the chair down again, splintering the console into pieces. Sweat dripped from his face, and his teeth bit into his bottom lip. With a final heave, he hurled the chair at the TV, sending it crashing to the floor.

"Malinowski!" a voice bellowed.

The store owner stormed into view—a short man with thinning brown hair, baggy jeans, and a black GoldenEye 64 T-shirt.

Malin stood panting, his green-and-yellow rugby shirt hiked up over his pale, hairy gut. He took a deep breath, slicked back his hair, and tugged his shirt down. The only sound was the swish of his brown corduroy pants as he walked toward the store owner.

The man threw up his arms. "What in the actual fuck, Malin?!"

Malin rubbed his right eye. "What?" he barked.

"What do you mean, 'What'?" the owner shouted, his face red. "Do you have any idea how much those PS2s cost?"

Malin groaned, a low, labored sound. "Well Phil, If I had to guess, half price—depending on which truck they fell off of."

The last thing Malin saw was a flash of white before his knees buckled. He crumpled to the floor.

Malin grabbed his jaw and winced, trying to shake off the cobwebs clouding his head. He looked up and saw Phil towering over him, right fist still in the air, cheeks burning cherry red.

"I will sue you!" Malin squealed, his voice cracking as he wiped at his face gingerly.

"Oh, really?" Phil cracked his knuckles, unfazed.

"You don't think I will?" Malin said, struggling to pry himself off the blue shag carpet. "I've got witnesses!"

Phil chuckled, folding his arms. "None of them like you."

Malin glared. "I'm calling Aunt Carol!"

"She doesn't like you either."

"FUCK YOU!" Malin shouted at his cousin, clenching his fists like a petulant child.

"Jeez and peas, Malin," Phil sighed, rubbing his temples. "I need you to leave."

"Fine!" Malin spat, wiping at the blood trickling from his nose. He turned toward the crowd of teenagers standing by the door. Several held up their phones, smirking.

Malin groaned. "And *they* say *video games* are the problem."

Phil shook his head. "Far from it." He stepped toward a kid in a brown checkered button-down and ripped blue jeans aiming a phone at Malin.

"You get enough for your Myspace?" Phil asked, his tone sharp.

The kid lowered his phone, eyes wide, and stammered, "Y-yeah. Sorry."

"Delete the pictures," Phil said, his smile icy.

"Y-yes, sir." The kid's hands fumbled over the phone.

Phil turned back to Malin, who was rubbing the side of his nose like a sulking toddler. "You OK?"

Malin nodded.

Phil let out a bark of laughter. "Sorry, but not sorry. You had it coming."

"Hey," Malin said, shifting awkwardly.

"What?"

"Can you spot me a twenty?"

Phil frowned. "For what?"

"Lunch."

"Twenty dollars? For lunch? Where the hell are you going? Champs?"

"They've got that nice one over at Southpoint," Malin said, eyes lighting up.

Phil groaned, shaking his head. "Malin, aren't you on your lunch break *now*?"

"Yeah, so?" Malin said, a nervous chuckle escaping.

"Your break was more than a half hour ago. And now you're planning to *sit down* for lunch?"

Malin scratched the back of his neck. "What are you, my dad?"

Phil pinched the bridge of his nose and sighed. "Mal…"

"Besides," Malin said, pointing at a group of teenagers trying to piece together the broken game console, "I don't see you telling them to get back to class."

"That's because tomorrow is Thanksgiving. They're on break, *fucktard*! And, unlike you, they're paying customers who don't wreck a tournament and then ask me for money!"

"Phil," Malin whined, dragging out the syllables, "Come on, man…"

"I'm not giving you another job, Malin," Phil said, jabbing a finger at him. "If you lose this one, don't come back to me."

Malin frowned, his face twisting into an exaggerated pout. "You'd really do that to me?"

Phil shook his head, folding his arms. "It's beyond me how you sealed the deal with Christine. She's your saving grace, my friend."

"You know what?" Malin said, throwing up his hands. "It's all good in the 'hood, cousin!"

He took a step back, promptly tripping over his fraying jeans. Phil watched, unimpressed, as Malin hissed under his breath and stumbled toward the exit. He paused long enough to glare at the teenagers and mutter a string of curses before kicking open the door and stomping outside.

As Malin walked out of his cousin's game store, he pulled the lapels of his tan leather jacket closer to his neck. The cold November air stung, instantly reddening his thick nose. He looked up at the black-and-white Gamer's Edge sign, snarling as he flipped it the middle finger.

"Hope it burns to the ground," he muttered.

A black Ford Expedition rolled past, its subwoofers thumping loudly enough to rattle the sidewalk. The SUV came to a stop in front of the store, and the engine's rumble cut out. A tall, burly man stepped out from the driver's side. Dressed in black from head to toe—sweater, slacks, a long leather coat, and suede Timberlands—he exuded an air of cold efficiency. Thick, calloused hands decked out in flashy gold rings adjusted his black yarmulke before he strode toward the store.

Malin's eyes widened. He waved eagerly, flashing a big grin.

"Guy!" he shouted.

Guy's eyes, narrowing in irritation, darted to Malin. He rolled them dramatically and tried to walk past without acknowledging him, but Malin darted ahead, blocking his path with a wide grin.

"Hey, hey, hey!" Malin chirped, his hands stuffed in his jacket pockets.

Guy sighed deeply. "What is it, Malinowski?"

"How's it been going?" Malin chuckled, rocking on his heels. "I haven't heard from you since I pitched that job."

Guy's brow furrowed. "You mean the job where we rob the toy store you work at?"

"Yeah."

"The toy store in Southpoint Mall?" Malin nodded eagerly. Guy rubbed his forehead and sighed again. "You wanted us to risk state charges… to steal stuffed animals and action figures?"

"I mean," Malin said, looking up at the gray sky, "you could get a great deal for some of those toys on the black mar—"

"Stop." Guy held up a hand. "Do you know how asinine that sounds?"

Malin's grin faltered. He scanned Guy's all-black ensemble and scoffed. "Nice look. What are you going for? Jewish Morpheus?"

Guy's expression hardened as he cracked his knuckles. "You've got half a second to get out of my way, or—"

"I'm sorry!" Malin said, holding up his hands in surrender. "Did you at least talk to him about it?"

"Talk to who about what?" Guy asked.

"Big man," Malin said, "Your boss."

"Braff?" Guy asked. "Yeah, I told him. As a joke. He laughed his ass off."

"You know what's a joke?" Malin shot back. "A middle-aged, balding Jew walking into a video game store dressed like he's in the Matrix!"

Guy's smile turned menacing. Without a word, he raised one of his size-twelve Timberlands and slammed his heel down on Malin's foot. Pain shot up Malin's leg, and both knees buckled as he collapsed onto the pavement, clutching his ankle.

"Didn't I just see you walking out of this game store?" Guy shook his head as he stepped over the writhing Malin. "Fucking idiot."

Malin groaned, rolling onto his side. He used one of the brick pillars to pull himself upright, then he hobbled toward his dented gray Ford Escort, muttering curses under his breath, his injured foot dragging against the asphalt.

❧

"Excuse me!"

Malin was hunched behind the counter, stuffing a stack of video games into the glass display case.

"Excuse me!" the kid shouted again.

Malin glanced over his shoulder at the freckled redhead standing by the counter, then grabbed a stepladder. Ignoring the boy, he climbed up and began rearranging a row of video game consoles, their black boxes stamped with a bright green X.

"Hey!" the kid yelled.

Malin sighed, closing his eyes for a moment. Slowly, he descended the ladder, his slightly faded black KB Toys T-shirt stretched over his round frame.

"Is it standard for all you people to ignore kids?" the boy demanded, spit flying with every word.

Malin winced as tiny flecks landed on his face. "How can I help you?"

The kid squinted at Malin's name tag. "For starters, you can answer my question… *Malin?*" He wrinkled his nose. "What kind of name is *Malin?*"

"It's a nickname," Malin replied flatly.

"What's your real name?"

"None of your damn business."

"Are you even allowed to talk to me like that?" the kid shot back, crossing his arms with mock authority.

Malin rubbed his forehead, muttering under his breath, "Give me strength."

"This is beyond rude," the kid huffed, shaking his head in exaggerated disbelief. "Where's your manager?"

Malin slapped his hand against the glass countertop, his voice rising before he could stop himself. "What the hell do you want, you little redheaded accident?"

The words echoed in the mostly empty toy store, bouncing off the shelves lined with action figures, stuffed animals, and board games. The distant hum of motorbike toys, train sets, and video game demos buzzed from the four narrow aisles, filling the silence from Malin's exchange with the boy. Malin closed his eyes, regret already pooling in his chest. He took a deep breath, patted his thinning brown hair, and wiped at his goatee as if trying to collect himself.

In a calmer tone, he said, "May I help you, young man?"

The kid raised an eyebrow, sizing him up with a smug grin. "I have a return." He pulled a CD jewel case from the white KB Toys bag and slid it across the counter.

Malin picked it up, turning the cover over in his hands. His brows furrowed. "*Power Stone*? Why would you—" he said before pausing and glancing at the kid.

"What?" the kid asked, his tone defensive.

"Of all the games, you chose this one to return?" Malin muttered, fanning himself with the game case, his voice shaking slightly. "Why would you even think of bringing this back?"

"It's not working."

"I was just playing this yesterday," Malin said, his voice rife with frustration. He could feel the veins in his neck pulsing as he continued fanning himself. "What's wrong with it?"

"I don't know." The kid's grin widened. He pulled a crumpled receipt from the pocket of his baggy black jeans and slammed it onto the glass counter. "But I've got a receipt."

Malin blinked, his eyes beginning to sting as frustration mingled with exhaustion. He exhaled sharply and grabbed the receipt. Without another word, he turned to the register, punching the keys with sharp, irritated movements. When the screen prompted for a manager override, he reached for his key, muttering under his breath as he unlocked the cash drawer.

Malin took out two hundred dollars in twenties and began counting the bills into the kid's outstretched hand. His fingers moved quickly, but by the time he got to one-sixty, he caught movement in his peripheral vision. His body tensed. Turning his head slightly to the left, he saw Ken, the store manager, and Ralph, the district manager, standing at the far end of the counter, their arms folded, their expressions unreadable.

Malin's stomach dropped, and his body jolted as if he'd been caught stealing cookies from the jar. His eyes darted back to the kid, his hand faltering for a moment before he finished counting.

Malin licked his thumb and smiled at the boy, sliding the cash across the counter. "One eighty… and two hundred. Here's your refund, young man. I'm so sorry about the game being defective. We hope you come back soon, OK, little guy?"

The kid snatched the money with a smug grin and strolled off without a word. Malin exhaled, forcing a polite smile as he turned toward two men standing near the entrance. Ralph was dressed sharply in a dark suit. Beside him stood Ken, looking smug with his crimson tie perfectly knotted.

Malin plastered on a grin and walked over, his voice overly cheerful. "Ken! Ralph! Happy early Thanksgiving."

Ken let out a sarcastic snicker, smoothing the front of his tie.

"Ralph!" Malin laughed nervously, clapping him on the shoulder. "What brings our illustrious district manager out here? Shouldn't you be in—"

"Shrinkage," Ralph interrupted, his tone flat.

Malin blinked. "What?"

"Shrinkage," Ralph repeated, crossing his arms tightly. "You know what that is, right?"

"Uh… yeah," Malin replied, scratching his cheek. "I think so."

"Stolen merchandise," Ralph clarified. "Right?"

Malin nodded, wiping a hand over his face. "Uh-huh. Sure. A damn shame."

Ralph's gaze didn't waver. "Malin, do you know what the average shrinkage is for a KB Toys store?"

Malin glanced up at the drop ceiling, sighing. "About… eleven percent?"

Ralph's lips pressed into a thin line. "Do you know what the shrinkage is for this store?"

Malin shrugged, trying to feign nonchalance. "I'd have to look at the data, but I think we're doing pretty—"

"Twenty," Ralph snapped, cutting him off.

Malin's eyes widened. "Whoa." He shook his head, trying to mask his alarm. "That's… high."

"Why do you suppose that is, Malin?" Ralph's voice rose slightly, his words sharp and deliberate. "Why do you suppose that this store—my store—doubles the national average?"

Malin stared at the lime-green carpet beneath his feet, his shoulders stiff. "I mean, it's hard to say."

Ralph leaned forward, his eyes narrowing. "Another fun fact. Of that twenty percent shrinkage, fifteen percent comes from the electronics department."

Malin scratched his earlobe, his throat dry. "You don't say."

"GameCube units falling off the truck. Fourteen Sega Dreamcasts vanishing from the shelves, as if jolly old Saint Nick swooped down from his sleigh and cleaned us out." Ralph's voice grew sharper with every word, his eyes boring into Malin. "How do you think any of this is possible?"

Malin bit his lip, his fingers fidgeting on the counter-top. "Ralph… I mean, I wish I could help you. Truly. But I haven't—"

"Got the foggiest," Ralph interrupted, nodding with a wry

smile. "I know. Don't bother hurting that little head of yours, son. After all, you're just the store manager, right?"

Malin's eyes darted around the room, locking on everything but Ralph's face. He cleared his throat. "Oh?"

Ralph shifted his gaze to the kid still standing at the counter. His smile was cold, almost too friendly. "Excuse me!" he called out to the boy.

The kid looked up, pulling his black headphones down around his neck. He paused his portable CD player and shuffled over, his baggy black pants dragging on the floor. The long silver chain attached to his wallet swayed with each sluggish step. He stopped a few feet from Ralph and Malin, his bored expression unchanging.

"How're you doing today?" Ralph asked, his smile stretching wider.

The kid shrugged. "OK, I guess."

Ralph chuckled lightly, glancing at Malin with mock amusement. "Today's youth!" he exclaimed, shaking his head. Then, muttering under his breath, "God help us when you fucks run the world." He straightened, clearing his throat. "So, what you got there?" he asked, pointing at the cash in the kid's hand.

The kid held up the wad of twenties, his face blank. "I dunno. Money?"

"I can see that, son," Ralph said, his tone overly patient. "You just got a refund, right?"

The kid nodded.

"What did you return?"

"*Power Stone.*"

"*Power Stone!*" Ralph repeated, his tone shifting to mock delight. His face brightened as he tapped a finger against his chin. "The cornerstone of any true gamer's Dreamcast collection."

He squinted at the kid, his smile turning sharp. "Say, how much did you pay for that game?"

"It was a gift," the kid said, his voice flat.

"Ah," Ralph replied, dragging out the sound like he didn't believe a word of it. He strolled over to the glass display case, his fingers skimming the surface until they stopped. "Let's see... *Power Stone, Power Stone...*" His finger froze. "There it is! *Power Stone*: forty-nine ninety-nine. Plus tax, of course." He straightened, turning back toward the boy. "How much do you have in your hand there?"

The kid glanced nervously at Malin.

"By my guess," Ralph continued, his tone growing colder, "and judging by the security cameras, it's close to two hundred dollars. Would that be right, son?"

Malin leaned against the counter, his handkerchief out, wiping away the beads of sweat forming on his balding head. "Fuck my life," he whispered under his breath.

Ralph leaned closer to the kid, his eyes narrowing. "You want to tell me what's really going on here, son?"

The kid froze like a deer caught in headlights. After a tense moment, he took two steps back and slapped the wad of cash onto the counter. His face flushed, and he spun toward Malin, shouting, "Dammit, Dad! You always get me caught up in your shit!"

Malin's entire body slumped as he watched his son sprint out of the store, the jangling silver wallet chain swaying with each step. Moments later, the store security team raced past, their radios crackling.

The silence that followed was heavy. Malin couldn't bring himself to meet Ralph's eyes.

Ralph finally broke the stillness, his voice dripping with contempt. "Just so I can grasp the full weight of how much of a cocksucking piece of shit you are—that's your son?"

Malin sighed, defeated. "Yeah."

"And you coerced him into stealing from the store you *manage*? Excuse me, *managed*."

"It would seem so."

For a moment, neither man spoke. The air between them was thick with mutual disgust, like two prisoners sharing the same tiny cell.

"You're not going to run, are you, Malin?" Ralph asked finally, his tone flat.

Malin scoffed, shaking his head. "Nope. Don't think so."

&

"Mom…" Brandon whined, his voice high-pitched and petulant.

Brandon and his dad stood behind Christine, who was unlocking the door to their apartment. Her long, dark brown hair tumbled into her face as she ruffled it in frustration. Christine opened the door. With a sharp motion, she tossed the car keys into a black Furby coffee mug.

"I don't get why *I'm* in trouble!" Brandon continued, pointing accusingly at Malin. "Dad made me do it!"

Christine turned, her green eyes blazing under the harsh fluorescent light of their dull galley kitchen. She crossed her arms, fixing her husband with a scowl that could melt steel. Malin clasped his hands behind his back and stared at the linoleum floor.

"Mom, I'm telling you—"

"I don't care, Brandon," Christine said while rubbing her temples, cutting him off.

"But he's my dad!" Brandon shouted, his voice cracking. "I was just following his—"

"Oh, yeah?" Christine said, her voice trembling with restrained anger. "And what did I tell you about following…" She shook her head and shifted her eyes to Malin before continuing. "Your own father." Christine wiped her face with one hand and whispered, "I can't. Brandon, bed."

"But I—"

Christine's face turned red as she stormed toward him. "Bed. Now!"

Brandon threw up his hands in surrender and shuffled backward toward his room, shooting a venomous glare at his father. He stomped down the hall and punctuated his exit with a door slam that rattled the kitchen.

The silence that followed was thick and heavy.

Malin clicked his teeth and let out a nervous chuckle. "I'm thinking… grounded?" he offered weakly. "No allowance for a month?"

Christine remained silent, her eyes glued to the floor. Then, without looking at him, she said coldly, "That would work for you, wouldn't it? After all, how are you going to give your son an allowance," she said, grabbing the nearest object, a stack of recordable CDs resting on the countertop, "when you don't have a fucking job?!"

She hurled the CDs like a fastball, hitting Malin squarely on the left cheekbone. He staggered backwards, stumbling over his own feet before falling flat on his back. Groaning, Malin cradled his face as he looked up at his wife standing over him, her fists clenched and her jaw tight with rage.

"What do you have to say for yourself?" she demanded.

Malin groaned again, rolling onto his side before pulling himself up. "First of all, *ow.* Second, I'm not an umpire, and you sure as hell aren't Randy Johnson, so could you—"

Christine let out a guttural grunt and reached behind the refrigerator, pulling out a nine-iron.

Malin's eyes widened. "—stop throwing things?"

Christine spun the golf club in her hand with practiced menace. "How about *Tiger-fucking-Woods*? Huh?"

Malin raised his hands defensively, taking a cautious step back. "Now, honey, let's not get carried away. You keep this up, and you're gonna end up on *Dateline*."

"Keep making jokes, Malin," Christine snarled, stalking toward him. "Maybe you can tell God a real funny one about how your wife bashed your skull in."

Malin's voice cracked as he blurted, "I-I don't understand why you're so mad! It's not like I haven't done this before. You *know* I pull an okey-doke around Black Friday. And let's not forget—you don't complain about the extra dough I make!"

Christine's grip on the club tightened. "You've never involved our son!"

"What do you want me to say, Christine? The con required two."

"Then find someone else!" she shouted, her voice breaking. "Not our fucking children!"

She dropped the golf club with a loud clatter, ran her hands through her hair, and let out a shaky breath. "You have to be better for them, Mal."

Malin furrowed his brow. "Have you gone nuts? Christine, we only *have* one kid!"

Christine shook her head slowly, her chest rising and falling as she lifted her gaze to meet his. Her green eyes glistened with unshed tears.

"For *them*, Mal," she whispered, her hand resting on her stomach.

Malin's face twisted in confusion. He squinted at her, his mouth half open. He pointed at her with a trembling hand. "You don't mean…"

Christine nodded silently.

"You're not…"

Another nod.

Malin's face went slack. His voice dropped to a whisper. "Are you telling me you're…"

Christine wiped at her eyes, exhaling a shaky laugh. "A little knocked up. Yeah."

Malin stared at her, his eyes glassy. His right hand, still trembling, lifted toward her as his lips began to quiver. "You've—" Malin's shaky hand clenched into a fist before slamming down on the kitchen table. "—got to be kidding me!" He slapped his bare forehead, letting out an exasperated groan before storming out of the kitchen and into the living room.

Christine followed close behind, her face a mix of disbelief and anger, her jaw slack. She found him pacing the tight, square living room, his sneakers squeaking against the dark brown floors with each frantic turn.

Malin planted his hands on his hips, his voice rising. "I don't get it, Christine! I don't fucking get it!"

Christine sighed, her lips trembling as she struggled to

contain her rage. In a calm but dangerous tone, she asked, "What don't you get, Malin?"

Malin spun to face her, his expression twisted with frustration. "What are you now? A fucking comedian? I don't get *this*! *How?*"

Christine crossed her arms. "Well," she said coldly, "when two people really love each other—"

"You were supposed to be on birth control!" Malin barked.

Christine's finger shot out, pointing at him like a weapon. "Asshole, it's not one hundred percent guaranteed! But you know what would've been? You keeping your damn condom on. And don't think I don't know you don't do it!"

"That," Malin said as he looked up at the popcorn ceiling and scratched the back of his neck, "has nothing to do with anything!"

Christine wiped at her tears with a trembling hand. "I thought you'd be happy."

Malin clasped his hands together, his voice dripping with sarcasm. "Christine, look at our situation here. I can barely take care of the one we *have*. And you want to what? Bring another fucking accident to term?"

"Don't call them that!" Christine snapped, her voice cracking. She sniffled and added, "I can get my old job back at the—"

"The one you had before we were married?" Malin's eyes widened. "Are you crazy? What did I tell you, hon? Before I put that ring on your skinny little finger, what did I say?"

Christine's gaze dropped to the floor. "That it's your job to put food on that table and provide," she mumbled.

Malin nodded, his tone condescending. "That's right."

Christine's head snapped up, her green eyes blazing. "Well,

you're doing a *real shit job* at your job, Malin!" Tears mixed with her mascara, streaking her cheeks as her voice trembled with fury.

Malin gasped, stunned into silence. He shuffled to the beige leather couch and collapsed into it, exhaling heavily. "We're not having it, and that's final."

Christine froze, her expression darkening. "What?" she whispered.

Malin met her gaze evenly. "The term has many names, Christine. In Polish it's called aborcja. In Spanish, it's *aborto*."

Christine stared at him, her face pale with shock, before spinning on her heel and disappearing into the kitchen.

Malin shook his head, grabbing the remote. He stared at the thirty-two-inch box TV, chuckling as an old sketch played. "I'm Rick James!" he whispered. "Classic."

The sound of approaching footsteps made him glance up. Christine stood over him, the nine-iron raised high above her head.

"Whoa, whoa!" Malin yelped, rolling off the couch just as the golf club crashed through the drywall, white dust flying into the air.

"Christine! What the hell?!" Malin shouted, scrambling backward on the floor.

Her face was stone as she swung again, slamming the golf club into the wall repeatedly, chunks of drywall flying with every blow until a gaping hole revealed the bedroom on the other side.

Panting, Malin froze, staring up at her in disbelief.

Christine dropped the golf club. It hit the floor with a heavy thud. Her chest heaved as she glared down at him. "The next time you suggest abortion," she hissed, her voice low and steady, "it's going to be your head I put a hole through."

She grabbed her keys from the Furby coffee mug and stormed out of the house, slamming the door behind her.

Malin sat motionless for a moment. Groaning, he pulled himself to his feet, brushed the drywall dust off his shirt, and folded his arms, glancing back at the wall. He grimaced and muttered, "Well, at least she didn't hit the TV." He groaned again. "Aww, shit! She's got me so mad I can't even watch *Chappelle*!" Malin slammed his thumb against the remote, flipping the channel to the news.

The image on the screen made him sit up straight. A young reporter stood bundled in a heavy coat next to a long line of people, their breath visible in the frigid air. Some were in tents pitched along the sidewalk while others sat in folding chairs, wrapped in thick blankets and wearing gloves, sipping hot chocolate. The bitter winter weather didn't seem to deter anyone.

Malin squinted at the TV. "The hell is going on?"

The reporter cleared his throat and began speaking. "We're live outside the Kmart on 15-501, where folks are braving the cold and preparing for what may be a long, wintry two days." He walked down the line, gesturing at the crowd. "Now, for those of you living under a rock, Vision Software has announced its latest console, *The Link*, which is set to debut in the US on Black Friday. Video game critics are already calling this 'the console to end all console wars.'"

Malin leaned forward, his eyes narrowing at the screen.

The reporter tapped a young woman on the shoulder. She turned around, revealing heavy black lipstick and mascara. The reporter visibly recoiled at the sight of her eerie white contact lenses. She grinned, showing off a pair of cheap plastic vampire fangs.

"Oh, h-hello," the reporter stammered, taking a step back. "Jimmy Jones with WTVD. Can you tell me and the folks at home what has you so excited about *The Link*?"

The girl's grin widened. "I'm only here to socialize. Nighttime's the only hours we get to hang out." She licked her white fangs slowly, her eyes unblinking.

An awkward silence followed. The reporter cleared his throat, visibly uncomfortable. "Uh… OK. Any thoughts on whether you'll actually get your hands on a console? I mean, you're pretty far back in the line."

She shrugged, flashing another plastic smile. "I'm here for the people more than the console." Her fangs suddenly popped out of her mouth, clattering against the sidewalk. She snatched them up, quickly shoving them back in. "You know what I mean?" she added with a wink.

The reporter tilted his head, exasperated. "Jesus wept," he muttered under his breath, stepping away. Facing the camera, he continued, "As you can see, these are the types of… *personalities* you'll find in these lines. Makes this reporter think maybe it's a *good* thing there's a limited supply."

He moved on, his tone shifting to professional. "Now, according to Jo Gabe, Vision Software's CEO, production delays tied to the Iraq War mean supplies will be extremely limited. The company predicts that additional consoles won't come off the assembly lines until late December 2006."

Malin shook his head, muttering, "Jo Gabe. Why they always gotta blame a war?"

The reporter continued. "Stores like Kmart predict they'll sell out of consoles within an hour. And aside from hardcore gaming fans, scalpers are already out in force; eBay estimates these $400 consoles could fetch as much as $5,000 each in online auctions."

Malin froze. His ears twitched. His toes began tapping against the floor. A familiar tingling sensation crept across his scalp, the unmistakable precursor to the sweat he always felt before an opportunity.

He sprang up from the leather couch, laughing. "I'll be," he said, shaking his head as his laugh grew louder. "I'll fucking be."

As he grabbed his car keys, his laugh escalated into something maniacal. "Jo Gabe, you beautiful bastard," he said quietly to himself, swinging open the door. With one last cackle, he slammed it shut behind him.

STAGE 5

"Mom, I can't just quit," Rick said, holding the Nokia phone to his ear as he pulled into another shopping center. His car's gas light blinked orange, its oil light glowed red. A sigh escaped his lips.

"Why not?" she asked, her tone sharp.

"You know how hard I worked to get that position. They told me back at Chapel Hill that if I could just get my foot in the door at Branson and Lloyd, I'd be set. Well, here I am." His voice cracked slightly as he cruised past an Electronics Boutique. The line wrapped around the building, people huddled in tents and sleeping bags, bracing for what was shaping up to be one of the coldest nights on record. Lacy crystals of ice clung to his windshield despite the defroster working overtime. He squinted through the streaked glass. "Dammit," he muttered under his breath.

"Excuse me?" his mother said.

"Not you, Mom," Rick said. "But why move my foot when it's finally in the door?"

"Because, honey, they're stepping on your toes."

"They're not stepping on my toes!" Rick snapped, gripping the steering wheel tighter.

"Really? Making you drive all over Durham to fetch a toy isn't stepping on your toes?" Her voice was tinged with disbelief. "Sounds like hazing to me."

Rick groaned, pulling into the next lot. "It's not hazing, Mom. It's… it's more like a rite of passage."

"Oh, a rite of passage, is it? Tell me, Rick, does that include being treated like a glorified delivery boy?"

Rick sighed, his eyes narrowing at the neon sign of Brendle's glowing across the street. A shiny diamond stamped between the "E" and "S" stood out like a relic of a bygone era. The line there was just as long as the one at Electronics Boutique. He scrunched his face in disbelief. *Those are still around?* he thought.

Pulling into a nearby gas station, Rick parked by the closest pump and hopped out of the car. He stuffed the nozzle into the gas tank. The pump clicked loudly as the fuel began flowing.

"You know, your brother—"

"Mom," Rick said, shaking his head. "Not the time to bring him up."

A long pause hung between them before she spoke softly. "I'm sorry. So… you'll be coming to Darryl's tomorrow, right?"

Rick winced. "Mom, I don't think I'll make it."

"What?" she said sternly. "Rick, there are some things more important than money. Your brother always taught you that."

Rick bowed his head, the weight of her words sinking in. "Well, guess who's not here to remind me of that."

"Rick…"

"I gotta go, Mom," he said, cutting off the conversation. He hung up and slipped the phone into his pocket, sighing heavily. "Up, up, down, down, left, right. Up, up, down, down, left, right," he chanted to himself, like a broken controller stuck on loop. Pulling the nozzle from the tank, he replaced it on the pump and climbed back into his car.

Across the street at the shopping center, tents were pitched, and people huddled around makeshift fires, their laughter and voices carrying through the night air. It looked more like a campground than a parking lot. Rick shook his head, biting back a curse.

Just as he was about to turn the ignition, a flicker of green light caught his eye. A laser, bright and sharp, danced across the night sky. Rick froze, his fingers hovering over the key.

"What the hell?" he whispered, his eyes narrowing as he leaned forward and winced.

A sharp green laser cut through the night, flashing from behind the shopping center. His curiosity piqued, Rick turned left, then right onto a half-paved road. The darkness pressed in around him, broken only by flickering fluorescent street-lights. A stray dog stopped in its tracks, growling at Rick's white Toyota as it crawled forward.

On either side of the road loomed a forest of bare winter trees, their skeletal branches clawing at the cold night sky. To his right, the trees thinned out, revealing an empty parking lot. At its edge stood a decrepit shopping center, looking as though it had been forgotten by time.

Faded white stucco covered its facade, cracked and peeling in places. A large red K perched on the roof, looming over the store like a relic of the past.

"Huh. Didn't know they still had one of these," Rick said. He pulled into the lot, eyeing the building. "Maybe it's closed or something." He scanned the empty expanse of asphalt. But his heart skipped when he noticed a small line of people gathered near the store's entrance.

He reached for the crumpled Black Friday newspaper on his passenger seat, flipping through the pages. "Come on, come on," he grumbled before finally finding the ad:

Big K: THE LINK—available at your nearest location. Limited supplies.

Rick parked and stepped out into the freezing air, zipping his jacket up to his chin. The night was unnervingly silent, the only sounds coming from the distant hum of the trees and his own footsteps crunching over loose gravel despite the line of people.

As he approached the store, he glanced at his watch: 9:30 p.m. The sign for the store's hours said 8 a.m. to 9 p.m. Rick's gaze shifted to the crowd. Unlike the festive chaos at other stores, this one was eerily subdued was eerily composed of a scattering of tents slumped against the cold, a few sleeping bags sprawled out, lawn chairs draped in comforters.

A group of frat boys stood nearby, dressed in matching red long-sleeve shirts, blue jeans, and golden Timberland boots. The Greek letters sigma, gamma, gleamed in gold across their chests. They were still setting up camp, their movements half-focused, sluggish from the cold. A young man with dark purple hair, a swollen bruised left cheek, and sharp Asian features barked orders, waving a hand as the others struggled to pitch a tent. On the cracked sidewalk in front of them sat a bulky thirty-two-inch box TV, the glass screen reflecting the glow of a plugged-in PlayStation, wires snaking toward a nearby generator.

At the very front of the line, a chubby man with graying hair lounged in a green-and-white checkered lawn chair. He adjusted his thick, black-rimmed glasses every few seconds, a contented smile frozen on his rosy, chipmunk-like cheeks.

Rick hesitated, then stepped closer. "Excuse me," he said, his voice breaking the stillness.

The man didn't respond, his smile unwavering.

"Excuse me," Rick repeated, louder this time.

The man sighed dramatically, pausing the handheld game in his lap. He set it on the ground and looked up, offering Rick a half-smile.

"Sorry to bother you," Rick said, but before he could continue, the man stood abruptly and declared:

"DASHING AND DARING…"

Rick blinked, stunned.

The man continued, louder now: "COURAGEOUS AND CARING!"

Rick glanced nervously at the others in line. None of them flinched. "Uh… OK," Rick said, forcing a polite smile as he shuffled backward.

The man cleared his throat theatrically and added, "Let's switch this to falsetto."

"He's not singing the theme song to Gummy Bears, is he?" said Rick.

"Sure, he is," a voice replied.

Rick glanced over at a young man and woman leaning against the wall, as if trying to soak up its warmth. The man stood with one foot propped against the bricks, hands buried in the front pockets of his black slacks. The wind tousled his bangs, brushing against the dark bruise circling his right eye. Beside him, a young woman in a black dress, black tracksuit pants, and white sneakers sat on the ground, knees curled up to her chest, shivering. Her pale skin glistened with perspiration, strands of long brown hair clinging to her damp forehead as she watched the scene unfold.

"You ever watched that cartoon?" the man asked Rick.

"Of course," Rick replied, smiling. "Used to pretend my juice was like the bears' and bounce around the house."

The man chuckled. "Me too. I miss Saturday morning cartoons—just a bowl of POPS and no cares in the world."

The three of them turned their attention to the man singing. His face turned shades of blue as he held the final note, staggering back as though about to pass out.

"Careful, Mannie!" the man called. "Don't think any of us can catch you!"

Mannie gripped the wall, his chest heaving. He fumbled for an inhaler, shaking it feverishly before taking two quick puffs.

"How… was… that?" he wheezed.

The line offered scattered reactions. Grimaces, a few weak claps, and others pulling comforters over their heads.

"Impressive, Mannie," the woman said, her voice dripping with mock praise. "I heard notes that not even Mariah could… *Carey*!"

"Or want to," the man whispered in Rick's ear, earning a chuckle.

Mannie grinned, oblivious, and picked up his handheld game.

Rick turned back to the young man and shivering young lady. "You don't know how many consoles they might have here, do you?"

The man shrugged. "I think twenty."

Rick's eyes widened. "Are you sure?"

"Yeah," the man said with a crooked smile.

Rick looked at the line, counting softly under his breath, "Ten, eleven, twelve." His stomach sank as his gaze landed on himself. "Thirteen," he whispered. A nervous laugh escaped him. "Oh shit, I'm thirteen."

"Lucky thirteen," the woman mumbled, her head still buried in her lap. Her voice was muffled but carried a biting edge. "Congratulations. Now you get to freeze to death with the rest of us."

Rick sighed, shoving his hands deep into his coat pockets. He took his place behind the two of them in line, his breath visible in the icy air.

"Welcome to the line of duty," the man said with a grin, extending a hand. "Got a name, soldier?"

"Rick," he said, shaking the man's hand.

The man pointed at himself. "Merlin. But you can call me Mer—it's easier when your lips are numb. And this here shivering disaster is my sister, Gwen."

Without lifting her head, Gwen gave a half-hearted wave, the blanket slipping slightly from her shoulders, though she barely stirred. She was still wrapped in the same black dress from earlier, its fabric crumpled, clinging to her like the weight of the evening. "Hey," she muttered, her voice laced with sarcasm. "Enjoy your stay in purgatory."

Merlin laughed, clapping Rick on the shoulder. "Don't mind her. She's cold, cranky, and about to start going through withdrawal.

Rick chuckled nervously. "With… withdrawal, you say?"

Merlin laughed, clapping Rick on the shoulder. "No worries compadre. Ain't her first rodeo. Ain't that right, Gwen?"

"Oh, man," Rick said, frowning, as he glanced at Gwen. "You must be freezing in that dress out here."

Mer let out a nervous laugh and kneeled next to his sister, whose back was convulsing from dry heaves that she was trying—and failing—to stifle. "She's just *really* excited about trying out the Kink!"

Rick raised an eyebrow. "It's called The Link."

"Yeah, that one," Mer said, waving a hand dismissively. He leaned in close to Gwen's ear and muttered, "Get it the fuck together, will ya?"

As Rick stood, his eyes lingered on Mer's fresh shiner and busted lip. Gwen trembled uncontrollably, her arms clutching her knees, bruises visible even in the dim light. *I don't know whether to ask who died or who won the fight*, he thought.

Mer caught Rick's bewildered expression. "What?" Mer asked, his voice sharper than intended.

"Nothing," Rick said as he shook his head and gestured to the empty space next to Mer. "Mind if I sit?"

"Please."

Mer stepped aside, and Rick slid down the wall, resting his back against the cold bricks. He pulled up his knees and sighed. "Looks like we're in for a long night, huh?"

"Yep," Mer said. His gaze darted nervously around the lot as he shifted between standing and sitting, his movements restless.

Rick watched him for a moment, then smirked. "So, you're a gamer, huh?"

"What?" Mer blinked at him, looking confused.

"A gamer," Rick repeated, tilting his head.

"Oh! Yeah, for sure. Totally!" Mer said, a little too enthusiastically.

Rick chuckled. "What are you playing right now?"

"Uh…" Mer's eyes flicked up to the dark red sky as if searching for divine inspiration. "I like that one."

Rick raised an eyebrow, amused. "That one, huh? Yeah, that one's a classic."

Mer laughed nervously. "No, I mean… You know. What's that game called?" He snapped his fingers, grasping for words. "The blue Mario hedgehog contra crisis!" He let out a forced chuckle. "Yeah, that game's pretty awesome."

Rick gave a knowing smile, the corners of his mouth twitching. A long silence stretched between them. He finally asked, "You don't play video games, do you, partner?"

Mer's expression crumpled into a grimace. "Hell, no," he admitted. "I'd rather rip my fingernails off with pliers." He glanced at Rick, narrowing his eyes. "How'd you know?"

"Your sister," Rick said.

Gwen raised her head just enough to reveal one glassy green eye, her face pale and clammy. A bolus of bile surged into her mouth, and she quickly swallowed it back down with a grimace.

"Hey, my friend," Rick said, giving a small wave to Gwen. "When's the last time you used?" All he got in response was a soft groan.

"I'm gonna tell you now," Rick said, his tone steady but firm, "you're in for a rough night."

Gwen moaned weakly, her voice cracking as she muttered, "Ugh… I hate sobriety."

"Don't we all," Rick replied, his gaze drifting back to the quiet parking lot.

"Surprised a gamer like yourself hasn't ratted us out to the rest of them," Mer said, breaking the silence. "You should've seen what they did to the last guy they caught selling his console. Stripped him bare-ass naked before tossing him in the dumpster out back."

Rick chuckled, then hesitated. The humor faded quickly when he realized Mer wasn't laughing.

"Just surprised you're not blowing the whistle is all," Mer added, his gaze steady.

Rick turned back to Mer, a small smirk tugging at the corner of his lips. "Now why do you think that is?"

Mer squinted, his brow furrowing as realization dawned. "You're flipping it too, aren't you?"

Rick chuckled, shaking his head. "I wish."

Mer studied him for a moment, as if weighing the sincerity in Rick's answer. "Look, friend, I know you know," Mer said, his voice dropping to a low whisper. "And I know you know this little toy made of plastic and circuits is gonna fetch a hell of a price on eBay."

Rick shrugged, his grin widening. "Smart man."

Mer nodded slowly, his wariness easing. He extended his right fist, his tone softening. "All right, then. Whatever your angle is, you look out for us, and we'll do the same. Deal?"

Rick met his fist with a gentle bump, locking eyes with him. "Deal."

❧

"This whiskey was made by the Lloyd Distillery out in Mebane," Lloyd said, swirling the amber liquid in his glass. Candace sat stiffly in the back of Lloyd's black Buick limo, her posture rigid as she compulsively tugged at the hem of her tan skirt.

"You ever been to Mebane, Candace?" Lloyd asked, his gaze lingering on her chest.

"No, I haven't." She pulled her black cardigan tighter over her white blouse, her voice edged with discomfort.

"The distillery's decent," Lloyd said, taking a slow sip of his drink. "But Mebane itself? That place is a fucking joke. Nothing but TPT pieces of—"

"I'm sorry, sir," Candace interjected, cutting him off. "Where exactly are we going?"

"My daughter, Zelda," Lloyd said, leaning back against the plush leather seat. "She's got a house off of 15-501."

Candace's brow furrowed, her expression twisting into one of disbelief. "Your twelve-year-old has her own house?"

Lloyd laughed, the sound sharp and grating. "Of course. I'm certainly not going to live with her." He leaned forward conspiratorially, his breath reeking of whiskey. "When we Lloyds hit our tweens, we turn into full-blown psychopaths."

Candace pressed herself against the car door, her nose wrinkling as the damp smell of Lloyd's hair wafted toward her. "You don't say?" she muttered, her tone tight.

"But it's also rewarding," Lloyd continued, his voice dropping to a low, almost predatory drawl. He slid a hand along her thigh, his fingers brushing against the fabric of her skirt. "You want children someday, right?"

"Umm..." The limo came to a stop. "Are we here?" Candace asked, her voice filled with a mix of relief and excitement. She wasted no time hopping out of the vehicle.

The driver quickly got out as well, hurrying to open the door for Lloyd. Candace's eyes widened as she took in the sight before her: a sprawling mansion, its red brick façade gleaming under the ambient lights. The biggest black entry door she'd ever seen stood at the center, flanked by elegant columns.

"What do you think?" Lloyd asked, stepping out with a self-satisfied grin.

"Impressive," Candace said.

"It's not as big as she wanted, but it suffices," Lloyd replied with a casual shrug. He slipped his hand around her waist. "I'd love to show you my place sometime."

Candace quickened her pace to free herself from his grip, moving toward a row of white and lavender roses planted near the door. "These are beautiful!" she said, her smile returning. She pressed the doorbell and stood back, admiring the blooms.

They didn't have to wait long. The door creaked open, revealing a staff member dressed in a charcoal boiler suit streaked with dirt, clutching a handful of oranges. Realizing who had arrived, the man wiped his sweaty brow and stood at attention.

"Mr. Lloyd," he said with a polite smile. "What a pleasant surprise."

Lloyd squinted at him. "Which one are you? Jorge? Ramon? Ronaldo?" He rolled the Rs deliberately.

"Jeff, sir," the man replied.

"Jeff," Lloyd repeated with a nod. "Where's my daughter?"

"She said to tell you she was… indisposed," Jeff answered, his tone careful.

"The hell does that mean, Jeff?" Lloyd snapped.

Jeff fished inside the boiler suit's pocket, pulling out a folded piece of paper. "She instructed me to read this to you exactly as written," he said, unfolding the note. Clearing his throat, he began: "Lloyd! Did you get my fucking console?"

"What?" Lloyd's face twisted in confusion.

Jeff looked up, raising an eyebrow. "Sir, are you going to answer that?"

"Where is my daughter!?" Lloyd barked.

Jeff continued reading without missing a beat. "I knew you were going to say that, which leads me to believe you've come up with fuck-all. So take your current fuck-buddy and fuck off."

Lloyd grunted in frustration, grabbing the door and mumbling, "This is bullsh—"

"Uh-uh-uh!" Jeff interrupted in a sing-song tone. "Take one more step, and I will burn all the data to the ground. Don't you think I see you, Lloyd?"

"No!" Lloyd shouted, spinning around to glare at the overhead security camera. "No! Please don't!" His voice cracked, and his arms shot into the air in surrender.

A heavy silence fell over the group. Candace stood back, arms folded behind her, face scrunched in disbelief at the absurdity unfolding before her.

Jeff cleared his throat, raising a hand. "There's more here. Should I continue?"

Lloyd lowered his hands, sighing heavily. He rested his palms against his forehead and muttered under his breath, "This can't be my life. " Lloyd held up a hand to Jeff, cutting him off. "*Por favor*, Jeff. You have the floor."

Jeff was still holding the crate of oranges with his right arm. He could feel the weight of them start to pull. He kneeled and placed the oranges on the ground, clearing his throat dramatically before reading aloud.

"I told you, Lloyd." Jeff's voice was ice-cold. "I told you that if you screwed me on this one simple request, it was going to be scorched motherfucking earth."

Candace shook her head, muttering under her breath, "The mouth on this girl."

Jeff sighed theatrically, rubbing his chin. "As punishment," he said, "I'm going to need your black Corvette."

Lloyd's head snapped up. "No. No way. The seats are signed by Richard Petty!"

Jeff gave a lazy shrug.

Lloyd squeezed his eyes shut, his fists clenching at his sides. Then, through gritted teeth, he let out a guttural, "Fuuuuuck!"

Jeff hesitated for a second but continued, his voice steady. "The next time I see you, dear father, you'd better have a 128-bit Link console with thirty-two megabytes of memory. By Black Friday. If not, then ask yourself: What is life like flying coach?"

Jeff paused, raising an eyebrow before finishing, "Just to prove I'm not messing around, I signed my name… in blood."

Jeff handed the letter to Lloyd. "Here you are, sir."

Lloyd snatched the paper, his jaw tightening as his eyes scanned the page. He closed his eyes for a moment, exhaling sharply.

"Will there be anything else, sir?" Jeff asked with a practiced smile. "Perhaps an orange?"

Lloyd stared at him, his face unreadable. "No, Jeff."

As Lloyd walked past Candace, he handed her the letter. She glanced at it, her frown deepening as her eyes caught the garish details. The signature read: Zelda Lloyd, written in what appeared to be blood. Around it were doodles of unicorns, glitter splashed in chaotic bursts of green and gold. Candace tilted her head, holding up the letter like it might bite her.

Lloyd sighed, burying his face in his hands. "God, help me."

STAGE 6

"You suck, Theo!" Jason shouted, his voice cracking with frustration. What was once a quiet line of nerds patiently waiting for the day after Thanksgiving became a gaming Colosseum. The Kmart crowd had come alive watching the two have a best-of-five tournament in Street Fighter Alpha, a game that usually drew attention.

Theo leaned back in his reclining lawn chair, exuding confidence, his auburn-tipped dreadlocks shifting as he stretched. The golden Greek letters on his red short-sleeved shirt caught the glow from the bulky thirty-two-inch TV in front of him. His dark eyes flicked lazily toward the screen, fingers idly tapping the controller with the ease of someone who had already won. His grin was slow, smug—like a man watching his opponent dig his own grave.

Despite the cold November air, Jason's long purple hair clung to his sweat-slick forehead, his jaw clenched. His knuckles turned white, his legs jittered beneath him, and the fabric of his red-and-gold frat shirt darkened with damp patches from his overheating body. His entire posture screamed desperation, and every button-mash made it clearer that he was losing.

The crowd in line had formed a semicircle around the TV,

their attention glued to the screen. The red, green, and yellow cables trailed from the back of the console to a roaring gas generator that filled the air with a low rumble and the sharp tang of exhaust. Rick sat a few feet away, his back against the Kmart's brick wall, hands clamped over his nose and ears in a futile attempt to block out the noise and fumes.

"Don't be mad at T-Money because you play like a noob!" Dustin hollered, barely containing his laughter.

Jason tugged at his skully, pulling it lower over his forehead as he let out a guttural groan. His lips clamped down on his bottom lip in frustration, his head shaking with disbelief.

The more Jason fumbled, the louder the crowd grew.

"Catch him with a fireball, Jason!" Brad shouted, cupping his hands around his mouth like a coach.

"Shut the fuck up!" Jason snapped. "You're as pale as ash on shit, Brad!"

His mouth twisting into a scowl, Brad rubbed his scalp through his spiked rust-colored hair with the heel of his hand, saying under his breath, "That's 'cause I'm Irish, asshole!"

Jason's thumbs pounded the controller as if sheer force would turn the tide. Spit flew from his mouth as his efforts grew more frantic.

Theo chuckled softly, his grin widening. He started humming an off-key rendition of "No Scrubs," completely unbothered as Jason flailed. Without breaking his rhythm, Theo calmly executed the final input on his controller before setting it down beside his gold Timberland–clad feet.

"He just did the super!" Dustin shouted, pointing at the screen.

Jason's face flushed crimson, matching the red long-sleeved shirts he and the other frat boys wore. His fingers throbbed from relentless button-mashing, his heart sinking as the screen flashed bright green. "Block isn't gonna help! You can't handle the chip damage!" Dustin added with a triumphant laugh.

The screen erupted with a glowing Perfect! The crowd roared in unison, cheering and laughing as Theo's victory sealed the match.

"A green screen *and* a perfect!" Brad announced, rubbing salt in the wound. Jason's watery eyes stayed locked on the screen as the cheers echoed around him.

Theo picked up his controller, resting it casually on his lap, and extended his hand to Jason with a friendly smile. "Good game."

Jason stared at Theo's outstretched hand, his jaw tightening. Without a word, he turned and spit on the ground, storming off, the crowd's laughter trailing after him.

Theo shrugged and stood up from his lawn chair, brushing off the imaginary dust from his jeans.

A few moments later, Jason marched back into the tent. Through clenched teeth he looked at Theo and said, "I want a rematch, you jabroni."

The laughter from Dustin and Brad cut off instantly. Theo's smile vanished, his posture stiffening as he locked eyes with Jason.

"Don't call me that," Theo said, his tone steady, but his fists clenched at his sides.

Jason smirked. "Oh, yeah?" He squared his shoulders. "I'm your big brother, bitch. I'll call you whatever I want."

Theo stepped forward, his voice rising. "Jason, don't fu—"

Jason cut him off with a mocking gesture, rubbing his thumb and fingers together. "Blah, blah—shut the front door!" He grinned, his tone dripping with condescension.

Brad and Dustin exchanged uneasy glances, their earlier amusement fading. Theo's jaw tightened. His nostrils flared, his breathing deep and slow.

Jason, oblivious or maybe just pushing his luck, gave Theo a light slap on the chest, his grin wide and insincere. "Take a chill pill, man. We're boys, right?"

Theo's eyes burned with restrained anger. Warm puffs of air fogged in front of his face as he exhaled sharply. Jason leaned in, his voice dropping into an almost sing-song tone. "C'mon, T. You want to throw hands over me calling you a jabroni?"

Rick, still sitting against the wall, noticed Theo's hands trembling at his sides. Theo closed his eyes for a moment, biting his bottom lip, before bowing his head with a long, heavy sigh. He nodded, his voice barely audible. "Yeah. Sure."

Jason slung an arm around Theo's shoulder, pulling him into a loose side hug. His grin widened as he squeezed just enough to make Theo tense.

"That's what I thought," Jason said smugly. "Sigma Gamma Alpha?"

"Sigma Gamma Alpha," Theo muttered through gritted teeth.

Jason finally let him go, grabbing the controller and holding it high. "All right, who's next?" His eyes scanned the crowd, lingering over the nervous faces until they settled on Rick.

"How about you?"

"Me?" Rick asked, pointing to himself. He held up his hands and shook his head. "Nah, I'm good."

"You scared?" Jason taunted.

Rick smirked, rubbing his arms for warmth. "I'm cold. You guys couldn't have brought a heater along with that big-booty TV?"

Brad smirked, leaning back in his lawn chair lazily. He flicked his red bangs out of his eyes and shot Jason a knowing look. "Priorities, my guy!"

Mer shook his head, letting out a breathy laugh. "A fucking *shanda* for your generation," he muttered under his breath.

"No kidding," Rick said.

"You want some of this?" Jason asked, pointing at Mer with a sly grin.

"What?" Mer raised an eyebrow, feigning confusion.

"Come on, Mer," Jason said, rubbing his hands together like a cartoon villain. "Let's see your *Street Fighter Alpha* skills."

"You do play *Street Fighter* , right?" Dustin chimed in, leaning forward. His red-and-gold baseball cap covering his face.

Mer let out a dry laugh. "Do I play *Street Fighter* ?" He stood up, dusting himself off, and strode over to the lawn chair. Picking up the controller, he smirked. "Let's go."

Jason sat down opposite him, gripping his controller confidently. Jason tilted his head, noticing Mer was holding the controller upside down. Mer quickly flipped it upright and pressed the X button.

"Oh," Jason said, raising an eyebrow. "You're using Guile?"

"Uh, yeah," Mer scoffed. "Who wouldn't? Army guy. Go Joe! Right?"

"Watch out, Jason!" Dustin said, nudging him.

"Don't tell me to watch out," Jason snapped. "Tell *him* to watch out."

The load screen appeared, and the two waited as the progress bar crawled forward.

"They really need to fix this," Dustin muttered.

"Hate load screens," Jason added, leaning back.

"They say The Link won't have any load times!" Brad chimed in, excitement lighting up his face.

The stage finally loaded. The announcer's voice boomed, "Ready… GO FOR BROKE!"

Jason grinned, immediately walking his character up to Mer's Guile and initiating a grab. Mer's fingers danced over the buttons, managing a perfectly timed input to break free.

"So," Jason said, snickering. "Tech throw. Well-timed, sir."

Mer smirked, pressing back on the directional pad, making his character retreat. As Jason closed the gap to try another grab, Mer's thumb shot to the trigger. Guile lashed out with a swift kick to Jason's character's face. Before Jason could recover, Mer followed up with a crouching sweep that sent Jason's fighter sprawling.

Rick, who had been slouched against the wall, perked up and crouched down by Mer's ear, grinning.

"Keep doing that," Rick whispered. Mer glanced at Rick briefly, then refocused on the screen. Every time Jason's character advanced, Mer countered with a low sweep. The match went on like this for the next five seconds. Drool was dribbling from Jason's mouth. His face cherry-red. The crowd erupted with laughter and cheers, only fueling Jason's frustration.

"Stop doing that cheap shit!" Jason yelled, gripping his controller tightly. Mer smirked, his focus unwavering. It wasn't long before the match ended. The screen flashed KO in bold letters, and Jason's character collapsed.

"Fuuuck!" Jason shouted, hurling the controller against the brick wall. It shattered into pieces, sending a collective gasp through the crowd.

"Dude!" Dustin shouted. His eyes locked onto Jason, his glare sharp enough to cut.

"Fuck off, Dustin," Jason shot back. "I'll buy you a new one. Now shut your pie hole and toss me another controller!"

Dustin muttered under his breath, rummaging through his duffle bag to retrieve a spare.

"You know this always happens," Brad said, laughing nervously. "We should keep a special 'Jason controller' just for when he rages."

"I don't recall asking you a fucking thing!" Jason shot back, rounding on Brad.

"D-dude," Brad said. "Chill. OK? It was just a joke."

"Here," Dustin said, passing Jason a new controller, "Please try not to break this one."

Jason snatched it from Dustin's hands and dropped into his chair. "Plug it in!" he barked. Dustin complied, attaching the joystick to the console.

The announcer's voice boomed, "GO FOR BROKE!" Jason grinned, immediately commanding his character Ryu to jump back and start hurling fireballs.

"Hadouken! Hadouken!" the game blared repeatedly as Jason's character unleashed a relentless barrage. Mer struggled, his frantic button presses doing little to counter as his character's health bar dropped from gold to red.

Jason leaned back, grinning smugly. "You thought you had the Guile… to take on the man with skills for miles? Even my fireballs got you coughing up bile."

Rick rubbed his eyes, suppressing a groan. *Please stop that,* he thought.

Jason glanced sideways at Mer, his grin widening. "What game are you gonna get with your Link if you score one tomorrow?"

"What?" Mer asked, distracted by his losing streak.

"What game are you getting tomorrow?"

"Shiiit," Mer sighed, his shoulders slumping. "Hell if I know. Haven't thought that far ahead."

Jason abruptly paused the game. The crowd fell silent, the only sounds now a faint murmuring of confusion and anticipation. An awkward tension spread, thick and unrelenting.

Jason let his controller drop into his lap. He scanned the faces around him before locking eyes with Mer. His tone was calm, but his eyes narrowed. "What do you mean you don't know what game you're gonna get?"

Mer's gaze flicked to the crowd. Dozens of post-pubescent, pimple-faced teens with clenched fists and twitching jaws stared back at him, their collective energy like a powder keg waiting for a spark. Mer stood slowly, glancing around for an exit. His eyes briefly caught Gwen still slumped on the ground, her head hovering over a bucket. Panic crept in as he patted his back pocket.

Shit. My gun.

Mer forced a laugh. "Of course I know what game I'm getting!" he said, a bit too loudly.

Jason tilted his head, his frown deepening. "Which one?"

Mer froze, his mind racing. His palms started to sweat. Finally, he blurted out, "M-*Madden*. Yeah, *Madden*."

The crowd groaned in unison, their faces twisting in disgust.

"You're one of them," Dustin sneered.

"One of what?" Mer asked, his voice rising an octave. "What did I say?"

"A sports gamer," Jason said, his tone dripping with disdain. He took a step closer, his presence looming. "It's fine. All gamers are the same. I respect that."

Mer let out a nervous chuckle, nodding quickly. "Exactly! All the same."

Jason's smile grew sharper. "It's the scalpers we don't like."

Mer's stomach dropped. His eyes darted to Rick, who stood against the wall, his face unreadable. "Sc-scalpers?" Mer stammered. "Why?"

"They kill the culture," Jason spat. The crowd murmured in agreement, their whispers building into a chorus. "Gaming's already expensive as hell. Those assholes snatch everything up, then jack the prices on eBay. They're the reason companies start screwing us too—raising prices and milking us dry."

"That's right!" someone shouted.

"Preach!" Brad yelled.

Mer's heart raced as the crowd roared their approval, fists pumping in unison. Before he could react, he felt two fingertips on his chin. Jason turned Mer's face back toward him, forcing their eyes to meet.

"I'm glad we had this chat," Jason said softly, his voice almost fatherly. But his eyes were cold steel. "Because if we find out anyone here is a scalper… they're dead."

Mer swallowed hard, his Adam's apple bobbing. The words hung in the air like a guillotine blade, the silence foreboding. After a long moment, Jason rolled his eyes and sat back down.

"You want to finish this game or not?" Mer asked.

"Betta believe it," Jason said.

Jason sat down and pressed start. Just as the two were about to continue round two the screen went black. Jason and the entire crowd started shouting.

Brad held his hands up and said, "Sorry! Sorry! He looked at Jason and said, "I think the generator is out of gas."

"Dammit, Brad!" Jason said. "We're in the middle of a game!"

"Chill, all right?" Brad said. "Gonna pop up to the gas station real quick. Be right back." Brad hopped out of the tent and jogged toward his truck.

"Hurry the hell up!" Jason shouted. Jason walked over to the generator and pulled the PlayStation console and TV plug. "Forget it! Video game on hold. Need a Snapple. To the gas station."

The tension broke as the crowd relaxed, murmuring among themselves.

Mer let out a shaky breath and gave Rick a subtle nod of gratitude. Rick's face remained neutral, but the slight raise of his eyebrow was all the acknowledgment Mer needed.

As he turned back toward his spot in line, his pocket buzzed. He reached in, fingers fumbling over the large ring of janitor's keys he had lifted from his father's house. His stomach twisted at the familiar weight of them. He pulled out his phone and glanced at the caller ID.

Mer scoffed and pressed the phone to his ear. "Was wondering when you were gonna call."

Silence.

"Pop," Mer said, his nostrils flaring, his grip tightening around the phone. "Will you stop it?"

Nothing.

Mer clenched his jaw, his face reddening. "You know what? Fuck you! These mind games are bullshit! I told you—we'll get you the money. And even now, you don't trust us. That's the problem, Pop. No trust."

The only response was the wet sound of chewing on the other end.

Mer frowned, his stomach knotting. "I hope you choke, Pop." He exhaled sharply, trying to steady himself. "Besides, you have no fucking idea where we are."

Braff's calm voice finally came through. Too calm.

"Hey, Merlin?"

Mer hesitated. "What?"

A slow swallow. A pause.

"When I find you," Braff murmured, his voice smooth as steel, "I'm gonna kill you myself."

Click.

A chill raced down Mer's spine. His fingers tightened around the phone as he stared at it, his breath shallow. He felt his hands shake as he shoved it back into his pocket. For a moment, he stood frozen. Then, wiping his face with both hands, he took a slow, measured breath and shook his head.

Keep it together.

Mer's gaze shifted to Gwen. Her sweaty hair was plastered to her back and the concrete wall, her head resting against the rim of the bucket. She panted heavily, her eyes half-closed as bile dribbled from the corner of her mouth.

Mer stuffed his hands in his pockets and sighed, shaking his head. "You must be God's most disgusting creature. You know that, right?"

Gwen grunted twice before lifting a trembling hand and flipping him off.

⤳

Mer turned the blue Honda Prelude into the gas station lot and pulled up in front of the convenience store. Next to him was a burnt-orange Nissan Xterra. Jason, Theo, Dustin, and

Brad stood in front of the SUV, laughing, hitting each other, and eating snacks.

Mer stepped out. The cold air slapped his face, instantly turning the tip of his nose red. He walked up to the group.

Jason folded his arms, a stick of beef jerky hanging from his mouth. "If it isn't the cheap-ass noob."

The others laughed.

When Mer got close enough, he smacked Jason upside the head.

"Ow!" Jason winced, rubbing his temple.

"What the hell was that?!" Mer snapped.

Jason's voice took on a defensive whine. "You told us to act like we didn't know each other."

"I said act like we don't know each other, not act like a complete dingleberry."

"I was acting, bro!"

"Yeah. Like a dingleberry."

"You were acting like a dick back there," Dustin added.

Jason turned to Brad and Theo. They both nodded and shrugged.

"Hey, fuck you guys," Jason muttered, still rubbing his head. "You don't know me."

"Look," Theo said, "we're sorry, okay? Jason got a little carried away."

"You want some Snapple?" Brad offered, holding out a half-finished bottle.

Mer sighed and pushed it away. "Where are we with the lines?"

"In place," Jason said. He crossed his arms and gave Mer a smug grin. "Did you get it?"

Mer just stared at him.

Jason laughed. "All talk. Bet he didn't even—"

Mer cut him off by pulling the janitor keys from his pocket.

The frat boys gasped in unison.

Jason's arms dropped. His jaw slackened. "You got it?"

"Do you know who those keys belong to?" Dustin asked, wide-eyed.

Mer's face twisted. "What's your major, Mr. Obvious?"

"Uh… pre-med."

Mer rolled his eyes. "Of course it is. Gentlemen, the lines. Where are they?"

"Chill out, OK?" Jason said. "Like I said, they're in place. RadioShack, Circuit City…" He scratched his chin, looking at the sky. "What was the other one?"

Mer's eyes widened. He planted his hands on his hips and stared at the pavement.

"You fucking kidding me?" he asked.

Jason looked around. "You guys remember the other spot?"

The group fell silent.

"From bikes to trains to fucking video games!" Mer yelled.

"Oh yeah, yeah—fo sho," Jason said quickly. "Toys 'R' Us. No doubt. That one too. There just might be a problem."

"What's that?"

"We, um…" Jason said, hesitating. "These boys may a be a little soft. You know what I'm saying? Putting in work."

Mer pinched his nose and asked, "Can someone please speak English."

"He's saying there might be some hesitation from our pledges carrying out certain parts of the plan."

Mer slid his hands into his pockets and nodded slowly. "Which part?"

Theo answered, "T-the illegal stuff."

"You mean the part that matters?" Mer snapped.

The four boys stood silent.

"Fuck my life," Mer muttered.

"Take a chill pill, homeboy," Jason said. "They're pledges. They'll do anything we tell them. We just say it's part of pledging and—"

"And what?" Mer cut in, resting his hands on the Xterra.

"It's kind of crazy when you think about it, right?" Dustin asked. "Join Sigma Gamma Alpha by breaking and entering, or get kicked out of school and do three to five in federal prison—for breaking and entering?"

"We have plans to talk to lines. OK?" Theo said.

Mer shook his head slowly at the four of them.

After a long pause, he clicked his teeth. "Fine. Please just tell me they're actually in line."

"We checked their MySpace accounts," Brad said. "They're there. Standing by."

"You hear about that thing they got at Harvard?" Jason asked out of nowhere.

"Yeah," Dustin said. "They call it *The* Facebook. Something like that."

"Enough with the fads," Mer snapped. He locked eyes with Jason. "Let me be clear—we both have a lot to lose. If Braff catches me, he catches all of us. And trust me, he won't settle for just busting up a few frat houses. He'll want a pound of flesh. The only question is *where* he'll rip it from. So, listen carefully: You will *not* fuck me over on this." Jason took a step back, almost tripping over his own sneakers.

"Now get your asses to the spots and make sure those lines are tight."

The four nodded timidly.

"Good. I gotta get back."

"Mer?" Theo called after him.

"What?"

"What do we say to your sister?"

"Homie raises a good point," Jason added. "What if she starts asking questions?"

"I'll handle Gwen," Mer said, walking back to the Prelude.

STAGE 7

Candace stood across from Lloyd's desk as he paced behind it, his black designer loafers echoing on the dark gray marble floor. Her eyes drifted briefly to the desk, where five perfectly lined up rows of cocaine gleamed atop a square mirror. She swallowed hard, forcing herself to focus on Lloyd's movements instead.

He stopped abruptly, planting his hands on the desk and bowing his head as if gathering his thoughts. "Candace," he said with a heavy sigh.

"Yes, sir?"

"Do you know why they call this meeting the Sight Beyond Sight Summit?" His voice carried the weight of someone about to deliver a revelation.

"To be honest," Candace replied, offering a polite smile, "I've never really given it much thought, sir."

"Where'd you go to school?" he asked suddenly, his gaze snapping up to meet hers.

"North Carolina State."

"Major?"

"Accounting."

Lloyd let out a dry chuckle, then leaned down, snorting a line of cocaine with practiced ease. As he straightened, he wiped his nose with the back of his hand and continued.

"Funny thing about making money—it's got very little to do with numbers. It's about vision. Seeing what's going to happen before it happens. You know what I mean?"

Candace nodded slowly, her hands clasped tightly in front of her. Lloyd's erratic pacing and sniffles were setting her on edge, but she kept her expression neutral.

Lloyd began pacing again, his energy building. "The best in the world—grandmasters in chess, quarterbacks like Joe Montana—they don't just react. They *see*. Five, eight, ten moves ahead. That's what separates the winners from the losers."

"Like Tom Brady?" Candace offered, attempting to keep the conversation light.

Lloyd stopped mid-stride, turning to glare at her. "That guy's a one-hit wonder. Be lucky if he lasts another season."

"Oh," Candace said quickly. "I'm sorry, Mr. Lloyd—"

"Candace," Lloyd interrupted, softening his tone as he leaned forward on the desk, "please. It's Adam."

He gestured toward the mirror. "I'm being a terrible host. You sure you don't want to… indulge?"

Candace's eyes widened. She held up her hands with a nervous laugh. "Oh, wow… That looks yummy… But I'm already high on life."

Lloyd chuckled, his sharp grin spreading across his face. "Suit yourself, but you don't know what you're missing." He bent down again, snorted another line, then straightened and wiped his nose. "Anyway," he said, his voice picking up speed, "vision. That's the key to everything. Numbers are nothing without someone who knows how to use them. You've got to see the game before it's even played."

Candace forced a nod, her hands tightening into fists behind her back. "That makes sense, sir. Vision is important."

"Exactly," Lloyd said, pointing a finger at her as if she'd just unlocked some profound truth. "It's why I'm where I am and why some people…" He trailed off, letting the implication hang in the air as he gestured vaguely toward the window. "Well, they're not."

Candace's polite smile didn't falter, though her stomach churned.

"Some people don't know what they're missing," Lloyd muttered, vacuuming up another line. He shook his head and wiped his nose, pacing in a tight circle behind his desk. "We move commodities, Candace. Everything. From the gold in this room to the frozen orange juice in your fridge."

He moved out from behind his desk, and Candace instinctively took a step back as he approached, her heels clicking softly against the marble floor.

"For the past five years," Lloyd continued, his voice swelling with pride, "the Sight Beyond Sight Summit has been a beacon for every major player in the commodities trade. For a cool fifty million, the *who's who* of the business world—everyone from Lehman Brothers to Warren-fucking-Buffett—comes to kiss the ring and see the future. Do you understand?" He placed his hands firmly on her shoulders, his gaze piercing.

"OK," Candace said cautiously, stepping back just enough to break his hold. "But don't guys like Lehman and Warren Buffett have their own forecasters?"

Lloyd let out a derisive laugh, shaking his head. "Not like mine." He turned away and strode over to the corner of the room, where a leather golf bag sat, and A.L. monogram stitched on the side. "That's why…"

He pulled out a gold-plated nine-iron, brandishing it like a weapon.

Before Candace could respond, Lloyd raised the golf club high above his head and slammed it against the edge of his desk. Shards of glass from the desktop scattered, and a puff of cocaine aerosolized, catching the light like glitter. Candace didn't flinch. She crossed her arms and muttered under her breath, "Here we go again."

Lloyd continued to hammer the desk, each swing accompanied by a grunt of effort. After ten seconds of furious destruction, he let the club clatter to the floor and leaned heavily on the desk, panting. Sweat dripped from his forehead as he wiped it with his sleeve and pulled back his thinning hair plugs into a makeshift ponytail.

"I'm sorry," Lloyd said between gasps for breath, "That was… out of hand."

Candace shrugged, unfazed. "It's Wednesday."

Lloyd's BlackBerry buzzed in his pocket, breaking the tension. He yanked it out and pressed it to his ear. "Yeah?" His tone shifted, suddenly sharp. "Rick! Where the hell are you? I told you—" He paused, his expression softening into something resembling hope. "You're what? You're in line to get one?"

The excitement in his voice was palpable. "Well, how much longer is it going to take?" Another pause, followed by a dramatic sigh. "What do you mean two days?!" Lloyd's hand slammed down on the desk, scattering glass shards. "Well, just go in there and *take* one! I'll cover your bail! A night in county ain't that bad—consider it a rite of passage!"

Candace raised an eyebrow but remained silent as Lloyd's mood spiraled further.

"What do you mean they're not in the store? They're *selling* them, aren't they?" Lloyd kicked the desk, his voice rising to a shout. "Then go to another fucking store!"

He noticed Candace's stoic face watching him and dropped to a whisper. "I'm so sorry."

He turned his back to her, his shoulders rising and falling with labored breaths. His fingers trembled as he pressed the phone harder against his ear.

"I don't think you quite understand the gravity of this situation," Lloyd growled into the receiver, his voice low and menacing. "So let me clue you in. The Sight Beyond Sight Summit is this Friday at 3 p.m. Eastern. If your confused millennial ass isn't at my door by one o'clock sharp *my time*—that's twelve-thirty *your* time—I will personally take a hanger and abort your fucking financial career before it even begins!"

Lloyd ended the call with a sharp click and hurled the BlackBerry across the room. It shattered against the glass wall of Lloyd's office, leaving a faint spiderweb crack.

The room went silent.

"Wow," Candace said finally, breaking the tension. "You really love your daughter."

Lloyd let out a bitter laugh, running a hand over his face. "No," he muttered, shaking his head. "She's just a highly intelligent pain in the ass." He walked to the door, pulling it open without looking back. "I need to be alone."

Candace grimaced and nodded. "Of course," she said, turning on her heel and walking out of the office, leaving Lloyd to stew in his chaos.

⌘

Brad pulled into the Toys "R" Us parking lot. A line snaked around the large standalone store, its walls a patchwork of white stucco and dark brown wood. Above the now-locked double doors, an orange giraffe with a wide, welcoming smile beamed down at the crowd.

He stepped out of Jason's burnt-orange Xterra and headed toward the middle of the line. Tents had already been pitched. Two Ford Explorers, one blue and one brown, and a Jeep wrangler were parked near the front, their trunk doors open with TVs hooked up to gaming consoles. Gamers lounged in lawn chairs, furiously mashing buttons. A crowd gathered behind them, cheering and heckling the players as matches unfolded.

Brad passed the makeshift gaming setups and continued toward the right corner of the building. This part of the line was different. Ten young men stood rigid, facing forward in dead silence. Each had "Master Chief" scrawled across their foreheads in black marker. Brad stopped to observe them.

At the front of the group stood a long-haired blond kid with thin-rimmed glasses and bloodshot eyes. He looked like he hadn't blinked in hours. An elderly man in a dark gray ushanka approached him.

"Excuse me," the old man asked.

Silence.

"Young man?" the elder pressed. "What are you standing in line for?"

Still nothing.

"You know, it's rude not to answer when someone's talking to you." The man stepped in front of the boy. "If I were ten years younger, I'd kick your ass."

Still nothing.

"Fucking long-haired hippie," the man muttered, walking away.

The blond kid's face lit up when he spotted Brad approaching.

"Master Chief Bradford on deck!" he shouted.

The entire group snapped to attention. "Master Chief, sir!"

People in line glanced briefly at the commotion, then returned to their comic books and handheld devices. The front of the line, where the music blared and *Smash Bros.* was in full swing, didn't even flinch.

Brad nodded in approval.

He looked the blond kid in the eye. "Executive officer," he said, trying to deepen his naturally high-pitched voice. "Have the men been briefed?"

"Sir, yes, sir!"

"Good."

"Sir?" the executive officer asked, stepping out of line. Head bowed, arms by his side, he shuffled toward Brad.

"Pledgie!" Brad snapped. "I didn't tell you to—"

"I need to talk to you," the officer interrupted, brushing his bangs away from his glasses.

Brad squinted, then gave a reluctant nod. "Fine. Talk."

"Sir, if you will…" the officer said, gesturing for Brad to follow. They moved past the tents toward the blue Explorer. The officer walked with his hands behind his back, twiddling his thumbs.

"Sir, I may be speaking out of turn, but…"

"You are," Brad cut in. "And the whole line will be punished for your insolence."

They stopped behind a crowd watching a thirty-two-inch TV in the back of the Explorer. Two gamers sat in lawn chairs, one with a purple controller, the other with a black one. *Super Smash Bros. Melee* blazed on the screen.

Brad squinted. "Her Mr. Game & Watch is legit." He nodded at the officer. "Speak."

"Sir," the officer said nervously. "We just… we want to thank you for this opportunity, and…"

"Can you pull your tongue out of my ass and get to the point?"

The officer sighed. "We don't want to do it."

Brad grimaced. "What do you mean you don't want to do it?"

"There's gotta be some other kind of hazing—"

"No there isn't! No there isn't!" Brad's voice cracked as it rose in pitch.

"Sir, I—I'm going to law school. The bar isn't too fond of its candidates…" He looked around, lowered his voice, and mouthed, "breaking the law."

Brad scanned the crowd, then grabbed the officer by the arm and pulled him toward a green Jeep Wrangler. A twenty-four-inch TV blared an *NBA 2K* game from its open trunk. The Neptunes thumped through the speakers. The players used Dreamcast controllers.

"Kobe!" someone yelled, just before a digital Kobe drained a three. The crowd erupted.

Brad leaned in. "I get that you're scared. But you're not going to get caught."

"How do you know that?"

Brad whispered, "Mer got the key."

The officer's jaw dropped. Brad smiled, then said, "I know. Shit just got real."

"He's gonna kill us."

"He won't," Brad said, weaving through the crowd. "As long as we don't chicken out."

They reached the brown Ford Explorer. Brad turned and pointed. "Just be in position when you get the call."

They both looked over at a plasma TV. A girl in a white hoodie with dragon balls stitched onto the front paced in front of the screen.

"No one wants none of this?" she shouted. The crowd stayed silent. "Are you not entertained?!"

She dropped into her chair, picked up a black PlayStation 2 controller, and muttered, "Bitch asses."

"Hard to beat a good Marshall Law," Brad said. He grabbed the officer and led him away from the crowd.

"Look, we're in it. No backing out now. The people we're dealing with…" He saw the fear in the officer's eyes. "We gotta see this through."

"Okay, but—"

"Your job is to keep the others in line."

"Okay, but—"

"Keep the pledges on ice. Wait for further instructions. Can you do that?"

The officer hesitated. "I don't know."

Brad stepped closer. "Keep the other pledges on ice. Right?"

The officer sighed and nodded. "Yes, sir."

"Good. I'm going to unlock the back door. Once the other pledges are in check, guard it. Make sure no one knows it's open. Last thing we need is someone finding it before we're ready."

"Wait… are the consoles already inside?"

Brad smirked. "Can I count on you, pledge?"

The executive officer nodded. "Yes sir, Master Chief, sir."

᷍

STAGE 8

RICK LEANED AGAINST the rough brick wall of the Big K, observing the chaotic scene unfolding in front of him. The sidewalk was illuminated by the flickering light from the large TV screen, on which Jason and his entourage continued their never-ending *Street Fighter Alpha* tournament. Nearby, Theo kneeled on the ground, wrestling with a black chest he'd dragged into the open, pulling out long metal rods and fumbling with them awkwardly.

Jason glanced at Theo between rounds, laughing as he pounded on his controller. "What's the ETA on that tent, T-Money?" Jason asked, his focus still on the screen.

Theo hesitated, holding up two metal rods that refused to fit together. "I don't know," he said, his voice low. "This seems kinda complicated. I've never—"

"Camped?" Jason interrupted, grinning as the game announcer declared another victory: "You WIN!" Jason smirked, tossed his controller onto the lawn chair, and stood up. He glanced at his freckled opponent, who looked frustrated. "You suck," Jason said, slapping the controller out of the guy's hand before laughing loudly. "Can *someone* please give me a challenge? That's all I ask."

The freckled player flipped Jason off and walked back to his spot in line without a word. Unbothered, Jason strolled over to Theo, who was now on the ground trying to force the tent poles together.

"I forgot," Jason said, his voice dripping with mockery. "You don't camp." He turned to his entourage, smirking. "Or swim."

Jason and his friends burst out laughing, the sound echoing across the empty parking lot. Theo looked up, his fists tightening around the metal rods. The forced faint smile didn't mask the rage in his eyes.

"Dude, it was a joke. All right?" Jason continued, doubling over with laughter as his friends egged him on.

Theo gritted his teeth. "I'm just trying to get this tent up," he said, voice steady.

Jason slapped Theo on the back, making him flinch. "I'm just messing with you, man! Lighten up!" He chuckled. "Finish that up, and I'll let you grab dinner. What you hungry for?"

Theo sighed and cracked a smile. "I could go for—"

"Cornbread?" Jason cut him off, laughing even harder. "You want some fried chicken with that, Mr. Bojangles?" He broke into an exaggerated tap dance, earning more howls of laughter from his crew.

Theo bit his lip hard, his jaw clenching as his eyes darkened. He stared at the rods in his hands, resisting the urge to swing them at Jason.

Jason finally stopped dancing and rubbed his chin thoughtfully. "Damn. Come to think of it, fried chicken *does* sound *dope* as hell." He turned to his crew, who nodded in agreement. "We're getting Bojangles after this."

Jason wandered back to the TV, leaving Theo hunched

over his half-assembled tent. Rick shook his head and muttered to himself, "What a little asshole."

"You're not wrong," a voice said. Rick turned to see Mer sitting next to him, his arms crossed. "Give me five minutes with that jabroni," Mer added, cracking his knuckles for emphasis.

Rick smirked, raising an eyebrow. "A tough guy, huh?"

Mer snorted. "Tough ain't got nothing to do with it. You seem like a pretty chill dude. But don't assholes like that make you want to…" He slammed his fist into his palm with a satisfying *thwack*.

Rick shrugged, a faint grin tugging at the corner of his mouth. "When I was twelve, I hit a punching bag, split open my knuckles, and needed four stitches. A fighter, I am not."

Mer chuckled softly. Rick leaned forward to see Gwen sitting on the other side of Mer. She was hunched over a bucket nearby, her pale face glistening with sweat as Mer rubbed her back gently. "Is she OK?" Rick asked, nodding toward her.

Mer sighed, shaking his head. "Nah."

"You don't think you should take her to a hospital?"

Mer glanced at Gwen, who groaned weakly into the bucket, then sighed again. "Nah."

Rick let out a sharp exhale. "Fair enough."

At that moment, both men's attention was drawn to the sound of heavy footsteps slamming against the pavement. A pair of mud-caked black army boots came to a stop in front of them. Rick and Mer looked up simultaneously to see a middle-aged man with a shaved head, dressed in khaki pants and a faded KB Toys T-shirt. He grinned at them, holding a box in one arm and a small stack of video games in the other.

Rick and Mer exchanged glances, their confusion mirrored in each other's eyes.

"You guys ready for that Link?" the bald man asked, his grin wide and expectant.

Mer and Rick stared at him, unblinking, their faces blank.

The man chuckled nervously, adjusting the box and stack of games he'd placed on the ground. "Well, I sure am! Can't wait for *The Link!*" He gestured grandly toward the box like a game-show host. "If I could just have a moment of your time—"

"You've already taken moments of our time," Mer interrupted, his arms crossed.

"Time we'll never get back," Rick added dryly.

The bald man laughed a little too loudly, pointing at them with both hands. "You two—couple of Wayans brothers over here. I love it. Anyway, listen, I've got a brand-new PS2 and a fresh set of games right here. You guys play the new *Oddworld* yet? It's a classic. Pure art!"

"Get to the punchline," Mer said, folding his arms tighter.

From her spot on the ground, Gwen muttered weakly into the bucket, "Who needs a punch in the face?"

Mer reached over and patted her head gently. "Go back to sleep."

The bald man scoffed, gesturing dramatically. "Why are you guys in such a rush to hear my angle? It's not like you're going anywhere."

"No," Rick said, "but we won't have to *listen* to you."

The man shook his head in mock offense. "That's not cool."

"You're the one invading *our* space," Mer said, his brow furrowing.

"And we're the assholes?" Rick added, raising an eyebrow.

The man threw up his hands, his face reddening as though

steam might shoot from his ears. Mer, meanwhile, leaned back against the wall, his shoulders bobbing as he stifled a laugh.

The man clasped his thick hands together and took a deep, audible breath. "Guys," he said, his tone calmer but strained, "my apologies. But you're not exactly making this easy."

"Then get to the point!" Mer snapped.

"Oh, you want me to get to the point?" he said, his voice rising, his hands slicing through the air. "Fine!" He jabbed a finger at them. "Give me your *fucking* place in line, and I'll give you *all of this!*" He gestured to the PS2 and games.

Mer's lips twitched into a grin. "There it is!" he said, shaking his head as if he'd just won a bet.

Nearby, Gwen let out a weak laugh, still hunched over her bucket. Between giggles, she managed to sputter, "He gets it!" before groaning and retching again.

Rick nodded toward her. "Even *she* gets it," he said, smirking.

The bald man scowled, his frustration mounting.

"What's your name, chief?" Rick asked casually.

"Malin," the man said, narrowing his eyes. "Why?"

Rick leaned back against the wall, nodding thoughtfully. "OK, Malin, what place are you in line?"

Malin hesitated, his expression darkening. "Forty-two."

"Okay," Rick said. "Mer, Gwen, and me are number eleven, twelve, and thirteen in line, which means as long as something cataclysmic doesn't happen, we'll have a Link in the next forty-eight hours. Why would we give up our spot for a past-generation console?"

Malin shook his head and said, "Yeah, but—"

"Not to mention the going price for a Link console on

eBay is gonna be as high as six thousand a pop," Mer added. "Maybe more. We could buy twenty used PS2s at that rate."

"Just in time for the holidays," Rick said.

Gwen chuckled, mumbling a hoarse, "Ho, ho, ho," from behind her vomit bucket. Malin's face tightened as he dropped his stash on the ground. He stood up, looming over Rick and Mer, his fists clenched at his sides. Pacing back and forth, he glared at them.

"You know what?" Malin said, cracking his knuckles. "Maybe I'm not asking. Maybe one of you gets your ass the fuck out of line before I bust your nose."

He took a step closer when Gwen lifted her head from the bucket. Her light green eyes sparkled under the fluorescent streetlights, her teeth clenched as green bile trickled from the corner of her lip. She pressed her hands against the wall and bent her knees, her feet flat on the concrete sidewalk. She looked ready to pounce.

"I wouldn't do that," she snarled, her voice deeper than it had been moments ago.

"Whoa," Rick said, his eyes widening.

Malin's body stiffened, a shudder running through him. He watched Gwen for a moment, then backed up, his shoulders relaxing as his fists retreated to his khaki pockets. He edged closer to his stash, snatched everything up, and muttered, "You know what? These fine stolen goods belong to better people anyway." He gave a mock salute with two fingers and said, "Gentlemen," then glancing at Gwen, "Little Miss Dope Fiend. Hope you folks have a shitty evening."

He strutted away, his swagger a weak attempt to salvage his pride, as he moved to terrorize the next group in line.

Rick glanced at Gwen, who was still watching Malin

until he was fully engaged with the next unfortunate group of people. Then her cheeks puffed out and her body jerked like she was about to explode.

"Some people," Mer laughed. "Ain't that right, Gwenny?"

Gwen's response was to shove her face back into the bucket. Rick crinkled his nose at the smell of bile and stomach acid wafting up. He fanned the air in front of his face and glanced at Mer.

"You sure she doesn't need to see a doctor or something?" Rick asked, pinching his nose.

Mer shook his head. "Nah, she's fine."

Rick pulled his phone out of his pocket, feeling it buzz. The caller ID read The Lord of the Flies. Rick sighed and flipped the phone open.

"Mr. Lloyd," Rick said, gripping his phone tightly. "I'm at the Big K on 15-501. I couldn't get in touch with you earlier." He paused, wincing. "Sir… Sir… please calm down."

"Rick!" Lloyd bellowed. "Rick, do you fucking hear me?!"

Rick pulled the phone away from his ear. "I'm here, sir," Rick said, taking a steadying breath. "Like I was saying, I managed to find a line. Yes, sir. I did. I'm number thirteen. This Big K, from what I hear, is projected to have twenty consoles, so with any luck—"

Rick grimaced. "What do you mean 'take one'? Sir, even if I *could* just take one—let me explain—the store is closed. It doesn't reopen until 4:30 a.m. on Black Friday." Rick shook his head, his patience thinning. "No, sir, I don't even know if the consoles are physically in the store right now. And breaking and entering? That's… I appreciate your offer to cover bail, but I like my clean record."

Rick placed his hand over the speaker and lowered the

phone, muttering to himself as he stared up at the sky. "This motherfucker…"

"Rick!" Lloyd's voice erupted from the phone.

Rick quickly brought it back to his ear. "Yes, sir. I'm still here." He sighed. "Mr. Lloyd, with all due respect, I wouldn't recommend leaving my spot in line. If I do, I can guarantee you won't have a console by Friday." Rick paused, holding the phone tightly as he doubled over as if someone had punched him in the gut. "Yes sir. 12:30. Got it. Please don't abort my career sir."

Rick drew a deep breath, trying to calm himself.

"Mr. Lloyd?" Rick said hesitantly, but Lloyd had already hung up. He let out a long, frustrated sigh, slipping the phone back into his pocket. He stared up at the night sky, hands on his hips. "This job is going to kill me."

Rick began softly chanting his calming mantra under his breath. "Up, up, down, down, left, right, left, right. Up, up, down, down, left, right, left, right."

"Sorry to interrupt your rosary there," Mer said with a smug grin as he leaned against the wall nearby. "But it seems I'm not the only one out here posing."

"I'm not posing," Rick shot back. "It's just… This isn't for me."

"I can hear that," Mer chuckled, nodding toward Rick's pocket. "Your boss sounds like a real piece of work."

"Yup," Rick said, nodding in agreement.

Mer crossed his arms, shaking his head. "People like that? They only take. Predators in business suits. You can't trust them."

Rick raised an eyebrow. "Great advice. How'd you come by this little nugget of wisdom?"

Mer smiled, his eyes glinting. "Because I'm one of them."

Rick let out a surprised laugh. "You? A suit?"

"Nope," Mer said, his grin widening. "A predator."

Rick shook his head, chuckling. "Sorry, Mer. I'm not seeing the fangs and claws."

"That's because they're both indisposed at the moment," Mer said, nodding toward Gwen, who was now fast asleep. He leaned in closer to Rick, his voice low and measured. "Listen, we're both here for more than just some toy. These testosterone-fueled, pimple-faced kids are just looking for something to play with between their sessions of jacking off to Stormy Daniels. All I'm saying is, we stick together and look out for one another. Deal?"

Mer held up his left fist.

Rick studied him for a moment, then nodded and bumped it with his own.

"So…" Mer said, folding his arms and rubbing his shoulders against the chill. "Got any siblings?"

Rick stared off into the empty parking lot, his breath visible in the cold evening air. "I'm an only child."

Dustin walked from the parking lot toward the line snaking up to the locked gates of a Circuit City. Its red-and-white logo glowed over the crowd, waiting patiently for Black Friday. The cold November air forced him to throw a black long-sleeved shirt over his red Sigma Gamma Alpha tee. It did little. The chill cut through his thin clothes like a knife through butter. He shoved his hands in his pockets, his braces cutting the inside of his mouth as his teeth chattered.

Multicolored tents were pitched along the sidewalk. Many

in line were dressed in cosplay. This group came prepared. Large beach umbrellas shielded round tables where line-dwellers sat playing card games. The music of choice was Daft Punk. Dustin passed one table mid-match—an elf and a dwarf bickering over whose turn it was in Pokémon.

At the next table, Sonic, Knuckles, and Amy played Dungeons & Dragons. A dark-skinned Robotnik served as dungeon master.

Further down, Dustin arrived at this year's cohort of pledges. They had brought no chairs, just an umbrella and jackets thrown over their red frat shirts. They sat cross-legged on the cold ground, balancing cups of hot chocolate in their laps. A black tower desktop was hooked up to two thirty-five-inch "big booty" TVs. In front of the glowing screens sat two gamers, fingers pegging away at black keyboards. Their mouse-pads featured half-naked anime girls with purple cat ears and tails.

One gamer was a round fellow with sky-blue hair and matching contacts. The other wore elf ears, his brown hair covering one eye.

The crowd watched in reverent silence, like spectators at a tennis match. So focused were they on the game, they didn't even notice Dustin standing over them.

"I tried to tell you, Hunter," the blue-haired pledge said, pushing his dyed bangs back, trying to speak without letting spit dribble past his braces. "Karadras is better than Iron Clad."

Hunter wiggled his elf ears and flicked his hair. "How can you say that? The game's about the Space Marines, Sterling. Not the Orks."

"That doesn't mean they're the best," Sterling snapped.

"Besides, you're such a shitty strategist, you could have an invincibility mod and I'd still mop the floor with you."

Hunter laughed. "I don't need to strategize. You don't know how to generate resources." He stuffed a Funyun in his mouth, yellow crumbs sticking to his brackets. "All I need to do is attack."

Sterling wiped blue dye from his chubby cheeks. "You don't know—" He froze. His expression dropped. "No. No. No. No." He chanted, feverishly tapping the keyboard. The other pledgees laughed, their braces flashing under the lights. Hunter took a long sip of hot chocolate and started singing *"Digital Love"* in sync with the speakers.

When the final explosion went off, Sterling stared at the screen, eyes wide, hands on his head.

"How?" he whispered.

"Looks like you guys are having a great time," Dustin finally said.

The pledgees immediately leaped to their feet and stood at attention, hands balled into fists at their sides, eyes skyward.

"Captain Gloval on deck!" Hunter shouted.

"Captain!" they echoed.

Dustin shook his head. "My Transformer line. What did we say? Normal clothes, gentlemen. Normal. No frat gear." His eyes locked onto Hunter's. "Hunter!"

"Yes, sir!"

"Come here."

Hunter stepped around the TVs and stood at attention, just inches from Dustin's face.

Dustin glanced around, then leaned in. "Have the men been briefed?"

"Yes, sir."

"Good." Dustin nodded. "Myself and the other house leaders are at the K-Mart in Durham off 15-501. If you need anything—"

"Sir?"

Dustin turned. Sterling was standing at attention behind him.

"Permission to speak?"

"You're already speaking, Sterling."

Sterling waved a hand. Four more members of Sigma Gamma Alpha stood and joined him, forming a line behind the setup. A mischievous grin spread across his moon face. Dustin winced at the metallic flash from his grill.

"Transformers!" Dustin barked. "Why are you standing? You're supposed to sit at attention until I or another big brother tells you to move!"

"We're past that, Dustin." Sterling said, flicking his hair. "I like that you named us the Transformer line. Did you know Starscream was my favorite? See, like him—and other characters of that… deceptive archetype, no pun intended—we're a treacherous bunch. Not to be trusted."

Hunter leaned in. "Sir?"

Dustin raised a hand. "What do you want, Sterling?"

"Not much," Sterling replied with a shrug. "Just five thousand dollars each and Link Consoles for our trouble."

"We're a brotherhood Sterling," Dustin said. "You'd do this to your own fraternity? You know our future is riding on this."

"I've opted not to give to a fuck," Sterling chuckled. "Consider this my resignation."

"Sterling," Dustin said, "this guy's a fucking gangster. Like, on some *Scarface* shit."

"Your problem, not mine," Sterling said, resting his fingers on his stomach. "I'm giving you four hours to talk it over with your guy. Otherwise, I go to my father. Then the police."

"S-Sterling!" Dustin shouted. "Come back! Now!" Sterling waved goodbye while walking backward, his chubby rosy cheeks jiggling as he laughed.

He and the other deserters laughed and strutted toward their cars. A feeling of horror washed over Dustin. He covered his mouth with his hands, blinking feverishly so Hunter couldn't see the tears welling.

"Shit! Shit! Shit!" Dustin mumbled, pulling out his phone.

"What now, sir?" Hunter asked.

"Get back in line with the others," Dustin said with a cracking voice, dialing. Hunter nodded and rejoined the group.

Dustin held the phone to his ear. "Theo!" Dustin shouted as he hit his head with the palm of his hand. "Shit, man! Oh, shit! We're in trouble."

STAGE 9

"Best character from *DOA*?" Maddox asked, leaning on the bar.

Rick smirked, swirling his tomato juice. "If I'm being honest—like, gun-to-my-head honest—it's Kasumi. All day."

They were sitting at a dimly lit bar, nursing greasy burgers with sunny-side-up fried eggs on top. The faint clink of glasses and muted chatter filled the air, classic rock humming in the background.

Rick glanced up at the rows of liquor bottles glistening like a rainbow against the mirrored shelves. Something in the warm amber glow of the bourbon caught his eye. He raised a hand, calling over the bartender who was refilling the ice bin.

Dressed in a snug sky-blue shirt and jeans, she straightened up, her sneakers squeaking on the black tile as she walked over. "What can I get you, hon?"

Rick tapped the bar. "A shot of vodka. Make it two."

The bartender nodded with a small smile. "You got it."

Maddox raised an eyebrow, his burger halfway to his mouth. "Dude…"

Rick turned to him with a blank look. "What?"

"We're supposed to be drying out."

Rick sighed, leaning against the bar. "I know. But a little vodka never hurt anyone." He turned back to the bartender. "Pour him a shot too, if you could."

Maddox groaned, shaking his head. "You're a bad influence, man."

"Quit being a candy ass and drink the damn shot," Rick said, laughing.

The bartender placed three clear shot glasses in front of them, the liquid inside reflecting the neon signs above the bar.

Rick raised his glass. "*Salud*, big bro."

Maddox sighed, picked his up and clinked it against Rick's. "*Salud.*"

They downed the shots, slamming the glasses onto the dark wood bar top in unison. Maddox's face immediately twisted, his teeth clenched as he wheezed and coughed. "This college life is gonna kill me."

Rick chuckled, wiping his mouth with the back of his hand. "Builds character."

Maddox leaned forward, pointing his finger. "You still haven't answered my question."

"What question?" Rick asked, reaching for his tomato juice.

"Best character from *DOA*. You said Kasumi, but I think you're lying. What about Ayane?"

Rick rolled his eyes. "Oh, come on. Ayane's just Kasumi with a chip on her shoulder and more purple. We both know Kasumi's the real MVP."

Maddox shrugged, taking another bite of his burger. "Fair point. But I think you're forgetting about Tina. Absolute queen."

Rick smirked. "You just like her because of the wrestling moves."

"And the cowboy hat," Maddox said with a grin.

The two laughed, their banter filling the space between them as the bar buzzed with life around them.

"So who's your character?" Maddox asked, leaning forward.

Rick paused mid-bite, chewing thoughtfully. He swallowed, took another bite of his burger, and mumbled through a mouthful of egg and beef, "Hitomi."

"What?" Maddox asked, his face scrunching in disbelief. "No."

Rick frowned, tilting his head. "No?"

"No," Maddox repeated, shaking his head firmly.

Rick sighed and set his burger down. "This guy," he muttered. After swallowing, he asked, "How are you going to tell me who my favorite character should be?"

"Simple," Maddox said, sipping his tomato juice. "You're wrong."

Rick laughed incredulously, gesturing toward Maddox with both hands. "OK, Professor *DOA*. Who *should* I like?"

"That's easy," Maddox said, shrugging nonchalantly. "Ayane."

Rick scoffed, picking up his burger again. "Yeah, right. She sucks."

Maddox gasped, clutching his chest dramatically. "How can you possibly form those chalky-ass lips of yours to say that?"

"She's fan service, dude," Rick said, waving his burger like it was a gavel. "They designed her with thigh-high white stockings, heels, and a scant little dress. Come on."

"Capcom dressed Chun-Li the same way!" Maddox fired back, slamming his glass onto the bar.

"Nope," Rick said, holding up his index finger. "Chun-Li's got white boots and is clearly wearing tights. Not the same."

Maddox shook his head, grinning as he leaned closer. "Shut the front door! You *know* damn well—"

"And may I also add, counselor," Rick interrupted, a sly smile creeping across his face, "that in later iterations—such as *Alpha*, for example—Chun-Li is wearing a very nice tracksuit and sneakers."

Maddox stared at him, then slowly raised his middle finger. "Counsel *this*."

Rick coughed mid-bite, laughing so hard he almost choked. "Oh, man," he wheezed, pounding his chest.

"How's that going, by the way?" Rick asked after regaining composure.

"The law school applications?" Maddox waved at the bartender, pointing at their empty shot glasses. She smiled and walked over, refilling them without a word.

"Yeah," Rick said, watching the clear liquid splash into the glasses.

"I sent them," Maddox said, picking up his fresh shot.

"How long ago?"

"A few weeks," Maddox replied, taking the shot in one smooth motion.

Rick clapped him on the back. "There you go worrying. Bro, it's only been a few weeks! Remember how long it took them to send your acceptance letter here?"

Maddox nodded, swirling his tomato juice. "You're right. It just feels like a lot's riding on this."

"You'll be fine," Rick said confidently, raising his glass.

"Thanks," Maddox said with a sigh.

Rick smirked. "Besides, you'll need an excuse when I beat that ass in *Street Figh*—" His words trailed off as he caught the sudden shift in Maddox's expression.

Maddox wasn't laughing. His face had gone slack, his mouth slightly open, eyes glazed and fixed on the TV above the bar.

Rick frowned, snapping his fingers in front of Maddox's face. "Come on, man, Bob Barker can't be that serious."

"A plane just crashed into one of the Twin Towers," the bartender muttered, her voice trembling.

Rick winced and turned toward the television just in time to see the second plane collide with the other tower. The impact erupted into a fiery explosion, sending plumes of smoke billowing into the air. The room fell silent. All that could be heard were the screams of horror echoing through the TV speakers.

Rick's arms went limp at his sides, his shot glass slipping from his fingers and shattering on the floor. A flood of emotions surged through him—anger, fear, confusion, and pain—all blending into an overwhelming wave he couldn't contain. He swallowed hard, feeling the lump in his throat swell, his vision blurring with tears.

The chyron at the bottom of the screen read: Airplane crashes into towers.

"I'll kill them," Maddox whispered, his voice trembling with fury.

Rick turned to face his brother. Maddox's eyes were bloodshot, tears streaming freely down his face. His teeth dug into his bottom lip so hard it began to bleed. With a sudden burst of rage, Maddox kicked over his barstool, the clatter startling everyone in the room.

"I'll fucking kill them!" Maddox shouted, his voice breaking as he stormed toward the bar's entrance.

Rick wiped his own tears with the back of his hand, rushing after him. "Maddox!" he called, his voice desperate.

They stepped outside into the downpour, the rain coming down in sheets. A chaotic storm was forming in the heavens, the sky a swirling canvas of gray clouds.

"Maddox!"

Maddox stopped in his tracks, his back still to Rick. His shoulders heaved with the effort of his ragged breaths.

"What?!" Maddox barked, his voice raw and broken.

"Don't go," Rick said, his voice cracking. The rain mixed with the tears streaming down his face, indistinguishable from one another. "Please, don't go."

"Why not?" Maddox demanded, his fists clenching and unclenching at his sides.

"Because, man," Rick said, his voice barely above a whisper, "you don't come back."

Maddox turned slightly, just enough for Rick to catch the anguish etched into his face. "You don't get it, Rick," he said, his voice thick with emotion. "I *had* to go."

Rick stared at his brother, the rain soaking through his clothes, but he didn't move. He couldn't find the words to argue—to stop him. All he could do was watch as Maddox turned around and disappeared into the storm.

Rick winced and whispered, "Had to?" His voice wavered as he stared down at his hands. A neatly folded American flag rested there, its edges crisp and precise. His fingers trembled as he brushed against its surface, the weight of it heavier than it should have been. When he looked up, Maddox was gone.

Only the swirling storm clouds and the sound of the relentless rain remained.

"This already happened," Rick murmured, his voice hollow. "I'm dreaming." He tilted his face upward, watching the rain cascade from the sky. The memory didn't align. "It didn't rain that day," he whispered to himself, his voice cracking. Rick inhaled sharply, and his eyes snapped open.

He was back—sitting on the cold sidewalk with his back against the brick walls of the Kmart. His damp khaki pants clung to his legs, and his sneakers were soaked through. The cold rain tapped relentlessly at his skin, sending shivers up his spine. His breath formed puffs of mist in the frigid air as his teeth chattered uncontrollably.

He didn't want to move. His body tensed, each muscle trembling as he wiped the water from his eyes.

When he glanced to his left, he nearly jumped.

Malin was crouched next to him, his yellow slicker bright against the gray, dreary backdrop. A big smile spread across Malin's pale face, and a black umbrella hovered over his balding head.

Rick jolted back, startled.

"Morning, sunshine," Malin said with a grin, his voice chipper despite the dreary rain. "You must be freezing!"

"Where's Merlin?" Rick asked, his teeth chattering.

"He went to get a tent on account of," Malin gestured upward with his free hand, pointing at the black sky, "you know, the monsoon."

"Shit," Rick muttered, straightening up. "He's gonna lose his place in line."

"No, he's not," Malin replied smugly, adjusting his

umbrella. "That's why I'm here. He said he might give me his sister's console."

"His sister's?" Rick frowned.

"Have you seen that girl?" Malin scoffed. "Video games are the least of her problems."

Rick stayed silent, his eyes narrowing as they flicked between Malin's irritating grin and the umbrella shielding him from the cold rain.

"You mind sharing that umbrella?" Rick asked flatly.

"You mind giving me your place in line?" Malin shot back.

Rick's jaw tightened. "You mind taking a long walk off a short pier?"

"Not at all," Malin said, his grin widening. "Just as long as you catch pneumonia first, asshole."

Rick squinted at him before pulling his jacket over his head with a frustrated sigh.

∽

Mer stepped through the sliding doors with Gwen lurching behind him. He paused just inside, closing his eyes and taking a deep breath. The smell of lemon-scented cleaning products and cheap leather wafting from the shoe department filled his nostrils, and he couldn't help but crack a small smile. The heated department store air wrapped around him like a warm blanket, and the soft hum of eighties pop music playing in the background brought a flicker of comfort. Red-and-green Christmas signs read: OPEN 24 HOURS EVERY DAY THIS WEEK!

Slicking his damp hair back with one hand, Mer turned to check on Gwen. Her black dress clung to her soaked frame, water and mud dripping from her combat boots with every step. One hand covered her mouth and nose, while the other clutched her belly.

"Will you hurry up," Mer said, his tone sharp.

Gwen snarled at him, limping past.

"I don't trust that Malin asshole," Mer continued, keeping pace beside her. "If we don't get back soon, he's going to try to claim our spot for himself."

Gwen groaned in response.

"I mean, I want to shoot that clown in the knee, but it wouldn't be a good idea," Mer said with a smirk.

Gwen groaned again, louder this time.

"Yes, yes, too many witnesses," Mer said, waving her off. Then he stopped, his expression shifting to a grimace. "Wait… is this really working? Am I actually understanding what you're saying, or—"

Gwen suddenly bent over, her mouth opening as a violent surge of bile and mucus erupted, splattering across the polished tan tiles. Mer pinched his nose and scrunched his face in disgust.

Wiping her mouth with the back of her arm, Gwen shot him a glare. "No, you dingleberry!"

"Oh," Mer said, glancing down at the mess on the floor. "Then what were you trying to say?"

"Nothing, you asshole!" Gwen snapped. "I was trying not to puke my guts out in the middle of Sears!"

Before Mer could respond, a store manager approached. He was a wiry man in tan pants and a white dress shirt, his black British Knights squeaking against the tile as he walked.

"Excuse me," the manager asked, his voice cautious. "Is she… OK?"

Mer flashed a tight-lipped smile and clapped Gwen on the back. "She's fine."

Turning to Gwen, he raised an eyebrow. "Aren't you, sis?"

Gwen gave a half-hearted thumbs up, muttering, "Peachy." She leaned over again, and a fresh spray of bile spattered onto the manager's tan pants. Gwen straightened up slowly, her face pale, and gave a weak thumbs-up. In a raspy voice, she croaked, "Right as rain."

Mer offered the manager an apologetic smile, nodding. "Clean up on aisle four, right?"

The manager stared back blankly.

Clearing his throat, Mer said, "Do you mind pointing me in the direction of sporting goods?"

"Seriously?" the manager asked, his voice dripping with disbelief.

Mer glanced at Gwen wiping her mouth with the back of her hand. "I think she got it all out this time," he said with forced cheer.

Gwen, still swaying slightly, shook her head. Rainwater and lavender hair gel was splattered across the manager's face. He flinched, blinking furiously as he wiped his eyes.

"Down that way," the manager said, pointing stiffly, "and make a left."

"Much appreciated," Mer said, giving him a finger-gun gesture. As they started walking away, Mer snapped his fingers and turned back. "Oh, hey, one more thing—any chance you guys are getting any Link consoles tomorrow?"

The manager shook his head curtly.

"Rats! Had to try, right?" Mer said with a shrug.

As they passed through the women's clothing department, Mer's eyes landed on a mannequin dressed in tan denim stretch pants and a long brown overcoat, dark faux fur lining the lapels and cuffs. He wrinkled his nose. "No FUBU? What kind of store is this?"

Gwen let out a dry, rasping laugh, still hoarse. "You wear FUBU?"

Mer nodded with mock seriousness. "Yeah. Why not?"

"Since when?" Gwen asked, smirking.

"Since I started dating Rachel," Mer replied casually.

Gwen's smirk widened. "Rachel who? You mean Amazon Rachel?"

"She's not that tall," Mer said, rolling his eyes.

"She's a *fucking giraffe*, Mer."

Mer gave her a deadpan look. "Now you're just being racist."

"What?" Gwen grimaced, her face pale. "How am I being…" She suddenly grabbed her stomach, cheeks puffing as she forced down another surge of vomit. She took a deep breath and steadied herself. "How's that racist?"

Mer shrugged, keeping his pace casual. "You know… she's Black."

"The hell does that have to do with anything?" Gwen snapped as they turned into the tools section, coming face to face with a life-size cardboard Bob Vila. The cutout, sporting a tool belt and a warm smile, stood tall near a display of power drills.

Mer pointed at the cutout and grinned. "Gotta love that guy."

"You didn't answer my question!" Gwen shot back, her voice rising.

Mer waved her off. "If you can't see how calling a tall Black woman a giraffe might be offensive, I don't know what to tell you."

"*Oy, gevalt!*" Gwen groaned, rubbing her forehead. "This generation. I swear, ten years from now, people are gonna call you racist just for eating a damn chocolate bar."

"*Oy, gevalt?*" Mer echoed, raising an eyebrow as they entered the sporting goods section. "What are you now? An eighty-year-old rabbi?"

The sporting goods area was decked out in holiday cheer. Rows of dark green Christmas trees adorned with white lights created a festive backdrop. Tents of various sizes and colors lined the walkway, each accompanied by mannequin families dressed in blue jeans, plaid lumberjack shirts, and tan Timberland boots. Every mannequin wore a Santa hat, completing the bizarrely cheerful tableau.

Mer stopped, surveying the setup. He began walking by each tent, grabbing price tags and studying them. "Hey, you want to help me here? Because—"

Before he could finish, Gwen swatted a price tag from his hand. She stepped in front of him, her eyes glassy and her smile unsettling, like she'd just swallowed another mouthful of bile.

"What?" Mer asked, narrowing his eyes.

"First," Gwen said, holding up a finger, "I take offense to you calling me a racist."

Mer rolled his eyes. "I didn't call you a racist. I said—"

"Second," Gwen interrupted, holding up a second finger, "you're a liar."

Mer laughed nervously, looking up at the ceiling. "What are you even talking about?"

Gwen's smile grew sharper. "Because Rachel—or Amazon Rachel, as we all call her—would never wear FUBU. Rachel is a proud member of the *Young Black Republicans of Durham*. She only wears Abercrombie & Fitch and is a die-hard fan of Hootie & the Blowfish."

Mer stared at her blank expression.

"That doesn't mean anything," he said, shaking his head.

"See?" Gwen nodded, her tone turning smug. "This is your problem. You lie. *Pathologically*. Make all these big promises…"

Mer hissed through his teeth and brushed past her, continuing to inspect the price tags on the tents.

"Daddy told you your heist ideas were terrible," Gwen said, crossing her arms.

Mer's shoulders tensed as he turned to glare at her. "I swear, Gwen. You're this close to getting left behind in this tent section."

"He thinks all my ideas are bad."

"Because they *are*!" Gwen shot back.

Mer stopped in his tracks and turned to face her. "If you thought they were such bad ideas, why the hell did you follow me?"

Gwen looked away, her gaze falling to the floor. She let out a long sigh, her voice softening. "You know why."

"Daddy's little junkie," Mer said, his tone sharp.

"Cut me s-s-some slack, asshole," Gwen snapped through clenched teeth. "I'm trying to get clean."

Mer shook his head, crouching beside a blue tent with black seams. It was shaped like an igloo and looked big enough to fit two people comfortably. He flipped the price tag over and winced. "Damn. Since when did camping get so expensive?"

"W-w-what's that supposed to mean?" Gwen asked, folding her arms.

Mer stood up, fixing her with a hard stare. Her red, tired

eyes met his. "It means, as we speak, Pop is making plans to put us in an early grave, and of all the times in the world to give up heroin, *this* is when you decide to get clean? I need a functional junkie! Not some sobering basket case."

Gwen's teeth chattered, her body shivering violently. Sweat dripped from her forehead. She closed her eyes and shook her head like a leaf in the wind. "I-it's n-n-nothing," she stammered.

"The hell do you mean, 'It's nothing?'" Mer asked, his voice rising. "Look at you! What the fuck is *this*?"

"It's w-w-withdrawal," Gwen said, waving a trembling hand dismissively. "Just c-c-continue."

"See?" Mer snapped, throwing his hands in the air. "T-t-t-this is what I'm talking about!" he said, mocking her. "How long is this *meshugana* going to last?"

Gwen's shoulders trembled as she shrugged. "I-I d-don't know!"

"Great!" Mer threw up his hands. "How do you think you can even hold a gun like this?"

Gwen's red-rimmed eyes hardened as she glared at her brother. Her voice dropped to a deep, steady tone, cutting through the tension. "What's your plan?"

Mer smirked, lifting the tent flap. "Simple," he said. "We wait until every one of those virgins has a console in their hands. Then we bring in the boys with three vans, stash the goods at that rental garage down the road. When those nerds walk out looking like they just hit the jackpot, we stick 'em up, and take the merchandise."

"T-t-throw the consoles in the v-v-van," Gwen stammered, her arms wrapped tightly around herself as violent shivers wracked her body.

"Then park 'em at the nearest storage center," Mer replied smoothly.

Gwen shut her eyes, pressing her lips together, trying to steady herself. After a moment, she forced out, "H-h-how…"

"How many can we grab before we make a run for it?"

Gwen nodded weakly.

"If there are five of us," he continued, "we each stick up six kids—"

"That's a terrible fucking idea!" Gwen snapped, shaking her head.

Mer frowned. "No, it isn't!"

"Basehead," Gwen scoffed. "Even if you manage to wrangle your so-called unicorn crew"—she made air quotes, her fingers stiff from the cold—"even if you can keep them from running away, how the hell do you plan to control a crowd of more than thirty people? In broad daylight? Outside?"

"I don't know!" Mer snapped. "Okay? But it's gonna have to do if Plan A fails."

"The hell's Plan A?" Gwen asked.

Mer sighed, digging into his pocket.

Gwen's eyes widened. She inhaled sharply, her stomach plummeting. Her eyes narrowed on the janitor keys dangling from Mer's fingers. "Is that what I think it is?"

Mer nodded.

"He's gonna kill us," she whispered.

"He won't if the money's right," Mer said, tucking the keys back into his coat.

Gwen exhaled, rubbing her temples. "OK…" She took a deep breath, steadying herself. "Let's say we don't do Plan A— because it's fucking suicidal. We move to Plan B. The one you just pitched. And your f-friend?"

"Who?"

"The one next to us."

"Oh." Mer's expression shifted slightly, a flicker of something unreadable in his dark eyes. Then a slow, wide grin spread across his face. "I like that kid. Stand-up guy. Just trying to make a living." His grin widened, his teeth flashing in the dim light. "But he gets it all the same."

Gwen swallowed hard. "N-nothing personal?"

"Just the law of the jungle," Mer said, his voice low and final. Mer felt a buzz in his pants pocket. He pulled out his cell phone and brought it close to his ear. "Yeah," Mer said, frowning. "Theo… Theo, slow down. They did what?!"

"What's going on?" Gwen asked. Mer shook his head.

"Listen," Mer said. "You said Brad works at North Gate Mall, right? Good. Set up a meeting with them. Theo. No. I'm not killing anyone, buddy. I just want to talk. OK. Meet you at the mall in twenty minutes." Mer stuffed the phone back in his pocket. He looked at Gwen and said, "I gotta go."

"Where?" Gwen asked.

"Get Dad's canines off of us."

"You want me to go?"

"No, stay here and find a tent. I'll pick you up at the front in an hour." Mer said. He started walking toward the exit and turned around. "Question."

"What's up?"

"The gun. It's still in the glove compartment, right?" Gwen nodded. Mer nodded and rushed out.

❧

"You leaving already, Ms. Candace?" the front desk security guard asked.

Candace smiled as she slipped on her dark blue peacoat and scarf. "I can only have so much fun in one day." Her brown high heels echoed against the dark blue hardwood floor in the vast, empty foyer.

As she adjusted her coat, her eyes drifted toward the janitor at the far end of the reception area, methodically buffing the floor. The sharp scent of pine cleaner filled the air.

"You working tomorrow?" she asked, nodding toward him.

The old guard chuckled, shaking his head. "Who, me?" He looked around dramatically before pointing at himself. "You mean this guy? Ha! No, ma'am. Tomorrow's Thanksgiving, and I'll be babysitting my grandbabies."

Candace raised an eyebrow. "Babysitting?"

The guard let out a tired sigh. "Their parents are spending the holiday out in the cold and rain, trying to get 'em that new video toy thing they keep talking about on the news."

"The Link?" she asked.

"That's the one!" The guard scoffed, crossing his arms. "Gonna waste a whole night camping out just to get my spoiled grandkids yet another toy they don't need." He shook his head. "My wife says she'll bring 'em a plate, but me? I say let those dummies starve!"

Candace let out a warm chuckle. "Ooh, you are wrong for that."

The guard grinned. "Anyway, you have yourself a lovely Thanksgiving, darling."

Candace smiled. "You, too." She felt a vibration, then pulled her cellphone from her pocket, and looked at the phone number on the screen: Prince of Darkness. Candace closed her eyes and mouthed, "Shit."

"It never ends does it?" the guard said, shaking his head.

"Nope," Candace said pursing her lips. "Never friggin' ends."

⟡

Knock. Knock.

"Come on in," Lloyd called.

Candace gingerly pushed the door open, stepping inside Lloyd's sleek black-and-gold-plated office. She kept her hands behind her back and head down, avoiding direct eye contact.

"Sir?" she asked.

Lloyd glanced up, momentarily surprised. "Oh, Candace. It's you."

Who else would it be, asshole? You summoned me.

"Please," he said, gesturing toward the black leather couch beside the gold-plated bar.

Candace crossed the room, smoothing the back of her dark tan skirt before sitting.

Lloyd exhaled, running a hand through his hair. "I want to apologize for earlier."

Candace forced a polite smile. "It's fine, sir."

"No, it's not." Lloyd shook his head. "I was taking my frustrations out on you, and that wasn't fair. For that, I do apologize."

Candace nodded, keeping her expression demure.

"Can I offer you a drink?" Lloyd asked, then smirked. "A legal refreshment this time?"

"No, thank you, sir." She shook her head.

"Aw, come on." Lloyd pouted, reaching for the bar. "You're really gonna make me drink alone on the eve of turkey-and-football day?"

Candace sighed, side-eyeing him before glancing at the liquor bottles.

"I make a mean gin and tonic," he added.

She rolled her eyes but gave a small nod.

"That's my girl." Lloyd grinned, grabbing two tumblers and dropping in the ice. "I knew there was a reason I hired you."

He filled both glasses, pouring the gin and tonic simultaneously.

Candace raised a brow. "I assumed because my ex-husband put in a good word for me."

Lloyd scoffed. "What? No." He frowned. "I get hiring requests all the time. Half the time I ignore them because the people are useless." He squeezed fresh lime wedges over the drinks. "The other half, I do it as leverage—an angle to get something from somebody. Even then, they're still useless."

He mixed the drinks with a wooden stirrer, handing one to Candace. Then he sat beside her on the sofa.

"But you," Lloyd said, raising his glass. "You, my friend, are *not* useless."

Candace felt warmth rise to her cheeks. She looked down, smiling. "Well…"

"No, I mean it." Lloyd shook his head. "You're a hard worker. You're sharp, and you keep up with some of my most seasoned employees when it comes to the market. The only reason I haven't offered you a financier internship yet is because HR hasn't greenlit another internship spot. That's why you're working as my secretary. But when they do?" He raised his glass. "You're up, kiddo."

Candace's lips curled into a wide grin. She tucked a stray black strand of hair behind her ear.

"Thank you so much, sir," she said, her gaze dropping to the floor.

Lloyd lifted his glass. "To success?"

Candace lightly clinked hers against his. "To success."

They each took a sip, setting their glasses down on the sleek black-and-gold coffee table, the yin-yang design etched into its surface gleaming under the light.

Candace coughed, laughing and clearing her throat at the same time.

"You OK?" Lloyd chuckled, patting her back.

Candace nodded, coughing lightly, then inhaling a steady breath.

"Good." His hand lingered for a second, rubbing slow circles against her back before he finally pulled away.

"You know who you remind me of?" Lloyd mused, studying her.

Candace shook her head. "No, sir."

"My wife," he said with a wry laugh. "Well… my wife five years ago."

"Is that so?" Candace asked, keeping her tone neutral.

"You're Oriental too, right?" Lloyd said casually.

Candace's stomach twisted.

She winced. "Wow. Didn't know we were still using that one. My dad's Italian American; my mom's Korean."

"Close!" Lloyd snapped his fingers. "To be honest, I thought you were half Jap."

The words hit like a gut punch, making Candace's head tilt slightly.

"Wow," she said flatly. "You talk like—"

"Like what?" Lloyd interrupted, taking another sip of his drink.

"Like… a man who's lived through a lot." Candace forced a smile.

Lloyd smirked, setting his glass down and leaning in. "Oh, but I have," he murmured.

His hand slid onto her knee. Candace's entire body tensed. A chill rushed up her spine, the fine hairs on her arms standing on end.

"I've lived a lot. Seen a lot." His gaze locked onto hers, his fingers pressing just slightly against her knee. "I could teach you a lot… if you'd let me."

A slow, devious grin spread across his face. "I don't know if you've noticed, but I've got a thing for Asians."

Candace's stomach churned. Her lips pressed together, her breath caught in her chest. Three slow blinks. She shot up from the couch.

"Whoa," she said, folding her arms tightly across her chest.

Lloyd's smirk faltered. "What?"

"Mr. Lloyd—sorry, Adam," she corrected, her voice steady but clipped. "I just want to thank you for the time and faith you've invested in me." She exhaled sharply. "I don't know what signal I may have given off, and if I did, I sincerely apologize, but—"

You're fucking disgusting.

"I'm fresh off a divorce, and there is absolutely no way— now or in the foreseeable future—that I could see myself with anyone."

She shut her eyes for a moment, inhaling. "Even a man as … sage, as tempered, as you."

Lloyd stared at her, his expression blank, the muscle in his jaw ticking. He poked the inside of his cheek with his tongue, finally saying, "OK."

"Adam?" Candace prompted.

Lloyd's tone was eerily calm. "Yes." Slowly, he got up, clasping his hands together. "I understand," he said, nodding once. "You want a purely professional, platonic work environment." He started walking toward his desk, his movements deliberate. "I get it." He held up his hands in mock surrender.

Candace let out a quiet breath, pressing a hand to her chest. Relief washed over her. "Thanks, sir," Candace said, scratching her scalp. "Trust me, I'm a mess."

"Uh-huh," Lloyd muttered, pressing a button on his desk.

Candace laughed lightly. "You wouldn't want to date me right now."

"Sure." Lloyd nodded, then suddenly snapped his fingers. "Hey, how about a little feedback time?"

Candace frowned, her body tensing. "OK…?" she said slowly.

Lloyd clapped his hands together. "Great." He scratched the side of his clean-shaven face. "First and foremost, I wouldn't change a thing about what I said earlier. I think you're talented as hell."

Candace smiled hesitantly.

"I do think, though…" Lloyd trailed off, staring at his desk, his tone shifting. "Your clothing can be a bit… provocative."

Candace's expression hardened. "I'm sorry?"

Lloyd nodded. "Yeah. Don't get me wrong—you're always professional. But sometimes, me and the guys… well, we don't know if you're coming in here to work or getting ready to do a spread for *FHM* magazine."

Candace's head snapped back as if slapped. She let out a sharp scoff. "Adam, I—"

"It's *Mr. Lloyd*, Candace." His voice turned cool, authoritative. "See that? These mixed signals. Are you doing that with the other guys too?"

Candace's arms dropped to her sides, her mouth slack.

Lloyd shook his head, sighing. "No, no, Candace. I'm married. *Happily* married." He leaned back, gesturing vaguely. "A lot of my guys here are in committed relationships, and I can't have you on my desk if this is the way you're going to present yourself in my company."

Candace stared at him, her vision blurring slightly. The floor beneath her felt unsteady, her stomach twisting as though she were in freefall. Lloyd's words buzzed in her ears, hollow and distant. She slowly raised her hands, her voice trembling. "So… so what? You're taking me off your desk?"

A venomous smile slithered across Lloyd's face. "No, Candace." His tone was almost amused.

The door creaked open behind her. Candace turned, her breath hitching. Two security guards dressed in black stepped inside. One of them carried a brown cardboard box. Her entire body locked up. The room seemed to shrink around her, the edges blurring as tears welled in her eyes.

Lloyd leaned back in his chair, watching her unravel with quiet satisfaction. "I'm taking you out of my office."

Candace barely registered the words before Lloyd turned to the guards. "Give her fifteen to pack her shit."

Her breath came in short, shallow gasps as she stared at him. He was already undoing his tie and picking up his golden phone, his expression shifting effortlessly, like the last five minutes had never happened. A deep, rumbling laugh left his throat as he greeted whoever was on the other end, launching into casual conversation while Candace stood there, her world collapsing around her.

STAGE 10

"W‍HAT'S TAKING HIM so long?" Sterling asked.

He and the other four deserters from Sigma Gamma Alpha stood outside a Suncoast Video, kicking around a red-yellow-and-green hacky sack. They passed it in a circle, the only sounds in the empty mall the slap of the ball against sneakers and the squeak of rubber soles on black porcelain tile.

Then, the store's metal gate began to rise.

"You jackoffs want to be any more conspicuous?" Dustin called out. "Hurry up and get in here."

"What took you so long, Dustin?" Sterling asked as they walked in.

"I was waiting for Mer to get here."

Inside, DVDs lined the black shelves. The store was dim, lit only by a few overhead flood lights. On a loop, a TV played clips from *Spider-Man 2*.

"You seen *this* yet?" Sterling asked, pointing to the TV.

"No," Dustin groaned.

"It's okay," Sterling shrugged. "Tobey Maguire's a good Peter Parker, but I don't know. I don't think this superhero movie thing's gonna last. You gonna see *Revenge of the Sith*?"

"Dude," Dustin said, shooting him a glare, "Are you serious right now?"

"What?" Sterling shrugged. "Just because I'm extorting you doesn't mean we can't have small talk."

"No, Sterling," Dustin said, shaking his head. "That's exactly what it means."

Sterling grinned. His eyes lit up. "Yo, you guys got the *Big O* box set?" he asked, pointing toward the anime section.

Dustin nodded, wary.

"You don't think I could just—"

"Please don't. They do inventory on the box sets," Dustin warned.

Sterling ignored him, grabbing the set and tucking it under his jelly-like arm.

"It's cool," he said, flicking his blue hair. "You got my back, right, big bro?" He let out a high-pitched laugh. The other four snickered.

"Matter of fact," Sterling added, turning to them, "help yourselves, boys."

They cheered and started grabbing DVDs off every shelf.

"Fellas!" Dustin shouted, throwing up his hands. "Stop! I was the last to close! If anything's missing, they're coming after me!"

Sterling flashed a braces-heavy grin, the blue rubber bands gleaming under the dim lights.

"Isn't this ironic?" a voice said.

Everyone turned to see Mer and Theo emerging from the back room. They walked up to the checkout counter, facing Dustin and his band of turncoat pledges.

"Funny," Mer said, "I've dealt with criminals my whole life. And I gotta say, you lot are quite the crooked bunch."

"You must be Mer," Sterling said, extending a sweaty hand. Mer looked down, unimpressed, and shoved his hands in his pockets. Sterling pulled his hand back and clasped it behind him.

"You know why we're here?" Sterling asked.

"I do," Mer said flatly.

"Good. So… do you have what we want?"

"No."

Sterling took a step closer. "Let's not play coy, Merlin—if that's your real name." He turned to his crew. "We got you dead to rights. We know your plan. We know those stores already have the Link shipments. What's to stop us from doing this ourselves? What we're asking for isn't unreasonable. Or, hey—you can always run to daddy."

They laughed. High-fives all around.

"I can't go to my father," Mer said. "He'd kill me."

"Tough break," Sterling smirked.

"Then he'd kill you."

The smile slowly drained from Sterling's face.

Mer stepped closer. "Can I call you by your Christian name?"

"What?" Sterling laughed nervously.

"Sterling's your line name, right? Based on some cartoon from the eighties or something. Right, Theo?"

"*Robotech*," Theo said.

"What he said," Mer hissed as he locked eyes with Sterling. "The thing is, Clarence," he said, stepping back, "I'm not into any of the shit you guys are into. Cartoons, video games—it's all just too weird for me, you know?"

Mer started pulling DVDs from a shelf.

"I'm a cinephile. You know what my favorite genre is, Clarence?"

Sterling shook his head.

"Rom-coms. *When Harry Met Sally, You've Got Mail, As Good as It Gets*—I eat that shit up. I hate action movies. And gangster movies. You like gangster movies, Clarence?"

Mer pulled a pistol from his waist and cocked it.

Everyone screamed. They dove behind counters and shelves—everyone except Sterling, who stood frozen stiff, eyes locked on the gun.

"You like gangster movies, Clarence?" Mer repeated.

Sterling's head shook like a leaf. He opened his mouth, but only breath came out.

Mer pressed the barrel against his forehead. "I asked you a question."

Sterling raised his hands. Tears rolled down his face.

"K-kinda," he whispered.

"You do?" Mer asked. "I get it. A guy like you, grew up in Raleigh. Address: 6207 Prescott Drive, right off Falls of Neuse Road. The high school you attended was a private school—Ravenscroft, right? Both parents, orthodontists. Two siblings, both dentists. Dog named Scooter."

Sterling gasped.

"I get it," Mer said, resting an arm around his neck, sweat beading on Sterling's double chin. "*Goodfellas, Scarface*—it's an escape. I'm like a cop who can't watch *NYPD Blue* or a doctor who flips past *House*."

Sterling whimpered. "Wh-what d-do you w-want?"

"Me?" Mer blinked. "Now you care what *I* want?"

He tapped the gun against Sterling's skull.

"Okay, Clarence. Here's what I want. I want you and your

little band of troublemakers to get back in line and do what the fuck we tell you to do. Can you do that, Clarence?"

Sterling's eyes clamped shut. He flinched with every tap.

"Good," Mer said. "Now, if you'll excuse us, your former big bros have some business to discuss."

"I can go back to Circuit City?" Sterling asked.

Mer nodded.

Sterling wiped his face with his forearm. He sniffled as the others followed behind him, each one glancing back at Mer, who stretched and waved them off.

Once they were gone, Mer slid the pistol back into his waistband.

"What the hell was that?" Theo asked.

They turned to Dustin, who was still in the corner, hands on his head, muttering to himself.

"What?" Mer asked. "We're in a mall. Security cameras outside would've caught any muzzle flash. And most importantly, do you think I'd count on you two *schlemiels* to help me move a body?"

Theo exhaled in relief.

"Oh… so you weren't planning to—"

"Please," Mer cut him off. "But *they* didn't know that. I bet those bums are already halfway back to Circuit City. You could tell them to stay in line for two months and they'd do it. They're scared shitless."

He took a deep breath. "I need a smoke. Come on. Let's get back to Super K."

Theo nodded, then walked over to Dustin, still curled up in the corner.

"Dustin," he said. "Dustin!"

Dustin jolted upright and whipped his head toward Theo.

Theo sighed. "You didn't hear a word he said, did you?" Dustin didn't respond. Theo kneeled down and helped him up. The three walked out of the store, pulling down a fence before leaving.

✍

Mer pulled into the Kmart parking lot and strolled toward the line. Mer was surprised to find himself in an upbeat mood, tapping an offbeat rhythm with his freshly manicured fingers. His steps were light, almost skipping, as he neared the line—until he spotted Malin crouched beside Rick.

Mer's grin vanished.

Rick sat slumped against the brick wall, motionless, his head hanging forward, his body trembling violently. Malin hovered over him, a black umbrella shielding them from the cold rain.

Mer's pace quickened. "Here," he said, shoving the tent into Gwen's arms. He stomped through the puddles, his black dress shoes splashing against the wet pavement. When he reached Malin, he snatched the umbrella from his hands.

Raindrops instantly splattered across Malin's bald head. He winced, squinting up at Mer.

"The hell do you think you're doing?" Malin snapped.

Mer ignored him and squatted beside Rick, holding the umbrella over him instead. "Hey, buddy," Mer said, shaking his shoulder. "Rick, you with me?"

Rick didn't respond.

Mer's frown deepened. "Rick!"

Malin chuckled. "Yeah, he's pretty out of it. Probably a fever. But you can't exactly call 9-1-1 for a fever, right?"

Gwen kneeled next to Rick and pressed the back of her hand against his forehead. Her expression darkened. "He's burning up."

Malin cleared his throat. "I was thinking I'd call if he, you know… stopped responding completely."

Both Gwen and Mer snapped their heads toward him, eyebrows furrowed, mouths slack with disbelief.

"Shit," Mer said. "I don't have time for this!"

"What the fuck do you care?" Gwen asked.

"We made a pact, Gwen. A fucking pact! You don't just—" He glanced toward the other tent, his jaw tightening. Mer got up and started walking backward in the tent's direction. He pointed at Gwen. "Start setting up that tent! Maybe one of these college kids is in biology or something."

Mer sprinted toward the tent. As soon as he unzipped the nylon door and stepped inside, a thick cloud of smoke hit him in the face. He coughed, covering his nose and squinting through the haze. The pungent, familiar scent of weed clung to the air.

Jason, Brad, and Dustin were lounging around a glass bong, laughing through red, glossy eyes. Jason and Brad were still mid-cough, their faces slack with amusement. Dustin clutched the bong, its shaft covered in stickers of different rap groups. A small battery-operated cassette boom box sat in the middle of the tent, softly playing "*Protect Ya Neck*" by Wu-Tang Clan.

Theo was in his lawn chair, hunched in front of the TV, fingers tapping at a purple controller.

Mer cleared his throat. "Are you guys fucking nuts?"

Jason lifted his head lazily, looking around. "What?" he chuckled.

"The fuck do you mean, 'what'?" Mer snapped. "They don't teach common sense at that hotshot school of yours?"

"I told them," Theo muttered, eyes still locked on the screen.

"Dude," Brad groaned, wincing. "What is your problem?"

"Well, dude," Mer mimicked, "it's illegal!"

"Who cares?" Jason grimaced, wiping ash off his red T-shirt. He leaned forward, taking another hit from the bong. Smoke curled from his lips as he coughed, muttering, "Shit's gonna be legal in ten years anyway."

"True dat," Dustin wheezed, slumped in his chair, his glassy eyes locked on the TV screen like he was in a trance.

"Crash dummies!" Mer barked. "How the hell does that help us today? Bottom line—if the cops smell that, they're breaking this up. And I don't know about you gentlemen, but I don't see another line forming anywhere to get one of these fucking consoles."

"I tried to tell 'em," Theo repeated, shaking his head.

Jason frowned. "Who the hell are you? My mother? Get the fuck out of my tent."

Mer exhaled sharply through his nose, nostrils flaring. "Which one of you is pre-med? Or nursing? Whatever."

Jason stood up, puffing out his chest. "You deaf? Get the fuck out before—"

"Hand to God, J," Mer cut in, pointing without even looking at him. "You say one more word, and I'm taking that little black cube over there and bashing your fucking skull in."

Jason's eyes widened. He swallowed hard, then slowly sat back down.

Theo paused his game and said, "I mean, I took a CPR

class, and my mom's a nurse. I don't know how much help that's gonna—"

"Sold!" Mer snapped his fingers. He motioned for Theo to follow him.

The two stepped out of the tent into the cold, steady rain. They walked over to Rick, who remained barely conscious. Gwen was still struggling with the tent. Malin stood on the sidewalk close by, holding his umbrella and pacing back and forth, watching the spectacle unfold.

Theo kneeled next to Rick and checked his pulse. "He looks like shit," he said.

"An astute deduction there, doctor," Mer said. "What the hell is wrong with him?"

"The hell should I know?" Theo said, smacking Rick's face lightly.

Rick winced, groaning as he weakly pushed Theo's hand away.

"I got the flu," he murmured. "I'm not dead."

"There's your diagnosis," Theo said, looking up at Mer.

"So what should we do?" Mer asked.

Theo shrugged. "I don't know! Look, if he doesn't want to go to the hospital or urgent care and still wants to keep his place in line…"

Theo then glanced over at Gwen and said, "Get that guy's umbrella and keep him covered while I finish setting this thing up."

Mer nodded. He got up and walked over to Gwen, who was crouched on the wet asphalt, assembling the tent. He bent down and whispered in her ear. She looked at him, nodded, and stood up. When her back was turned, Mer slipped a hand into his pocket and pulled out the janitor keys. His fingers curled around the cool metal, feeling the weight of them. He cracked a smile, jangling them once before stuffing them back into his damp coat pocket. Without a word, Gwen walked over to Malin, cracking her knuckles.

"Your umbrella," she said calmly.

"Fuck off, lady," Malin sneered.

Gwen exhaled through her nose. "My next response will be an action, not words."

"Well," Malin scoffed, flipping her off, "let me—"

Before he could finish, Gwen grunted and drove her forehead into Malin's nose. Blood sprayed across her long hair. As he staggered, she hooked her foot behind his heel and sent him tumbling backward. Before he even hit the ground, Gwen snatched the umbrella from his grasp and walked away.

She sat next to Rick, tucking the umbrella close to cover them both. Rick turned his head slightly, his bleary eyes squinting at her.

"Hey," he murmured.

"Yeah?" Gwen asked.

"You got blood on your cheek."

Gwen's face flushed. She quickly wiped her face with her damp sleeve. "Good look," she muttered.

Rick smirked, his voice barely above a whisper. "Don't mention it."

STAGE 11

Candace sat in her rusted green Volvo, the engine sputtering like it was on its last breath. Across the circular driveway, past the grand lion fountain, Lloyd's sleek black Corvette sat gleaming in front of his daughter's mansion, untouched by the cold, unlike her.

Candace pulled her thick wool sweater tighter around herself, her old blue jeans doing little to block the morning chill. Her eyes were heavy, rimmed with smudged mascara, dried tear tracks staining her cheeks from a night of intermittent sobbing. She could see her breath in the stale air, shivering as she rubbed her hands together before reaching for the dashboard. The heat was already cranked to max, but all it managed was a weak, pitiful stream of lukewarm air.

She sighed hugging herself, her body rocking slightly to the rhythm of N.E.R.D.'s *PROVIDER*…blasting through the portable CD player resting on her lap. A long black cord trailed from the player to the cassette adapter wedged into the ancient tape deck—a relic of a time when things had felt simpler.

Her gaze dropped to her wristwatch: Thursday, November 27: 8 a.m.

Candace scoffed. "Happy Thanksgiving to me."

Moments later, four pickup trucks rumbled up the driveway. Candace sat up, gripping the steering wheel, her pulse quickening. One of the drivers climbed out and rang the doorbell, his breath visible in the cold air. A servant in a crisp black tie answered, nodded once, and shut the door again.

The driver turned and motioned to the others. One by one, the trucks veered off the main drive, bouncing over the manicured lawn toward a dirt path that led behind the house.

Candace's fingers tightened on the wheel. *What the hell are you up to, Lloyd?*

As the last truck disappeared behind the estate, she turned her ignition. *Whrrr-click, whrrr-click.* It finally sputtered to life. She winced at the noise, quickly shutting it off. No way she could follow them by car.

She took a deep breath, put on a wool jacket, and stepped out. Keeping low, she trailed the tire tracks through the trees, boots crunching against frost-covered leaves. The farther she went, the stronger an acrid smell grew, curling her nose. *Fertilizer?*

Emerging from the woods, she crouched behind a row of hedges, peering at the trucks now parked behind the mansion's west wing.

A loading dock.

Her eyes narrowed. Slipping out of cover, she made her way to the back entrance, easing open the heavy door. A rush of heat hit her like a wave as she stepped inside.

The kitchen was a five-star operation: cooks in white aprons and puffed hats moving in a synchronized dance, prepping the Thanksgiving feast. The air was thick with the rich scent of butter, roasting turkey, and caramelized onions.

"Hey!"

Candace's entire body jolted. For a split second, her mind screamed—*Run!*—but her feet stayed frozen in place.

"You!" the voice barked again.

Candace turned slowly, forcing a polite smile. A burly chef stood with his arms folded, eyes narrowed in suspicion.

"Who are you? What are you doing back here?"

Candace blinked, then pointed to herself innocently.

"Me?"

The chef nodded, his expression laced with skepticism. "Yeah."

"Oh," Candace said, blinking rapidly. "I work for Mr. Lloyd."

The chef arched an eyebrow. "You *work* for Mr. Lloyd?"

Candace nodded eagerly. "Yup."

"And his *Satan spawn* let you in?"

"Umm…" She hesitated, forcing a confident smile. "Yeah. Why wouldn't she?"

The chef chuckled, folding his arms. "Yeah, *why wouldn't she*? So, is this *official business*, or did the Lloyds invite you to dinner?"

"That one!" Candace blurted, snapping her fingers like she'd just solved a puzzle.

The chef gave her a slow once-over, taking in her jeans and worn coat. "You're a little underdressed for dinner—and a lot early. The guests won't be arriving for another twelve hours."

Candace's mind scrambled. *Think, think, think.* She stuffed her lips in her mouth, then blurted out the first thing that came to mind. "Well, I thought I'd stop by early and… help with the cooking?"

The chef's grin widened. "I'm sorry, was that a *question*?"

"No." Candace cleared her throat, forcing herself to sound more confident.

"Thanksgiving is *a lot*, you know? All the cooking and cleaning, all that work. And I thought—since Mr. Lloyd has been *so good* to me this year—I'd come by early. See if you needed an extra hand in the kitchen."

The chef studied her for a moment, his smile turning thoughtful.

"Well, now," he said, tapping his chin. "That's awfully generous of you."

Candace forced another smile, trying not to look as nervous as she felt.

The chef grimaced as he slowly turned, his gaze sweeping over the thirty-person staff hustling around the massive kitchen, each focused on their own tasks in preparation for Thanksgiving dinner. He exhaled sharply, then turned back to Candace with a raised eyebrow.

"*Help?*" the chef repeated, his tone dripping with skepticism. "No, I think we're *good* here. Besides, if Mr. Lloyd was having a dinner, he would've invited you to his house not his daughter's." He squared his shoulders, stepping toward her with slow, deliberate movements. "You could stop wasting my time and just *tell* me why you're really here."

Candace's stomach tightened, her nerves twisting into a knot, her heart pounding in her chest. The chef kept closing in, his expression darkening.

"I-I *just* told you!" she stammered, forcing a smile as she rubbed her sweaty fingertips together.

"*Stop lying!*" the chef barked through clenched teeth. "I got a whole damn bird waiting to be basted—I don't have time for this bullshit!"

Candace's head whipped around, legs tensed, ready to sprint for the exit. She didn't make it a single step.

Something *slammed* into her forehead—hard.

Her arms went slack. Her vision blurred. A sharp pain flared across her skull. The chef's furious shouts faded into the distance as everything around her *swirled* into darkness.

❧

Framed *cartoon drawings* lining the walls. A *massive* 200-inch plasma TV positioned against the far side of the room. Candace's gaze drifted downward. Under the TV sat *every video game console ever made*, each one neatly encased in glass, hardwired into the entertainment system. Candace's eyes flicked to a separate glass display beside it. Inside was a *Nintendo Power Glove* illuminated by soft neon-blue lighting. Surround-sound speakers filled the air with light ambient music, wrapping the room in an almost surreal calm.

Then she noticed them.

Two *suits* stood by the door, their backs half-turned as they muttered quietly to each other. Candace let out a low groan. Both men immediately stiffened. One of them nudged the other, and they turned toward her.

"Hey," one of them said, starting toward her.

Candace's instincts *snapped* into action. Her fingers curled around a gray-and-purple *controller* sitting on the coffee table, clutching it like a weapon. She *whipped* it up over her head, coiling her body in preparation to *launch* it at the first one who got too close.

"*Whoa!*" one of them shouted, both men raising their hands in surrender. "*Hold on!*"

"Don't take another step!" Candace barked, her pulse pounding.

The taller of the two spoke cautiously, his hands still raised. "Ma'am, you need to calm down."

"Calm down?" Candace spat. "You *goons* knocked me out, and now you want me to *calm down?!"*

The shorter guard's brow furrowed. "Knocked you out?" he repeated, confused. "The hell are you—"

Candace let out a sharp laugh, cutting him off.

"Oh, you guys are *so* busted," she sneered. "When I get out of here, I'm calling the police, and they're going to—"

A voice interrupted her.

Soft. High-pitched.

A *little girl's* voice.

"No one touched you, Candath."

Candace froze. Her grip on the controller loosened slightly as she turned toward the source of the voice. Her eyes flicked back to the two guards, neither of whom had spoken. Confused, she looked beyond them, toward the far end of the room. Candace pushed back her sweaty black bangs, her breath still uneven.

"Who said that?" she demanded.

From behind one of the guards, Zelda stepped forward.

She was small, but her presence filled the room. Stoic, her blue eyes catching the halogen light with an eerie sparkle. She folded her arms, the pink glitter dusting her wiry forearms catching the glow.

Candace's gaze flicked down. Sailor Moon's oversized cartoon eyes stared up at her from the front of Zelda's gray T-shirt. Below that, she wore designer blue jeans that flared at the bottom, just enough to reveal the sleek black toe box of high-end sneakers.

Zelda tilted her head slightly. "No one touched you, Candath."

Candace winced, pressing her fingers against the newly forming lump on her forehead. "Bullshit," she muttered, clenching her teeth. "You guys just don't want to get sued."

Zelda cocked her head. "You ran into a wall."

Candace blinked. "I-I what?"

"You tried to run," Zelda said, her voice calm but patronizing. She lightly smacked her own forehead for emphasis. "Inthtead, you went fathe-firtht into a column."

One of the guards snorted. "If we had hit you, lady, what the hell would you even sue Lloyd for?" He crossed his arms. "You're trespassing."

Candace opened her mouth, scrambling for an excuse. "I-I was summoned here, at the, um… behest of Mr.—"

"He fired your dumb athth latht night," Zelda cut in flatly.

Candace's mouth snapped shut. Her arms dropped to her sides. Shoulders slumping. Resignation settled over her.

Zelda slowly walked toward Candace, her eyes locked onto hers, unwavering. Candace blinked at Zelda's intense stare and quickly looked away. Zelda squinted her eyes and said, "He tried to thleep with you, didn't he?"

Candace folded her arms, covering her body the best she could. Her face flushed. "I know what you're doing here," Candace murmured.

Zelda flicked a glance at the guards, then back at Candace, her lips curving into something that wasn't quite a smile. "What ith that exactly, Candath?"

"The… those domes out back!" Candace blurted out, eyes darting wildly. She let out a pained groan, rubbing her forehead. "What the hell are you planning? This is some kind of terrorist cell, isn't it?"

Zelda tilted her head, her expression unreadable. "Excuthe me?"

"The fertilizer!" Candace pointed toward the back of the house, her voice rising. "I know what's going on here. I've been on the net, you know. The dark web. This has all the signs of a…" she lowered her voice dramatically, "…bomb-making operation."

Zelda's blank stare didn't waver.

"You're just kids," Candace continued, nodding to herself. "But kids can be radicalized. Brainwashed. I saw it on that show with the guy from the teen vampire movie—"

Zelda blinked. "Kiefer Thutherland?"

"Yes! That show with the terrorists."

Zelda's lips pressed into a thin line. "*24.*"

Candace snapped her fingers. "Yes! Great show, right?"

Zelda sighed. "Unbelievable thhow."

"Have you seen season two?"

"No."

Candace clutched her head dramatically. "Oh, man! You are missing out! Jack Bauer just—"

"Candathe." Zelda's voice was quiet, but firm.

Candace shut up immediately, sitting up straighter. "Right. Sorry."

Zelda studied her for a moment, then exhaled through her nose.

Candace shifted uncomfortably. "So… what happens now?"

Zelda didn't answer right away.

Candace licked her lips nervously. "Look, I… I get it. You

have to keep the domes a secret. And I probably shouldn't have snooped. But come on; you have to see how this looks. Fertilizer? Massive structures in the backyard? The way those trucks just…"

She mimed an explosion with her hands.

Zelda just shook her head.

Before Candace could say another word, the little girl stepped forward, her movements eerily precise. Candace whimpered and instinctively curled up on the couch, squeezing her eyes shut. Something cold pressed against her forehead. Candace cracked one eye open.

Zelda stood over her, pressing an ice pack against the lump forming on her head.

"Hold thith," Zelda muttered.

Candace hesitated before taking it from her, pressing it against her bruise.

Zelda straightened, adjusting the sleeves of her T-shirt. Then, without looking at her, she turned for the door.

"Come on," she said over her shoulder.

Candace swallowed hard.

"Let'th go for a walk."

Candace and Zelda walked down one of the estate's many long hallways. Zelda strode ahead, hands clasped behind her back, her movements precise, almost rehearsed. Candace, on the other hand, could barely keep a straight line, her eyes darting from one piece of decor to the next. Then her ears twitched at a familiar sound—soft harp music drifting through the overhead speakers. Candace winced and asked, "That song. Is that 'The Legend of—'"

"You have quite the ear," Zelda said, stopping in front of a framed photograph.

Zelda stood in the photograph grinning in a sparkling white dress, black dress shoes, her hair tied into neat little pigtails. A pair of missing front teeth only added to her infectious smile.

In her tiny hands, she held a plaque that read: MENSA INDUCTEE 1999.

Candace's brow furrowed. "Wait… you're a member of—"

"Yeth." Zelda sighed without turning around. "My IQ ith two-seventy. I could beat you in cheth before you even move your sixth piethe."

Candace stared at the picture a moment longer, before shaking her head and continuing down the hallway. Mounted on the walls were Nintendo consoles of different colors and sizes, each displayed like a museum artifact. She stopped again. Her eyes widened at the sight of a gold NES mounted halfway down the corridor. Carefully, she reached out, tapping the console's surface with the tip of her index finger. "That isn't—"

"Of courthe it ith," Zelda said, her tone carrying the weight of someone explaining basic arithmetic. "Tholid gold. I had it made to commemorate the firtht time I beat *The Legend of Zelda*."

Candace exhaled in disbelief, reluctantly tearing her gaze away from the console as they moved forward. Halfway down the hallway, a series of figurines stood on floating glass shelves, each spaced with precision.

Candace paused again, pointing at one of the figures.

"Who's the muscle guy in the orange jumpsuit with blond hair?"

Zelda stopped abruptly. Slowly, she turned to face Candace, her hands still tucked behind her back. Her icy blue eyes locked onto Candace with an intensity that made the air feel heavier.

"If that wath an attempt at humor," Zelda said, her expression unreadable, "you are not funny."

"I-I mean, I just don't really know these things," Candace stammered.

"Everyone knowth that," Zelda said, shaking her head in disapproval before she resumed walking.

Candace exhaled, rolling her eyes before hurrying to catch up.

"Hip-hop evolved in the eighith and ninetith into a permanent fixture of pop culture," Zelda continued matter-of-factly. "Anime will do the thame in ten yearth."

Candace smirked. *That lisp,* she thought. *You'd think with all that money…*

"You an anime fan?" Zelda asked.

"Uh, not really," Candace admitted. "To be honest, my ex-husband was the big nerd when we met."

Zelda glanced at her. "Wath? What do you mean *wath?*"

Candace hesitated. "Well…" She cleared her throat, scratching the back of her neck. "Life happened. We're not together anymore."

Zelda stopped. "Huh."

Candace shifted uncomfortably. "I don't think you would—"

"Why didn't you sleep with him? Adam, I mean." Zelda asked.

Candace blinked. A flush of heat crept up her neck. She glanced down at the black carpet beneath them, a repeating pattern of Atari logos stitched in red and white.

"Don't bother infantilizing the quethtion," Zelda continued, her voice light but firm. "I have an IQ of two-seventy."

Candace frowned, her head pulling back slightly.

"Bethideth," Zelda said as she took a slow step forward, stopping just inches away. She tilted her chin up, standing on her toes to meet Candace's gaze. "I already know the anthwer."

The child's lips curled into a devilish grin.

"You know what you and my mother have in common?" she asked, her voice sweet as honey.

Candace felt her stomach twist.

Zelda's grin widened. "You were both hith former thecretary."

Candace recoiled, wincing at the comment.

Zelda let out a soft chuckle, then turned and started walking again, her laughter growing louder as she waved Candace along.

"Come," she called. "Come."

As they walked down a white-bricked path toward the three massive white-domed structures, Zelda asked, "What wath your intention coming here?"

Candace trailed four steps behind, watching the girl in front of her blow wide apple-green bubbles that popped softly against her face. Candace winced. "My intention?"

"That'th right," Zelda said casually, not even looking back. "You're already fired for not putting out. Tho, were you trying to get thome dirt on Lloyd?"

Candace barely registered the question. The hairs on her neck prickled as she became aware of footsteps behind her. She turned her head slightly, just enough to catch a glimpse of two men in dark-gray suits, thick navy-blue peacoats draped over their broad shoulders. Candace's stomach dropped. She pulled the lapels of her charcoal-gray winter jacket tighter, stuffing her trembling hands deep into her pockets.

"Hey!" Zelda snapped her fingers.

Candace flinched. "Wh-what?"

"I athked you a quethtion."

"What do you mean?" Candace stalled.

Zelda sighed, finally stopping in front of the first dome. "It'th dithingenuouth to anthwer a quethtion with another quethtion, you know."

The two men halted just inches behind Candace. She turned her head fully this time, her breath catching as she looked up at them. They were huge. The sun framed their faces in shadow, obscuring their expressions, making them seem even more menacing. She forced a tight-lipped smile before looking away, her eyes darting for an escape route.

Zelda caught it. "They're pretty big, aren't they?" she said conversationally, tilting her head. "Ethpecially the one on the right. I think Lloyd thaid he uthed to live in Vegath—taking bodieth to the dethert."

Zelda turned her face skyward, thoughtful. "You ever thee *Cathino*? Great film. Clathic. Really giveth you a thenthe of how bodieth just… dithappear out there."

Candace's breathing grew shallow. Sweat prickled her spine despite the cold.

Zelda clapped her hands in front of Candace's face. "Hello? Focuth."

Candace jolted.

"I know what you're thinking," Zelda said, shaking her head. "Not happening. To your left? Nothing but denthe foretht. To your right? The interthtate. But between you and it?" She made a sweeping gesture. "A hundred acreth of open land. And let'th be real, Candace."

She stepped closer, resting a delicate hand on Candace's shoulder. "Do you honeshtly think you can outrun them?"

Candace shuddered. She squeezed her eyes shut, her lips trembling as she whispered, "What do you want?"

Zelda inhaled deeply, her face lighting up. She exhaled. "I want you to thee what we do here. I mean, that'th totally why you're here, right?"

Candace's eyes brimmed with tears. She bit her bottom lip hard enough to taste iron and gave a small, broken nod.

"Good."

Zelda turned to the towering glass doors of the first dome, a brown-black triangle painted across the glass.

"Would you like to thee what'th inthide?"

Candace's tongue darted across her lips, licking at the salty tears trailing down her face. She shook her head.

Wrong answer.

"Let'th try again," Zelda said, a trace of amusement in her voice. "Would you like to thee what'th behind door number one, or…" She motioned toward the two men standing behind Candace. "Would you prefer the alternative?"

Candace trembled with every breath. She swallowed hard, glancing from the door to the men behind her. There was no choice. She sniffled, then nodded toward the entrance.

Zelda grinned. "I knew I could perthuade you."

With that, she pushed open the door.

A gust of warm, coffee-scented air rushed past them, carrying the soft hum of classical music. Candace winced, her instincts screaming at her to keep her eyes shut.

"Candace?" Zelda's voice lilted.

Candace exhaled shakily and, with a heavy heart, forced her eyes open.

"L-listen," Candace stammered, her eyes squeezed shut again. She raised her hands slowly, palms out in surrender. "I haven't seen anything, OK? If you let me go, I swear—I won't say a word to anyone."

"Candace."

"And if anyone—like, I don't know—the cops, or whatever you kids say these days, the, um, five-oh, if they bring me in for questioning—"

"Candace."

"I-it won't matter! Because I don't know anything! Because I haven't seen anything!"

"Open your eyeth, Candace."

Candace shook her head, her breath hitching. "I don't need to. I don't want to. Just tell your goons to move—"

"Enough!" Zelda said, snapped her fingers.

Candace flinched at the sound, her entire body trembling like a puppy caught in the rain.

"Lady, what'th your problem?" Zelda said. "Open your fucking eyeth, or they'll pry 'em open."

A heavy, calloused hand landed on Candace's shoulder. The weight of it made her knees threaten to buckle. She inhaled sharply, whispering, "O-OK. OK."

Candace stood as though she were balanced on a landmine. Her face contorted, her stomach twisting as she forced her eyes open—just a sliver at first, then fully. She blinked. Her grimace eased slightly. Her breath slowed. Confusion replaced fear.

There were no poppy fields. No buck-naked workers shoving white powder into little plastic bags. No cartel-like operation playing out before her.

Instead, before her stretched two football fields' worth of lush green plants, neatly arranged in row, their roots nestled in light brown dirt enriched with dark fertilizer. Workers, their straw hats shielding them from the heat, moved methodically, plucking ripe red berries and dropping them into dark-blue wheelbarrow. Some had headphones on, their heads nodding along to the music blasting from their portable CD players.

Candace exhaled, her gaze drifting to a nearby black-and-red digital thermometer: twenty-seven degrees Celsius.

"What do you think?" Zelda asked.

Candace stood with her mouth slightly open, blinking rapidly at the farm. "I-It's only twenty-seven degrees in here?"

"Thelthius," Zelda corrected, rolling her eyes. "Ew, you are *tho* American."

"I don't understand," Candace muttered, shaking her head. "You wanted me to see—"

Before she could finish, the overhead lights flashed red. A mechanical hiss filled the air. Both men behind them snapped open large black umbrellas,each adorned with the design of a man in an orange *gi*, blue boots, and wild yellow hair.

Then, a monsoon.

Water poured from the sprinklers in thick sheets. The sudden downpour sent a shock through Candace's body as cool rain met the heated earth. The air turned thick with steam, rising in a dense mist around them.

Zelda leaned in close, her voice low but sharp. "Colombia hath one of the highetht prethipitation rateth in the world. The beanth need a thit-ton of water. The thity tried thutting uth down, but Lloyd greathth the right palmth. Giveth them a piethe of the action."

"Action?" Candace echoed, her voice barely above a whisper.

Zelda smirked. "Let'th get out of here."

The four of them stepped out of the dome and back into the cold November air. Candace shivered violently, the shock of the sudden temperature shift making her limbs feel even heavier. Water dripped from their clothes, turning into ice-cold droplets against her skin. Zelda casually shook off her FUBU sneakers, brushing water beads from her jacket like it was nothing.

"It'th going OK in there," Zelda muttered, more to herself than anyone else. "I think I'm getting good at thith. Wouldn't you guyth agree?"

The two men nodded without hesitation.

Zelda grinned. "A thingle cup of coffee from thothe beanth? Jutht thy of three hundred milligramth of caffeine. With numberth like that? Hot damn, we could give Juan Valdezth a run for hith money."

Candace furrowed her brows. "Wait, you're—"

Zelda suddenly gasped, cutting her off.

Candace turned to see an older woman making her way down the bricked path, a black cart rolling in front of her. She was dressed in a traditional maid's uniform peeking out from beneath a long charcoal trench coat. Steam rose from the clear pot of coffee on the cart, the rich aroma curling into the crisp air.

Zelda inhaled deeply, her expression softening into something almost dreamy. "Don't you juthht love the thmell of coffee in the morning?" Her eyes flicked downward—then hardened.

"Dammit, Ethmerelda!" Zelda hissed, stomping a foot against the pavement. "I told you I'm on a diet!"

Esmerelda barely flinched, shaking her head as she placed a silver serving plate neatly stacked with donuts onto the cart. "You are always on a diet, *señorita*."

Zelda sighed dramatically, throwing up her hands. "True dat, true dat."

She started toward the cart, then suddenly paused.

Turning on her heel, Zelda locked eyes with Candace, who was still standing stiff, her body trembling. Her cheeks were cherry red, her breath shallow. Fear and cold had frozen her in place.

Zelda's nose scrunched. "What'th wrong with you?" she asked, annoyed. "I'm trying to be hothpitable."

Candace cleared her throat. "So… you're not going to kill me?"

Zelda grimaced.

"Because," Candace continued, her voice shaky, "my ex-husband knows where I am, and if I don't call him in the next thirty minutes, he's going to call the police, and then—"

Laughter. First Zelda. Then the guards. Then Esmerelda.

Esmerelda clutched her chest, laughing so hard she had to wipe tears from her eyes. The two guards behind Candace leaned on each other, their chuckles turning into full-bodied cackles. Zelda, red-faced, collapsed to the ground, laughing until she could barely breathe.

Candace's stomach twisted. "What!?" she shouted.

Zelda finally stood, wiping the smile off her face like flipping a switch. She walked right up to Candace, looking her dead in the eyes.

"Why on earth would I have you killed?"

Candace hesitated, glancing around at the others before muttering, "Because…"

"Go on," Zelda nodded, waiting.

Candace swallowed. "Because I saw too much?"

Zelda raised an eyebrow. "And what did you thee exthactly?"

Candace just stared. Her head tilted slightly, lips parting in the perfect embodiment of *What the hell?*

Zelda sighed, shaking her head. "You are sthuch a fucking jabroni." She grabbed a cup from Esmerelda's cart and held it out. "Here."

Candace hesitated before taking the coffee, sniffing the rich aroma. The steam curled up in soft wisps. She blew on it gently but didn't sip.

"Tho now you think it'sth poithon?"

Candace glanced at her, then down at the cup. Slowly, she raised it closer to her lips.

Zelda scoffed. "Your imagination getsth away from you, doesthn't it? Maybe chill out on all the Lifetime moviesth."

Without thinking, Candace flipped off Zelda while finally taking a sip.

Zelda snorted, rolling her eyes so hard Candace could practically hear them shifting in her skull.

The moment the coffee hit her tongue, Candace stopped walking. Her breath hitched as the bold, velvety bitterness coated her mouth. She gripped the cup tighter, cradling it against her chest like a sacred relic. The warmth spread through her frozen fingers, up her arms, melting away the last remnants of cold and fear.

Zelda smirked. "I aththume you like it?"

Candace pulled the cup away, wiping her lips on the sleeve of her jacket.

She met Zelda's gaze, her voice barely above a whisper. "Sublime."

Zelda nodded. "I gueth you have quethtionsth about what we do here."

Candace nodded.

Zelda gestured for Candace to follow her toward the next dome. "On to Triforthe Number Two."

Candace kept the coffee close to her lips, taking slow sips. Esmerelda and the two guards trailed a few paces behind.

"Me and Lloyd—" Zelda started.

"You mean your father?" Candace asked.

"Yeah, that guy," Zelda nodded. "How can I put thith plainly? It'sth not that I don't like him." Zelda sighed. "It'sth not really like I hate him either. He'sth…"

Zelda turned around, walking backward now, watching Candace as she spoke.

"A man who dethervesth neither my rethpect nor my despithe."

She turned back around, continuing toward the second dome.

Candace frowned. "That's a bit harsh, don't you think? Especially coming from a little girl?"

Zelda scoffed. "With an IQ in the strathostphere, the only way I can look at anything ith… harsth. Cold."

She gestured vaguely with one hand.

"Lloyd wath finna run the family company into the ground. I mean, how dumb can you be? You didn't even need to go to high thchool to keep that plathe going. Granddad thet that racket up bulletproof. All you had to do wath do whatever the hell the trusteesth tell you to do."

They stepped through the sliding doors of the second

dome. A field of orange trees stretched before them. Workers in blue overalls climbed steel ladders, plucking ripe oranges and dropping them into wooden crates. Once inside, the temperature had dropped. Candace could see her breath. She hugged the steaming coffee cup, soaking up what little warmth she could.

"Why is it so cold in here?" Candace asked, rubbing her arms.

"The Florida and California wintersth have been uncharacteristically cold thith fall," Zelda said, blowing into her hands for warmth. "Tho far, it would appear the abnormally cold weather hasn't affected production thith theathon."

She turned to Candace with a pointed look.

"Although, you interrupted me. Don't do that again."

Candace squinted at the kid, her grip tightening around her coffee. *Watch it, Tinker Bell. I'll throw this hot coffee right in your smug little—*

"What wath I thaying?" Zelda tapped her chin, then snapped her fingers. "Oh, right! All Adam Lloyd had to do wath jutht thign whatever the hell they tell him to thign, then he could go off to Epthtein'sth little island and bumfuck till his heart'sth content!"

Candace blinked. "Epstein?" she asked. "Who is that?"

Zelda rolled her eyes. "You'll know him. Jutht a matter of time."

Candace shook her head, stepping closer. "Zelda, I'm not sure I'm following you. Or any of this."

"You know the company filed for Chapter Eleven? Twithe in the path five yearsth."

"Bullshit," Candace shot back.

Zelda stopped walking. She turned her head slowly, giving Candace a long, blank stare.

Candace frowned. "How? That's public information. The board—"

"He paysth yearly to have that information buried."

Candace exhaled sharply, shaking her head. "That's impossible."

"Very few thingsth are impothible when you're rich, Candace." Zelda approached one of the trees and plucked an orange from a low branch. She returned to Candace, tearing into the peel with her fingernails. Once it was cleaned, she held it out to her. "Go on,"

Candace hesitated before popping the slice into her mouth. The tangy citrus burst over her tongue. She sighed.

Zelda smirked. "I know. The bomb, right?"

Candace licked a bit of pulp off her fingers. "Zelda, your story doesn't add up. This is a shit time to graduate, you know. I have a degree in business and advertising from Duke."

"Boo," Zelda snorted. "Wolfpack, baby!"

Candace rolled her eyes. "You'd think I'd be able to find a job in my field. Or at least an internship. Lloyd and Sterling was the only company in the Triangle that would hire me. For secretarial work, no less. How is a company that has filed for bankruptcy twice still able to…"

Zelda groaned, throwing up her hands. "You adultsth are, like, the wortht fucking listhtenersth."

Before Candace could react, Zelda grabbed her face, scrunching her cheeks together like a stress ball.

"Candace! Look around! What do we buy and trade?"

Candace winced. "C-commodities," she mumbled through squished cheeks.

"What commoditiesth hath Lloyd been blabbering about monitoring for the past two yearsth?"

Candaces eyes darted around. "Coffee and frozen orange ju—"

She froze. Her gaze dropped to the dirt ground beneath them. Her brows knitted together. A slow gasp escaped her lips.

She looked up at Zelda, her mouth slightly open. "Wait."

Zelda grinned. "Thothe dotsth connecting yet?"

Candace yanked herself free from Zelda's grasp, taking a shaky step back.

"This… this place… you're recreating the environments!" Her voice gained speed. "The temperature, the humidity."

"Right down to the insectsth."

Candace stared in awe, her brain piecing it together in real time. "Each biodome matches a real-world location where oranges or coffee beans are grown. You're not just predicting the market—you're controlling it."

"Bingo." Zelda twirled a strand of hair around her thin index finger, her lips curving into a satisfied smirk. "We collect yearsth worth of data, compile it, and feed it to the bankersth before anyone else can even thmell the trend."

Candace shook her head in disbelief. "You really are a genius."

"Totally," Zelda said, beaming. Then, just as casually, she added, "Good thing you didn't thee what we're doing in the dometh a few acres away." She giggled. "Then we'd really have to kill you."

Candace chuckled nervously—until she noticed Zelda's blank, unwavering stare. The laughter died in her throat.

Zelda turned on her heel and walked past Candace toward

the exit. "I like you, Candace." She tossed a glance over her shoulder, flashing a devilish grin. "Like you more than Adam. Thaths why I'm gonna burn the company to the ground."

Candace's stomach dropped. "W-wait. What?" She spun around, trailing after her. The two stepped outside into the crisp morning air. "What are you talking about?"

"I'm not dithclosing thith year'sth information to anyone."

Candace gave a polite, uneasy smile. "What do you mean?"

Zelda stopped walking, and sneered, "Lloyd, like, totally fucked up. That'sth what I mean."

Candace tilted her head, pressing a hand against her temple. "I'm… not sure I'm following."

"There'sth nothing to follow." Zelda kept walking, her sneakers crunching against the gravel. "If you wanna live," Zelda called over her shoulder, "don't follow me."

"Wait!" Candace shouted.

Zelda turned around, her glare sharp and unamused.

Candace held up her hands in surrender. "I-I'm sorry. OK? Lloyd is an asshole. Huge zit on humanity. I get it. But please tell me why you're willing to run an entire company—families, pensions, 401(k)s—into the ground?"

Zelda sighed. She looked up at the clear blue sky, exhaling. "You really wanna know?"

Candace nodded.

"The Link. You got one?"

"The video game thing?"

"It'th not a…" Zelda took a deep breath, pulling her hair back in frustration. "It'th an experience. OK? An experience that I want and detherve! He promithhed me one! He promith- hed me…" Zelda trailed off, her voice tight with emotion. She held up her hands, eyes locking onto Candace's. "Do you have one?"

Candace shrugged, shaking her head. "No one does."

Zelda clicked her tongue and turned around, already walking away. "Then I gueth you don't have a company."

Candace's arms flopped to her sides. Her head tilted as the sheer absurdity of the situation sank in. The initial shock wore off fast. Heat crept up her neck, spreading like wildfire. Her jaw tightened, her teeth grinding so hard it sent a dull ache through her skull. Her hands curled into fists, nails pressing into her palms.

She stomped forward and shouted, "Are you fucking kidding me?! Over a video game?! You ignominious little shit!"

Zelda and her guards kept walking, Zelda waving her middle finger goodbye without a second glance.

❧

"You feeling any better?" Mer asked.

Rick sat slouched in a lawn chair, swaddled in a blue-and-black comforter. His hands were wrapped in boxing tape, shoved into a pair of brown wool mittens. Color was just starting to creep back into his cheeks. He tugged at the New England Patriots beanie on his head and nodded, his gaze sweeping across the spacious, grayish-blue nylon tent with its high ceilings. Despite his clogged sinuses, the sharp scent of plastic still lingered in the air.

Gwen sat cross-legged, cradling a steaming cup of coffee. She had finally gotten out of that damp black dress with matching tracksuit bottoms. The sleeves of her new red-and-black tracksuit were rolled up, exposing the purple track marks, the jagged scars from suicide attempts, the bruises on her knuckles. She stared at them, her tongue flicking out to catch a tear before it fell.

"I don't think I am," she murmured.

"Wasn't talking to you," Mer said. He looked at Rick and said, "Didn't peg you for a Patriots fan," Mer handed him a cup of coffee, "You're welcome by the way."

"I hate the Patriots," Rick muttered, poking at the cap on his head.

Gwen frowned into her cup. "I wanted cream."

"Out of cream," Mer said.

She glared at him, her eyes burning holes through his face. At first, he ignored it, sipping his coffee. Then he finally noticed. "What?" he asked, shrugging.

"It's not my fault!" Gwen snapped. "I was detoxing! I didn't know—"

"Whoa!" Mer threw up his hands. "I never said it was your fault. Chill."

Gwen's grip tightened around her cup. The Styrofoam buckled and collapsed, coffee spilling between her fingers. She shot to her feet and walked toward the brick wall of the Big K. Her fists curled, knuckles whitening, trembling. Then she swung.

The first punch hit the wall with a dull thud. The second, harder. The third, cracking against the bricks, rattling through the cold night air.

The line went still. People stopped mid-conversation. Controllers, Game Boys, and PSPs were lowered in unison as Gwen kept swinging. Her fists moved like she was fighting something no one else could see—something only she could feel.

A chunk of brick crumbled at her feet. A murmur rippled through the crowd.

Gwen stopped. Her breath came in ragged gasps. Her hands throbbed, raw and bleeding. She looked around, eyes darting over the silent sea of onlookers.

"What?!" she barked.

No one answered. The crowd simply parted as Gwen stalked past them.

"Where are you going?" Mer called.

"Around the corner," Gwen said.

"Why?"

She didn't answer. She just kept walking.

"Gwen!" Mer shouted.

"To squat and piss in private!" Gwen shouted.

Even as Gwen disappeared around the corner of the Big K, heading down the alley, the entire line remained silent. From the zit-popping teenagers to the chubby, four-eyed middle-agers who refused to grow up, they all just stood there, exchanging glances.

"That," Malin muttered, still rubbing his bleeding head, "was hot as hell."

Everyone turned to Malin, nodded in agreement, then quietly returned to their places in line.

Mer clicked his teeth, stuffed his hands into his pockets, and dropped into his lawn chair next to Rick. The two of them sat in silence, watching the sun shine bright in the cold winter sky.

"Mer?" Rick asked.

"'Sup?"

"You gonna tell me how your sister became a fucking Power Ranger?"

Mer chuckled, staring down at the concrete sidewalk. "You want the long story or the *Reader's Digest* version?"

Rick shrugged. "I don't have anywhere to be. You?"

Mer sighed. "Yeah… Gwen's always been a problem for our father. Petty theft, running away from home. Your typical delinquent shit. But one night she and her friends decided to play a little game called 'Dare.'"

Rick smirked. "What was the dare?"

Mer exhaled sharply, shaking his head. "Stealing a cop car."

"Bullshit."

Mer smirked. "Nope. We come from a pretty well-to-do family, and with that comes a certain level of status. That means kids like me and Gwen don't look at jail the way most people do."

Rick cocked his head. "And how do people like you look at jail?"

Mer let out a deep breath, his gaze drifting toward the sky.

"Ever played *Monopoly*?" Mer asked. "In real life, jail is bad, but for us? It's just 'can't collect $200.' Doesn't really mean anything."

Rick raised an eyebrow. "Did she do it?"

"Did she?" Mer scoffed. "Not only did she do it, but her and her mean-ass, bad-ass, trick-ass girlfriends took the damn thing and drove it to a Durham Bulls game. That's how they got caught."

Rick burst out laughing.

"My old man was *furious*," Mer continued. "But then my mom said something that, to this day, my old man would have your head if you ever repeated."

"What's that?"

"She told him, 'Think outside the box. That's where the

magic happens.' And my old man thought and thought—until he came up with an idea I *know* he rues that he ever had. They sent her to military school in Hokkaido."

Rick grimaced. "That actually sounds… reasonable. I mean, she *did* steal a cop car."

"Yeah, well, what my dear late parents *thought* was that she'd get a grade-A education and some structure in her life. What they *didn't* think was that she'd end up running with rich girls who were all daughters of the Yakuza, learning Shotokan karate, and turning her arms and legs into fucking *steel*."

"Shit." Rick frowned, shaking his head.

For a moment, the two sat in silence. Rick took another sip of his coffee. "Your mom and dad have got to be the unluckiest set of parents ever."

"Tell me about it," Mer sighed, shaking his head. "Since we're sharing and shit, can I ask you a question?"

Rick shrugged. "Shoot."

"How the hell do you know all this geek shit?"

Rick chuckled. "What?"

"You heard me," Mer smirked. "You don't think I *see* you?"

Rick shook his head. "I don't have a clue what you're talking about."

"No clue, huh?" Mer asked.

"Not the foggiest."

Mer leaned forward. "OK, then. How'd you know what to do to beat that kid?"

Rick blinked. "What?"

"The kid in the tent," Mer said, mimicking throwing a fireball with his hands. "How'd you know?"

Rick cracked a smile, looking down at the pavement. He took another sip of his coffee and sighed. "I, uh—"

A black car swerved into the parking lot. The word *SECU-RITY* was plastered in red on the side doors. Tires screeched, burning rubber streaking black across the asphalt as the car skidded to a stop just inches from the sidewalk. The driver's side door swung open. The group scattered in a frenzy, leaping and scrambling over each other to get out of harm's way.

A man stepped out wearing a uniform barely containing the thick ropes of muscle threatening to tear through the gray button-down shirt. He slid on a pair of aviator sunglasses, shoved a toothpick between his lips already bulging with chewing tobacco, and took a slow look around. Then he walked toward the group.

Malin stormed toward him, chest puffed, face twisted in rage.

"Are you out of your mind? You could have killed someone, you—"

The security guard's arm snapped out like a whip, backhanding Malin across the face. The crack echoed. Malin let out a shrill gasp, stumbling backward and crumpling to the ground, where he lay, out cold.

The guard kept walking. His size-fourteen boots stomped against the cracked pavement like a war drum. People stared at him, petrified. They had all encountered bullies before—just not ones built like tanks.

Mer glanced up at the man, squinting. His breath hitched. He quickly turned his head. "Great," he muttered under his breath. "Just great."

The four frat boys gawked, mouths half-open. Jason absentmindedly popped his retainer in and out of place, nudging Theo.

"Aren't you gonna do something?" he whispered.

Theo grimaced. "Why me?"

"I-I don't know," Jason stammered. "I thought all you Durham guys carried firearms."

"No."

"Well…" Jason shook his head, eyes darting between Theo and the behemoth marching toward them. "Aren't you at least gonna fight him?"

Theo looked down at his own thin arms, then back at Jason. "How?" He gestured toward the approaching brute. "Look at him. He's huge—he's like the last boss in *Double Dragon*. Like the guy you pick in a fighting game just because he takes up half the screen."

The giant finally stopped walking, standing tall on the sidewalk just across from the line. His heavy breaths flared his nostrils.

"Afternoon, the name's Brute," he said slowly. "I know you little weeaboo fucks are in line to get your pieces of electronic plastic, but the proprietor of this strip wants you off."

Brute held up his hand. His palm was slick with sweat. His fingers trembled slightly. Then, a twitching smirk stretched across his face. "Please, though," he whispered, almost giddy, "give me a reason." Brute closed his eyes, as if savoring the moment. "I'm begging you." His hands came together, rubbing against each other in anticipation. "Please don't step off this sidewalk. Please don't get in your cars and drive away." He held up a single trembling finger. "Because for once in my life—just this once—assault," he said, pacing and cracking his knuckles, "and battery," he exhaled slowly, eyes gleaming, "are legal today." He continued. "You know why? Because I'm security, and I just asked you to get the hell off the property!" The giant cracked his knuckles, his grin stretching wider. "So please, stay. Stay in your little warm tents. Do whatever you cheese-faced, basement-dwelling dorks do." His voice lowered to a near growl. "Because if you're not off this property in the next ten seconds…"

Brute stopped.

The line fell silent.

Mer stepped out from the crowd, walking toward him, cigarette pack in hand.

Brute's eyes widened. "Merlin?"

Mer nodded, sliding a cigarette between his lips as he approached. Even standing on the raised sidewalk, he barely reached Brute's shoulders. The two locked eyes while Mer lit his smoke.

Brute scoffed. "So what? You ain't gonna give me one?"

Mer exhaled a slow stream of smoke. "Don't you think chewing tobacco and smoking is a bit overkill?"

"Are you mental?" Brute snapped. "Your old man put a mark on you. And this is where you've been hiding? One of his shopping centers?"

Mer shrugged. "Hiding in plain sight, I guess."

"Dumb sight is more like it," Brute muttered. "I like you, Mer. You know I do. But you're putting me in a real precarious situation here."

Mer smirked. "Look who's been using his thesaurus."

"Yeah, yeah, screw you." Brute scowled. "Your daddy put a bounty on your head, and here you are making wisecracks. You think this is funny?"

Mer took another drag and exhaled through his nose. "Nah. But you know what *is* funny? You, playing mock execution with my old man, licking his boots like some loyal lapdog."

Brute's jaw tensed. "Cry me a river, rich boy. You know the game."

Mer spat onto the pavement. "Yeah, I know it."

Brute flexed his fingers, rolling his neck. "So, what's it gonna be, Mer? You getting in the trunk, or am I folding you into it?"

Mer smiled. "Where's my sister?"

Brute's smirk faltered.

Mer took another slow drag of his cigarette, his grin widening. "Oh, yeah," he said. "You're about to find out."

Brute barely had time to register the words before he heard the pounding of footsteps rushing up behind him. He turned, but too late. A tire iron slammed into the back of his neck with a sickening *thunk*. He staggered forward, knees buckling, his massive body lurching toward the pavement.

Before he could brace himself, the tire iron swung again, this time cracking against the back of his right knee. Brute let out a guttural grunt and collapsed onto all fours, his hands slapping the concrete. He managed to lift his head slightly before the sun blinded him, casting the attacker's face into shadow. But he didn't need to see. He already knew.

"Gwen," Brute muttered, shaking his head.

"Brute," Gwen said—right before she swung the tire iron like a baseball bat, catching him square across the face.

Brute's massive frame crumpled onto the pavement, his limbs sprawled, his tongue slack, eyes glassy and unfocused.

Mer and Gwen exchanged a look, then each grabbed one of Brute's heavy boots, dragging him across the empty parking lot.

For a moment, the entire line stood in stunned silence. The only sound was the scrape of Brute's dead weight sliding against the asphalt, mingling with the crisp whistle of the winter wind. Then someone shouted.

"That was fucking *awesome*!"

The entire line erupted, a frenzy of cheers and laughter. Mer and Gwen smirked at each other as the crowd began chanting their names.

They reached Brute's car, popped the trunk, and with one big *heave*, dumped his body inside.

Mer slid into the driver's seat, Gwen beside him. The engine roared to life, tires screeching as they peeled out of the lot. Behind them, the crowd erupted in cheers.

Malin joined in, hopping up and down, throwing his fists in the air like he was just another excited bystander. He slowly edged his way out of the group, careful not to draw attention. Once he was far enough, he pulled out his cell phone, pressed a speed dial, and held it to his ear.

"What?!" a voice barked on the other end.

"Guy! Don't hang up!" Malin said, rubbing the rolls of fat at the back of his bald neck. "I got something."

A frustrated sigh crackled through the receiver. "Why the hell did I ever give you my number?"

"Because I'm your brotha from anotha motha!" Malin grinned.

"Malin," Guy growled, his voice tight. "I don't have time for this bullshit right now, OK? The boss has his hand so far up my ass trying to find—"

"Would that be Mer and Gwen?" Malin said, his voice smug.

Silence. "How do you know that?" Guy finally asked.

Malin's grin widened. "I'll fill you in on every detail just as soon as you set up a meeting with the big guy. *Capisce*?"

❧

For about a half hour, Brute's burly body rolled limp in the trunk of Mer's black Lincoln. He'd regained consciousness, but when the car came to an abrupt stop, his throbbing head banged against the roof of the trunk. He could hear the engine cut off. Two car doors slammed shut, followed by the sound of footsteps moving toward him.

Brute squinted when the trunk popped open, light flooding in and momentarily blinding him. He raised his left hand to shield his eyes, barely making out two blurred silhouettes, and asked, "This where you're gonna kill me?"

"Shut up," Mer muttered, shaking his head. He and Gwen each grabbed one of Brute's arms and hauled him out of the trunk. "Kill you? What are you talking about? I was at your Bar mitzvah for crying out loud. Stand up."

Brute stumbled forward, his face smeared with blood, which was still dripping from the bridge of his cracked nose.

"Let me take a look." Mer stood on his tip toes, gripping Brute's face in one hand and tilting it to inspect the damage. "Yeah, she broke it."

Brute shot a glare at Gwen and lunged at her.

"Calm down!" Mer barked, stepping in to hold him back.

"You fucking junkie!" Brute spat, his voice raw with rage.

"I ain't afraid of you," Gwen said, scratching at the track marks on her right forearm. "Butterface motherfucker."

Brute grunted, trying to push past Mer, who wrapped his arms around his waist in an attempt to hold him back. The two of them slid slightly on the black asphalt of the empty parking lot.

Mer shot a look at Gwen. "Not helping."

Brute took a few heavy steps forward, still dragging Mer with him.

"You're lucky she didn't shoot you," Mer said.

"Yeah," Brute muttered, licking the salty blood from his lips. "Why didn't she?"

"What do you mean by that?" Mer asked, tightening his grip. "We're all friends here."

Gwen shrugged. "Too many witnesses."

Brute bit his lip, breathing hard. He pushed Mer off him and wiped at the tears stinging his bloodshot eyes. Turning away, he paced a few steps before stopping to look up at the black-and-yellow sign hovering over a small diner.

"Of all the places you could have taken me," Brute scoffed, pointing at the glowing yellow sign overhead, "you took me here?"

"What?" Mer shrugged. "It's safe."

"It's a fucking Waffle House!"

"So what?" Mer asked. "I'm lying low, Brute. It's the only place Pop won't be looking for me. Besides…" He shoved his hands into his pockets and looked away.

Brute narrowed his eyes. "Besides what?"

Gwen cut in, shaking her head. "It's the one place we can drag a guy out of a trunk without anyone giving a shit."

Brute gently prodded at his broken nose and muttered, "Figured you'd be halfway to Canada by now."

"Working an angle."

"You should be hiding."

"I am."

Brute let out a sharp exhale and shook his head. "Don't say that 'plain sight' bullshit."

"I'm trying to make things right."

Brute's face darkened. "Merlin, your twenty-four hours were up forty-eight hours ago."

Mer threw his hands in the air. "He's just grandstanding. On my mother's grave, he wouldn't—"

"He put a bounty on your head."

The words hit like a hammer. Mer inhaled sharply, his jaw tightening. A twitch flickered at the left side of his face, his shoulders slumped, and he leaned back against the trunk of his Lincoln. The tension thickened between them, the cold wind howling as crisp autumn leaves skittered across the pavement.

Brute exhaled through his nose and looked at Gwen. "Both of you."

Silence.

Then Gwen let out a dry laugh, clutching her stomach. "Bring us in alive, right?"

Brute and Mer exchanged glances. Then both turned to stare at her.

Gwen felt the panic rising fast. Her breath quickened, chest tightening like a fist closing around her lungs. She folded her arms and started pacing, her nails digging into the track marks on her left forearm, scratching until thin rivulets of blood bubbled to the surface.

"I-I…" She struggled for air, her voice ragged. "I can't do this. I need a fix. A bump. A needle. *Something!*"

Brute and Mer watched as her panic spiraled. Her pacing faltered, her legs wobbled, and then she was on her knees, vomiting onto the cracked asphalt of a Waffle House parking lot.

Brute grimaced. "She OK?"

Mer didn't even look. "She's fine."

Brute scoffed. "Yeah, she looks great."

Mer ignored him. "How much time do we have before you let the old man know where we are?"

Brute exhaled heavily, pressing gingerly against his broken nose. "I don't know. Soon."

Mer frowned. "Like how soon?"

Brute shook his head, frustrated. "Tell you what. First thing I gotta do is make a trip to the hospital and get this checked." He gestured toward his swollen, bloodied nose. "'Cause little Miss UFC over here busted my shit."

Mer smirked. "She does that."

Brute rolled his eyes. "Yeah, hilarious. Listen, I ain't got insurance, which means Durham Regional. Fucking cesspool. That's gonna take at least eight hours."

Mer's smirk widened.

Brute pointed at him. "Don't smile. 'Cause before I do that, I'm going into this fine establishment of gourmet dining and getting my hash browns covered, chunked, and peppered." He rubbed his fingers together. "Which means I'm gonna need some financial assistance."

Mer chuckled, pulled a fifty from his pocket, and pressed it into Brute's palm.

Brute grinned, tucked the bill into his pocket, and the two bumped fists before parting ways.

STAGE 12

MALIN WALKED BEHIND Guy, flanked by his entourage as they stepped inside the restaurant. At the coat rack, the maître d' stood poised in a flowing black dress. She flashed a polite smile as her gaze landed on Guy.

"Mr. Goldman," she greeted smoothly. "Welcome back."

Her eyes flicked to Malin, noting how he was dwarfed by the five men surrounding him, each easily a foot taller, dressed in sharp black suits.

"Will your… party be dining with you this evening?" she asked carefully.

"No table needed, hon," Guy said with a casual grin, rubbing her shoulder as he passed. "Just here for Mr. Braff. He in?"

"Yes, he is," she said with a slight nod. "May I take your coats?"

"No thanks, hon." Guy waved her off and led the group deeper into the restaurant.

Malin glanced around, taking in the opulence. Crystal chandeliers dangled from the ceiling painted deep blue, casting soft pools of light across the otherwise dusky dining area. Waiters maneuvered through the space, pushing carts loaded with bottles of aged wine. Patrons turned their heads as Guy's crew strode through, whispers rippling in their wake.

All eyes on me. Malin smirked to himself.

The double doors to the kitchen swung open, revealing Braff seated at a table in the back. He faced the entrance, his posture relaxed but calculated. To his left, an open Torah lay marked with a folded ribbon. To his right, a gleaming 9mm rested beside a glass of wine. In front of him, a perfectly plated salmon and sweet potato entrée sat untouched.

Guy stepped aside as Braff's men moved in, giving Malin a thorough pat-down. Braff, unbothered, took his time swallowing a bite of salmon before leaning back, casually crossing one leg over the other.

"This him?" Braff asked, his voice cool and detached.

Guy nodded.

Braff took a slow sip of his wine, savoring it before placing the glass down. He dabbed his lips with a red napkin, his eyes scanning Malin from head to toe. Malin, shifting uneasily, flicked glances at the men flanking Braff—each of them clad in dark suits, hands resting near the grips of their guns, holstered beneath their lapels. Their cold, silent stares made goosebumps rise on Malin's neck. A thin film of sweat formed along his forehead.

Malin swallowed and forced a nervous chuckle. Taking a careful step forward, he extended a hand. "Mr. Braff, Happy Thanksgiving. It's a—"

Braff raised a hand, cutting him off. The gesture was calm, controlled, but carried the weight of command.

Malin stopped mid-step. Braff gave a small flick of his fingers, motioning him to move back. Malin obeyed, lowering his head, his arms folding across his chest as though he were naked in a snowstorm.

The silence stretched.

Braff sighed—a slow, layered exhale—shaking his head as if disappointed. Malin felt the seconds drag, each one heavier than the last.

Finally, Braff leaned back and licked his incisors. "So," he said, his voice smooth, almost amused, "you're a Patriots fan, huh?"

Malin glanced down at his jersey. "Yes, sir," he nodded quickly.

"Oh," Braff chuckled. "Good for you."

Malin forced a smile, shifting his weight.

"You're not one of those bandwagon types, are you?" Braff continued, his tone light, his eyes anything but.

"Who, me?" Malin feigned offense, shaking his head. "Nah, sir. Like the gangstas say—ride or die, right?"

Braff's smile faded. "We don't say that, Mal."

Malin's eye twitched. He stared down at the pristine white tile, his lips pressing into a thin line.

Braff leaned forward, cutting into his salmon. "Funny thing, though—you say you're a diehard fan. You born in New England?"

"Uh…" Malin hesitated. "No, sir."

"Huh." Braff stabbed a piece of fish with his fork, lifting it to his mouth. "OK, then. Quick question: Where's Foxborough?"

Malin blinked. "I'm sorry?"

"Foxborough," Braff repeated, still chewing. "Where is it?"

Malin's brows knit together. "Where is that?"

Braff chuckled, shaking his head. "You know, Mal…" He

took another sip of wine. "It's not the fact that you don't know where Foxborough is that gives you away." He gestured lazily with his fork, pointing at Malin's forearm. "It's that damn Cowboys logo tattooed on your arm that does."

Malin's stomach dropped. He instinctively pulled his hands behind his back.

Braff smiled, finally setting his fork down.

"You know where my progeny are?"

Malin swallowed hard. "Y-yes, sir."

Braff studied him. "And you're willing to divulge this information?"

"Yes, sir." Malin wiped the sweat from his forehead.

"I assume there's a price tag," Braff said, watching Malin carefully.

Malin swallowed, his hands damp with sweat. "W-well, um…"

"Speak up!" Braff laughed, leaning back in his chair. "Guy's been telling me you wanted a sit-down. Here we are. So, tell me—what do you want?"

Malin's stomach twisted into knots so tight he thought he might throw up. He glanced around the room at the cold, assessing stares of Braff's men, at the weight of the moment pressing down on him. He clenched his fists, squeezed his eyes shut, and inhaled deeply. When he opened them again, he met Braff's gaze head-on.

"This," Malin said softly.

Braff tilted his head. "Come again?"

Malin straightened his spine. "I want this." His voice grew steadier. "Your shoes. Your seat at this table. Your suit. Your connections. Your women. I want to be you."

Braff stared at him for a long moment, then let out a

slow chuckle. He rubbed the stubble on his chin as he stood and walked toward Malin, his hands casually tucked into his pockets.

"Wow," Braff mused, shaking his head. "That's a first." He let out another laugh. "You know that saying? 'Give a man a fish, he eats for a day. Teach a man to fish, he eats for a lifetime'?"

Malin nodded eagerly.

"I used to believe that," Braff continued. "I thought it was true every time I said it, for every situation. But today, Malin…" He grinned, a sharp, almost predatory expression. "You have, without a doubt, proven to be the exception."

Malin's smile faltered.

Braff sighed theatrically, shaking his head. "You see, Malin, there are people—hundreds of thousands of people—smarter than you, stronger than you, sharper than you, who have tried to become me. And do you know where they ended up?"

Malin's throat was dry. He didn't answer.

"Dead. Or rotting in a prison cell," Braff said smoothly. "Which, let's be honest, are fates far worse than the parasitic joke of a life you're living now."

He leaned in, their noses almost touching. Malin could smell the smoked salmon on his breath.

"Let's be real here. You don't have the loyalty. You don't have the fangs. And you sure as hell don't have the intelligence to pull off this life." Braff smirked. "And because I like you—just a little—I'm going to do you a favor. I won't give you the blueprint to becoming me, because if I did, Malin," he said, his voice dropping to a near-whisper, "you'd choke on your first meal."

Malin's mouth hung open, his breath shallow.

Braff pulled back, exhaling like he'd just done Malin a favor. "Now," he said casually, smoothing out the front of his jacket, "let's lower our standards, shall we?" He smirked. "You want one of those video game machines?"

Still in shock, Malin nodded.

"Maybe two?"

Malin coughed, cleared his throat, and forced out, "Y-yes, sir."

Braff smiled wider, his teeth gleaming under the dim lights. "Then where the fuck are my children?"

STAGE 13

"WHAT'S THE PLAN, bro?" Gwen asked, scratching the back of her neck.

They rode in Brute's car, pulling into the Big K parking lot. Mer was silent, gripping the gray steering wheel with white-knuckled intensity.

Gwen glanced at him. "Mer." Her voice rose slightly.

No response.

"Merlin!"

Merlin sighed. "I don't know, Gwen."

"You know he knows where we are now, right?" she pressed.

"Yes, Gwen, thank you for reminding me," Mer snapped.

"Then why are you so calm?"

"I don't know, Gwen!" he barked, slamming his palm against the steering wheel. "Maybe because I don't have a next move! Maybe because I'm not some fucking chess master you keep projecting on me! Maybe you hitched yourself to a complete loser, and now we're both gonna end up at the bottom of Jordan Lake!"

He threw his head back against the headrest and covered his face with his hands.

Gwen stared at her brother, her brows furrowed, lips

pressed into a tight line. She exhaled sharply, then turned her head, looking out the windshield toward the sidewalk in front of the Big K.

Music thumped from the frat boys' tent. People stood outside their nylon shelters, hanging their wet clothes under the pale Thanksgiving afternoon sun. The whole line had turned into a makeshift celebration, holding up slices of pizza as they sang along to *Raise Up* by Petey Pablo.

Gwen slapped Mer's shoulder.

"What?" he asked, his voice raw.

"You want some pizza?"

Mer lifted his head, looking out the window. His eyes tracked the communal chaos—nerds, college kids, loners, and diehards bonding like they had just won a football game. He tilted his head and whispered, "I could eat."

The two hopped out of the old sedan and walked toward the line.

Theo's eyes widened.

"It's them!" someone shouted.

The entire camp erupted in cheers. Mer and Gwen waved and smiled, playing along.

Gwen leaned in, whispering in Mer's ear. "So, do we tell them?"

"Tell them what?" Mer frowned. "That our psychopath dad will be down here in ten hours to gun us down—along with anyone else standing in this line?"

The crowd, oblivious, jumped and chanted in unison: "We ready! We ready!"

Rick stepped out of Mer's tent, scanning the scene. His eyes met Mer's, then Gwen's. He gave them a casual two-finger salute, which they returned.

A fellow lineman tapped Rick's shoulder. "Hey, man, you want a slice?"

Rick smiled, shaking his head. "No thanks. It's a Gatorade Thanksgiving for me."

The guy shrugged and rejoined the crowd, now forming a loose circle around Mer and Gwen.

Rick paused. His gaze drifted beyond the celebration, past the shifting bodies. On the far side of the lot, he spotted a woman in a thick peacoat, her arms folded tightly in front of her.

His brow furrowed. "Candace?"

He stepped around the crowd, making his way to her. They met beside her old green Volvo, its engine still smoking from the last drive.

Rick cleared his throat. "Hi."

"Hi," she said, scanning him from head to toe. "You look like hell."

"Flu, actually." He snapped his fingers. "Good eye."

"You OK?" she asked, her voice softer now.

Rick smirked, shaking his head. "Never been better." He tilted his head, studying her. "What brings you out to our little neck of nerdom?"

Candace sighed. "We gotta talk."

"Shit," Rick muttered, his eyes widening. His mouth hung half-open as he sat beside Candace on the hood of her car. The setting sun cast pink and purple hues through the leafless trees across the street, long shadows stretching over the pavement.

Candace picked at a leftover pizza crust from her greasy

napkin, tearing off a piece and popping it into her mouth. "Yup," she said. "You can't make this shit up."

"Certainly not." Rick shook his head. "You sat at his desk. Any clue to any of—"

"Not a single vowel."

Rick winced. "That's why he fired you?"

"No." Candace stared down at the half-burnt crust. "He fired me for other reasons."

Rick exhaled sharply. "You didn't press him again for a spot, did you?"

Candace turned to him, face blank.

"Yup," Rick nodded. "That's what I thought. I told you, Candace—we might be getting divorced, but I can still help you if you'll let me."

Candace chuckled. The sound grew, rolling into a laugh—offbeat, hollow, unsettling.

Rick frowned. The laughter died down, but her face fell, her eyes glistening. She ripped a piece of napkin and dabbed at them.

Rick edged back slightly. "Hey," he said carefully. "That's no reason to feel bad. We've all been there."

"That's not it, Rick." Her voice was barely above a whisper.

"Look, it sucks to get rejected, but you just gotta—"

"It's because I wouldn't let him fuck me, Rick! OK?!"

Rick flinched. His breath caught. His jaw clenched so tight he could hear his own teeth grind. He looked down at the black asphalt. His hands curled into fists on his lap, knuckles white. A rush of heat spread through his chest: rage, disgust, shame for ever doubting her.

A long silence stretched between them.

He clicked his teeth. "How long has he been doing this?"

Candace laughed again, this time, dry and bitter. She stared at Rick through red, puffy eyes, shaking her head.

"What?" Rick asked.

"You don't ever listen, do you?"

"What?" Rick frowned.

Candace threw her hands up in the air. "Never mind."

"No," Rick said, holding up a hand. "Please, continue." He practically rolled his eyes through his words.

"Don't worry about it." Candace wiped her eyes with the back of her hand, her expression hardening.

Rick scoffed. "Fine. But don't ever wonder why we didn't work out." He hopped off the hood of the car. "Thanks for the heads up. Your services are no longer needed."

"There he goes." Candace let out a bitter laugh. "Walking away."

Rick stopped. His shoulders stiffened. He turned around, glaring at her. "What do you want from me, Candace?" He threw his arms wide. "The guy's a scummy toad! I told you that when you decided to take his desk. I told you about the complaints, the rumors—"

"So it's my fault, then?" Candace cut in, her voice sharp.

"I didn't say that!" Rick's voice cracked with frustration. He ran a hand through his hair and shook his head. "I'm just saying—"

"Why can't you ever be on my side?" Candace asked. Her voice was quieter now. Her face was streaked with tears, but her expression was blank.

Rick exhaled sharply, looking away for a moment before stepping back toward the car. "You never listen to *me*."

Candace blinked. "What?"

"You see?" Rick jabbed a finger at Candace. "This is exactly why we didn't work. 'Candace, don't eat the old meat in the fridge. It's bad—throw it away.' What does Candace do? She eats it and winds up in the ER. 'Candace, your firm is strict about punctuality, and you're just a junior advisor. Set your alarm an hour early so you can get there on time.' What do you do? Set it for the usual thirty minutes before, and guess what happens? You get fired. And the only job you can find is on Lloyd's desk—because, as we now know, and as I've been trying to tell you—Lloyd didn't hire you for your stellar typing skills!"

Candace wiped her eyes, her expression hardening. "You see that? That is why I never listen to you."

Rick scoffed. "Oh, here we go."

"Because every single one of your so-called suggestions comes wrapped in a beautiful little insult."

Rick threw his hands up. "Did we graduate from the same business school, or didn't we? I swear, your skin has zero thickness to it!"

Candace let out a bitter laugh and hopped off the hood of her car. "Didn't think I needed thick skin to be around my own husband."

Rick folded his arms. "Oh? Then why'd you leave?"

Candace shook her head. "That should be an easy one, Rick."

"Enlighten me."

"You stopped talking." Her voice softened. The fight drained from her eyes, replaced with something raw. "You shut me out completely, and I had no idea why."

Rick's smirk faltered. His jaw tensed, his gaze falling to the ground. He let out a slow, strained sigh, shaking his head as he bit his bottom lip. "Tell you what," Rick said, staring at the ground. His eyes were too tear-filled and his neck was too heavy to make eye contact with her. "When your brother dies in some bullshit war, see if you want to have a conversation about the fucking drapes." Rick turned around and started back for the camp. He could hear Candace's footsteps get closer and pick up speed behind him.

"Hey," she said.

Rick turned around just as Candace tackled him with a hug. Rick's body laid limp in her arms as she rubbed the back of his head with her perfectly manicured fingers. He placed his arms around her waist. Candace could feel his body shake. She didn't know whether it was him coughing or sobbing.

"OK," Rick said, quickly pulling away from her and turning around. "Back to line for me." He walked away, getting halfway across the street, then turned back. "Oh, and Candace."

"Yeah?"

"Thank you."

Candace smiled. "Yeah."

STAGE 14

Rick stared up at the stars. He sat back in his lawn chair, wrapped in a thick blanket, sipping Gatorade. The hum of generators filled the cold night air, long extension cords snaking from the hoods of cars to power them. The sharp scent of gasoline mixed with the lingering dampness of the asphalt. Bass thumped from stereos propped inside tents, punctuated by bursts of cheers and profanity as the line of campers turned into a makeshift festival.

Rick shivered, feeling the fever creeping back. He reached into his pocket, popped two ibuprofens into his mouth, and swallowed them dry. He spotted Mer talking with Theo across the way, their voices lost in the noise.

A voice beside him broke his trance.

"Penny for your thoughts?" Gwen asked, settling down next to him.

"That's all they're worth?" Rick asked.

"A nickel, then?"

Rick chuckled, shaking his head. "She finally speaks."

"You could've said hi first," Gwen teased.

Rick's eyes widened. "And risk getting my ass kicked? No thanks. With you, I wait to be spoken to."

"Not a man of risks, huh?" Gwen asked.

"Risks are overrated."

Gwen leaned back, gazing up at the sky. "It's all a risk, though. Isn't it?"

Rick glanced over at her. "What is?"

"This," she said, gesturing to the chaotic scene around them. "Life. Family. Going after something worthwhile. It's all a risk, right?"

Rick shrugged, exhaling a slow breath. "I don't know."

"I'll tell you how risky all this is," Gwen said, locking eyes with Rick. "None of us are making it out alive."

Rick laughed, shaking his head. "Touché. Touché."

"So, you gonna tell me how you're so damn good at those video games?" She smiled. "Don't worry; I won't tell Mer."

Rick exhaled, tightening his grip on his Gatorade. "Me and my brother, Maddox—we used to hit putt-putt every day. Mostly for the go-karts. We were, like, ten years old. Saved up all week just to ride during the summer. Then, summer of ninety-two, a game showed up in the arcade that changed everything. *Street Fighter.*" He chuckled, shaking his head at the memory. "We were hooked."

"Whoa," Gwen said, leaning in. "You guys still play?"

"Nah," Rick muttered, turning his gaze to the stars.

"Why not?" Her brow furrowed.

"He's up in Arlington."

"The city?"

"The cemetery." His voice was flat.

Gwen inhaled sharply, her body subtly jolting back. A pause settled between them. "How?" she finally asked.

"An IED." Rick's eyes stayed on the sky.

Gwen nodded slowly, watching the flickering red lights of airplanes blink across the night.

"So," she said after a moment, "what are you gonna do with your *Link*?"

Rick scoffed. "It's not mine. It's for my boss—or should I say, my boss's sociopath of a daughter."

Gwen arched a brow. "Didn't know standing outside in the freezing cold was part of a financial advisor's job description."

"There's a *lot* of shit that asshole has me doing that ain't in my job title."

They sat in silence for a moment. Then Gwen let out a dry laugh.

Rick glanced over. "What's funny?"

She shook her head. "Life's supposed to be better playing it safe, right?" She nodded toward him. "Yet here you are, playing it safe, working for a guy who's got you waiting in the cold for days, catching the flu. How's that working out for you?"

Rick looked down the sidewalk, clicking his teeth as he nodded. Gwen smirked, watching him process her words.

Then a voice from the line cut through the night.

"Yo, who the hell is that?"

Rick and Gwen snapped their heads up. The hum of distant engines grew louder. Low, rumbling, steady, like a slow-moving thunderstorm rolling in. A parade of black Escalades rolled into the parking lot, their tinted windows swallowing the glow from the streetlights.

The crowd in line stirred. Some murmured in confusion, while others instinctively backed away from the curb. A few shifted their weight uneasily, eyes darting to each other.

Inside the nearest tent, a stereo kept thumping—bass-heavy hip-hop shaking the fabric walls—but the energy outside had shifted. The usual laughing and trash-talking died out as tension slithered through the air.

The line of Escalades rolled to a stop in front of the crowd. Multiple doors swung open in near-perfect unison. Men in dark suits with gold chains and black gloves stepped out, their movements crisp, their presence imposing.

Jason let out a nervous chuckle, elbowing a rigid Theo. "Man, this is some straight-up *Men in Black*–type shit."

Nobody laughed.

The last Escalade's back door opened. Guy stepped out. He moved with purpose to the opposite door, pulling it open. Braff emerged, wearing a charcoal gray trench coat. He stood motionless for a moment, letting the weight of his presence settle over the crowd. The streetlights barely touched him, leaving only the sharp, icy glint of his baby-blue eyes visible.

Braff stepped forward.

"Good evening," he said, glancing at his watch. His expression twisted with mock surprise. "*Oy gevalt!* It's four in the morning?" He let out a small, amused laugh. "Scratch that. *Top* o' the morning. And of course, a very happy Black Friday."

He took a slow step forward, scanning the crowd.

"For those of you who don't know me—and I assume that's most of you, given that your generation's knowledge rarely extends beyond pop culture—my name is Braff Goldman."

Silence.

Braff sighed, shaking his head. "I've been informed by my security that you lot have been… let's just say, *uncooperative*. Violent, even. Over what? A *toy*?" He exhaled heavily, as if the absurdity physically weighed on him. "You know, the Torah— what you Christians might refer to as the *Old Testament*—is very clear on certain matters. An *eye* for an eye. A *tooth* for a tooth." He turned slightly, addressing his men. "Boys."

Like clockwork, his entourage of thirty men pulled metal baseball bats from beneath their coats. The reaction was instant. A few people screamed, sprinting toward their cars. Others stood still, wide-eyed, their legs refusing to move. Some clenched their fists, their faces twisted in a mix of anger and fear.

Braff held up a hand. "Shh," he cooed.

The crowd stilled, trembling, barely breathing.

"Now, children," Braff said, voice soft and almost fatherly. "I could let my boys here—who, mind you, left their *families* on this fine holiday—blow off a little steam." He smiled and clapped his hands together once, the sound cracking through the air like a gunshot. "*But*, we're not gonna do that today."

The bats were *lowered* but didn't disappear.

"You *do*, however, have five minutes—*five*—to pack your shit and get the fuck off my property."

They didn't hesitate. People rushed back to their tents, their hands moving on instinct, tearing down everything they'd spent hours setting up. The music stopped. Curses were muttered under breath. Some fought back tears. Others glared at Braff, their eyes burning with unspoken rage.

Braff simply smiled and gave them a little wave.

The line was no longer. Dead.

"*Pop!*" a voice called out.

Braff turned to his right. Mer and Gwen were approaching, their heads low, steps slow, like children being dragged to the principal's office.

Guy and the others moved in immediately, forming a circle around the siblings. Mer finally raised his head to meet his father's cold, disappointed gaze. Gwen kept her eyes locked on the ground, her shame weighing her down.

"Merlin. Guinevere," Braff sighed, exhaling as if the very sight of them exhausted him.

They stood a few feet away, silence stretching between them like a canyon.

"Daddy?" Gwen said hesitantly.

"What is it, pumpkin?" Braff asked, though his eyes never left Mer.

"I'm four days clean."

Braff didn't even blink. "Afraid that's not good enough, pumpkin."

Gwen's shoulders slumped.

Mer clenched his jaw. "And what *is* good enough for you, Pop?"

Braff rubbed his forehead. "We're not doing this here, Merlin." His voice was tired, as if he'd had this conversation too many times before. "Pretty sure I already know the answer, but… do you have my money?"

Mer exhaled through his nose. "Working on it."

"Oh, *yeah*?" Braff scoffed, his grin sharp and humorless. "Where? *Here*?" He gestured around them. "You were gonna… what? Lift twenty of those things? Rob every nerd as they walked out the store? *At my strip mall*?"

"A little more nuanced than that, but yeah. Something like that," Mer said.

Braff's face darkened. A vein pulsed at his temple as his breathing grew heavier. He flexed his fingers, clasping them tightly together, like he was trying to keep from putting them around Mer's throat.

"My own offspring," Braff muttered, shaking his head. "A fucking *shanda*, the both of you."

Without warning, Malin stepped out from the sea of Braff's men, grinning as he sidled up beside him.

Gwen's eyes snapped to the bald man. Her teeth clenched.

"Hate to interrupt this beautiful family moment," Malin said, smirking, "but Mr. B., if it's all the same to you, I'm just gonna go ahead and put up shop right by the front door. If you could let your guys—"

Braff cut him off, his patience running razor thin. "*What?*"

"You know," Malin mumbled, suddenly less confident. "The, uh… deal we had?" The smirk on his face flickered.

Gwen's hands curled into fists.

Braff's gaze turned to Malin.

The air went still.

"Oh, *that*," Braff muttered under his breath. He lifted a single index finger. "Guys," he ordered, "get him to the front of the Big K. Make sure he gets his two consoles."

Malin grinned ear to ear, his chest puffing with self-satisfaction. Gwen's fingers twitched. She could feel the fire churning in the pit of her stomach, slowly rising to her chest, tightening her throat.

Merlin noticed her stance shift: the slight pivot of her foot, the subtle adjustment of her hips. Slow, deliberate breaths. He'd seen it before.

She was picturing it. A bat.

A brick.

A solid concrete block.

And her right foot smashing clean through it.

Then came the grin—a flash of something wicked.

"Hey, Malin," Gwen said, her voice too smooth, too calm.

Malin scoffed. "What do you want?"

"You know Dave Chappelle's Rick James joke about what the five fingers said to the face?" she asked, tilting her head. "Well… you ever heard what my shin said to your neck?"

Malin's brows knit together. "What—?"

Gwen moved.

A textbook roundhouse, the top of her foot and shin slamming into the side of Malin's thick neck with a sickening *crack*. The force sent him flying backward, crashing into Braff. The two of them went down hard.

One of Braff's men lunged for Gwen, but she moved fast, chopping him in the throat. The man staggered back, wheezing.

"Run!" Mer grabbed Gwen's arm. They bolted.

Gunmetal flashed. "Those little…" Guy growled, pulling a pistol from his coat.

The crowd *erupted*. Screams rang out as people abandoned their tents, scrambling for their cars. Folding chairs overturned, pizzas hit the pavement.

Gwen and Mer sprinted toward their car.

"Come on!" Mer yanked on the locked door handle. "*Open the door!*"

Gwen patted herself down, frantic.

Mer shook his head, his voice breaking. "No, no, no."

Beep, beep. A car unlocked.

Rick.

He ran past them, gripping his key fob, and dove into the driver's seat.

Mer and Gwen didn't hesitate.

They sprinted after him, flung open the back doors, and *threw* themselves inside. The parking lot of the Big K was chaos. The abandoned tents flapped in the wind, half-collapsed, their neon colors stark under the buzzing floodlights. Shopping carts lay overturned, scattered in the frenzy of people scrambling for cover. The black Escalades lined the curb like sharks in the water, their engines humming, ready to attack.

"Go!" Mer shouted.

"Get the hell out of my car!" Rick snapped.

"What?" Mer frowned. "Why?"

"Why?" Rick scoffed. "Take a wild fucking guess! They're after you!"

"We just saved your life!" Gwen shot back.

"And that has exactly what to do with—" Rick's words were cut short as two bullets ricocheted off the roof of his car. All three flinched, ducking instinctively.

Rick's eyes widened as he spotted Guy and his men charging toward them, guns raised.

"You want to have this conversation somewhere else?!" Mer shouted.

Rick clenched his jaw, cursing under his breath. "Shit."

He turned the key, and the engine roared to life. Throwing the car into drive, he slammed the gas. *Up, up, down, down,* Rick chanted to himself. More gunfire erupted, shattering the rear window as the car spun onto the gravel backroad, tires kicking up dirt as they disappeared into the darkness of early morning.

⁂

"Damn, this is amazing!" Mer laughed, his mouth full, bits of sausage biscuit crumbling onto his tray as he squirted grape jelly onto what was left of his sandwich.

"This is amazing," Gwen agreed, her plastic fork stabbing

into a Styrofoam container of macaroni and cheese. She shoveled a bite into her mouth, chewing with satisfaction before glancing at Rick, who sat hunched across from them, his arms folded tight against his body. His face was pale, his skin slick with fever sweat, but his expression was stony.

"Hey!" Gwen snapped her fingers at him. "What's the name of this place?"

"Timeout," Rick muttered flatly.

Rick tucked himself closer to the window, trying to fight the shivers rattling through his flu-ridden body. His eyes drifted downward, catching the glimpse of the handgun nestled beneath Mer's half-open dress shirt.

When he looked up, Mer was watching him, one eyebrow raised. "You're not planning any funny business, are you?" he asked, voice casual.

Rick scoffed and shook his head.

"You sure?" Mer pressed.

Rick closed his tired eyes and nodded.

"Good." Mer leaned back, stretching an arm over the back of the booth. "Because I'd hate to have to… well, you know."

Rick exhaled through his nose, shaking his head. His fingers curled into fists under the table.

"If you're not planning anything funny, why are you looking at my piece?"

Rick scoffed. "Where am I running, Mer? Your dad isn't just after you two anymore; he's after all three of us." He jabbed a finger at each of them in turn. "The three of us, Mer."

"Why are you so mad?" Gwen asked, wincing at his tone.

Rick let out a bitter laugh. "Because up until you two jumped in my car, he was only trying to shoot *you two*."

"You can leave," Gwen shot back, her tone sharp.

Rick slammed his palm against the table, rattling the trays. "How? *How*, Gwen? They've got the criminal equivalent of an APB out for my car. *My car*, Gwen. So please, enlighten me. Where the *fuck* am I supposed to go?"

"Hey," Mer interjected, his voice edged with warning. "Don't talk to her like that."

Rick exhaled through gritted teeth, then held up a hand in surrender, reaching for his water. He took a slow sip, his fingers tightening around the Styrofoam cup.

Gwen kept stuffing her face with macaroni and cheese. "Who'd have thought they had this kind of goodness on Franklin Street?" she mused between bites.

"You know they got chopped barbecue over there too," Mer added, nodding toward the counter.

"For real?" Gwen laughed. "Why don't you get some?"

"Why don't *you*?" Mer shot back.

The siblings locked eyes for a beat before bursting into laughter, their amusement so genuine it made them nearly double over. Rick just stared at them, his expression blank.

Mer caught his look and grinned. "We're Jewish."

Rick nodded, expressionless. "Good to know."

"Hot *damn*," Gwen sighed, pushing her tray away. "I feel so much better."

"See?" Mer turned to Rick. "I told you she was all right."

"Good for Gwen," Rick said flatly.

Gwen eyed his untouched chicken biscuit. "You gonna eat that?"

"No," Rick replied, still staring at Mer.

Gwen gingerly reached for it. "May I?"

"You may *not*," Rick deadpanned.

Gwen pouted.

"Who put the thorn up your candy ass?" Mer grimaced.

"You two did, Mer," Rick said, pointing at the siblings. "*You two*. The second you jumped in my car, you made me an accessory to… *something*. Something neither of you have even *bothered* to explain. What the hell did you *do*?"

Gwen shrugged. "Well, we—"

Rick clamped his hands over his ears and shouted, "Hey! *Hey!* Never mind! Come to think of it, I *don't* want to know!"

Mer's smile faded. He adjusted the grip of his gun, subtly repositioning the holster under his jacket.

Rick's breath hitched. He pressed himself deeper into the wooden bench as Mer leaned forward, resting his elbows on the table.

"You know what's funny, Rick?" Mer said, clasping his hands together. "I'm the guy with the gun, and yet you're the one sitting here airing out grievances like I'm your *damn* therapist." His voice was quiet but with an edge. "You don't know if I'm a killer. You don't know what I did to the last person who talked to me like that."

Rick swallowed hard. His fingers curled around his water cup as Mer's stare bore into him.

"And yet," Mer continued, his jaw clenching, "you still talk to me like we're *equals*. Like you didn't just get a firsthand look at the *circles* I move in." His baby-blue eyes stayed locked on Rick. "So tell me, Rick—why *is* that?"

Rick sighed heavily, his shoulders slumping. He looked down at the scuffed linoleum floor.

"Well," Rick muttered, "because you're definitely not going to shoot me here." He took a slow sip of water before setting the cup down with a quiet *thunk*. "Look, I just need this," he said, gesturing vaguely between them, his fingers steepled beneath his chin. "I just need *you both* out of my life so I can get back to *mine.*"

Mer chuckled, shaking his head. "*Get back?*" He turned to Gwen, grinning. "You hear that?"

Gwen snorted. "Poor guy just wants to *get back* to his life."

Mer grabbed a fry, popped it into his mouth, and grinned. "He don't know about the black swans."

"They don't teach that shit in finance," Gwen said, swirling the straw in her chocolate milkshake.

"Well, they *should,*" Mer replied.

Rick pinched the bridge of his nose and exhaled sharply. "What?"

Mer smirked and leaned back. "Back in the 1600s, European explorers landed in Australia and saw black swans for the first time. Up until then, everyone assumed swans were only white." He picked up another fry and pointed it at Rick. "It became a metaphor."

"For what?" Rick asked, already regretting it.

"For the fact that no matter how *perfect* you think things are—how *stable*—something can always come along and completely fuck up your *entire* world," Gwen said before slurping down the last of her shake.

Mer grinned. "For people like us, it don't matter how good the grift is going; there's always a black swan waiting in the wings. The mistress with the ice pick. The partner who gets greedy. The up-and-comer looking to make a name for himself. One minute, you're on top. The next? You're a news story."

Rick shook his head, stabbing a finger against the table. "Yeah? That's real touching, Mer. But I'm not a criminal."

"Right," Mer chuckled. "Yet here you are, breaking bread with two borderline sociopaths."

Gwen wiped a bit of chocolate shake from her lip. "Sounds like a black swan to me."

Mer rubbed his hands together. "Come on, we'll walk you to your car."

Rick shot him a look. "Do I have a choice?"

Mer ran a hand through his hair. "I have your keys, so…"

Gwen stared at Rick, unreadable. When he finally met her gaze, she winked before pushing back from the table and heading toward the exit. Rick sighed, shaking his head as he stood. Mer gestured for him to walk first.

As they moved through the crowded restaurant, Rick bumped into patrons waiting in line, jostling past them. His mind raced. *Maybe I could sprint out of here. Find a police station.* The thought barely had time to settle before he felt Gwen's calloused fingers scratch the back of his neck. He flinched, turning just enough to catch her smiling and shaking her head.

Rick swallowed hard and kept walking.

Once outside, Mer and Gwen flanked him as they made their way toward Rick's car. The early-morning air carried the scent of fried food.

"You two are letting me go, right?" Rick asked, trying to keep his voice level.

"Just keep walking," Gwen said.

"You gonna call your dad?" Rick pressed, stumbling over a yellow parking barrier.

"Will you shut up?" Mer snapped.

They reached Rick's beat-up white Toyota Corolla. Mer dangled the keys in his fingers before sticking them in the trunk lock. He looked at Rick, shaking his head with mock sympathy. "Rick, you're a smart guy. Sucks it has to end this way."

Mer popped the trunk. Gwen shoved Rick forward.

"Wait! Wait!" Rick shouted, panic setting in. "How the hell are you gonna throw me in the trunk with all these people around—"

"Will you shut up and just look at the damn trunk?" Gwen snapped, grabbing Rick's head and turning it toward the open interior.

Rick winced at first, squinting with one eye, half-expecting to find something illegal or worse, if that was possible. But as his vision adjusted, both eyes slowly widened. His mouth dropped open.

Inside the trunk sat a sleek black box. Neon green-and-yellow lettering in a retro nineties font read: The Link.

Rick's breath hitched. He looked from the box to Gwen and Mer, who were grinning like they'd just won the lottery.

He reached for it, but both of them grabbed his arms before he could lift it.

"Whoa," Gwen warned. "People are still in line for these things. Best not to flash it around."

Rick swallowed and nodded, running his fingers reverently across the top of the box.

"How did you—when—" he stammered.

"Not important," Mer said, shaking his head. "The real question is, what do you plan to do with it?"

Rick barely heard him, still mesmerized by the console. "What do you think?" he scoffed. "As soon as I give this to Lloyd—my boss—I'm in, man."

Mer's grin faded. "Until he needs you for something else?"

Rick's eyes gleamed, locked on the prize in front of him. "What?"

"Guys like Lloyd don't reward you, Rick," Mer said. "They dangle the reward in front of you, like a carrot on a stick."

"Maybe in your world," Rick countered, shutting the trunk of his Corolla. "But in my world? The legal world? You work hard, and you get rewarded for it."

"With more hard work," Mer shot back. He stepped in closer, lowering his voice. "The black swans aren't always a bad thing. Sometimes when shit hits the fan, it's just the universe realigning what's important."

Rick studied the two of them for a moment, then sighed and shoved his hands in his pockets. "You guys need a ride?"

"Nah," Mer said, glancing down the street. "We got one coming." As if on cue, a black SUV rolled up, slow and silent. Guy and two other men dressed in black stepped out, their hands folded in front of them.

Rick quickly slid into his Corolla, watching through the rearview mirror as Gwen and Mer were shoved into the SUV. Rick gripped the steering wheel, forcing himself to look away. He hit the gas and kept his eyes on the road.

Braff stood with his hands tucked into the deep pockets of his charcoal-gray trench coat, staring out over Jordan Lake. His cheeks and nose were raw from the bite of the cold November air. Wisps of his breath curled into the stillness, vanishing as quickly as they formed. He exhaled slowly, the scent of tobacco mingling with the crisp morning breeze.

The wooden dock stretched before him, lined with his men dressed in dark suits and black gloves, standing at attention. At the far end, two of them worked on the sleek jet-black speedboat, its four outboard motors rumbling low against the quiet. The name *Marla* was painted across the bow in bold, blood-red letters. Braff winced at the glare of the sun as it climbed higher into the sky, then slid on a pair of black aviators.

A black SUV rolled into the empty lot, tires crunching against loose gravel. Braff retrieved a Cuban cigar from his coat, slicing off the end with a gold cutter. He lit it up and took a slow drag as the vehicle came to a stop.

The driver stepped out and yanked the back door open. A moment later, Mer and Gwen were pushed out onto the pavement, their hands instinctively raised. They didn't resist, didn't speak, just watched as Braff's men flanked them, hands resting close to their holstered weapons, waiting for a command.

The siblings walked toward their father, the sound of their footsteps the only thing breaking the silence. The faint, sweet scent of Braff's cigar filled their noses as they drew closer.

"That's far enough," Braff said, the cigar balanced between his lips. He removed it with two fingers, exhaling a slow stream of smoke as he pointed toward Gwen. "That one likes to kick people."

Mer and Gwen didn't react. They stood still, their eyes locked onto their father's.

Braff studied them in silence, shaking his head slowly. A twitch flickered in his left cheek, his lips pressing into a hard line. Disappointment radiated off him like heat from the pavement.

"What have I done?" he muttered, almost to himself. "I put you in the best schools. Showered you with gifts. Did everything humanly possible to keep you out of *this* life." His voice was calm, but the weight behind it was heavier than a shout.

Mer shrugged. "Shit happens. It's like that—"

"*Don't* start with that black swan bullshit, Merlin," Braff interjected, jabbing a finger in his direction.

"Well, *Daddy*," said Gwen, folding her arms and tilting her head sassily. "Maybe you should've thought of that before giving us *your* last name. We're Braff's kids." She smirked, eyes gleaming with something between defiance and acceptance. "It's in our DNA."

"Yeah?" Braff shook his head. "*That's* the problem."

He started to pace around his children, slow and deliberate, like a predator sizing up its prey.

"You think I got all this because I was *smart*?" He scoffed. "*Oy vey*, child. No. Somebody was *praying* for me." His eyes flickered with something distant, almost haunted. "I can't tell you two numbskulls how many times I found myself staring down the barrel. In this life, it *don't matter* how smart you are—sometimes things just *go wrong*."

He flicked his wrist, and his men stepped in behind Mer and Gwen, pressing cold steel against their backs.

"As it has just gone wrong for you two now." Braff sighed, tilting his head like a disappointed teacher. "You know our policy. After twenty-four hours, we collect *one* of two things. Money…" He paused, then exhaled slowly. "Or a head."

"Pop—" Mer started.

"It's been *more than* twenty-four hours."

"Pop," Gwen cut in, shifting uncomfortably against the gun at her back.

"Children or not—"

"Pop!" they both shouted at the same time.

Braff rolled his eyes to the sky and muttered, "*Got hob rakhmones, you two are stealing my thunder.*" He pinched the bridge of his nose, inhaled, and finally grumbled, "What?!"

Mer nodded toward Braff's pocket. "You need to answer that."

Braff frowned, hesitated, then pulled out his buzzing flip phone. He opened it, pressing it against his ear. "Yeah?"

A pause.

His breath hitched. His entire face tensed as his grip on the phone tightened.

"What do you mean *stolen?*" His voice was low. "*How many stores?*" He squeezed his eyes shut. "Fifteen?!"

Mer and Gwen exchanged a glance.

Another pause. Braff rubbed his temple. "OK. OK."

He snapped the phone shut, stuffing it back into his coat pocket. For a moment, he just stared at the ground, his breath coming out in slow, measured exhales. "Three of my retail properties were hit this morning."

"Oh," Mer said.

"Was anyone hurt?" Gwen asked.

Braff glared at them, his lips pulling into a tight line. "No. The stores are completely trashed inside."

"What stores?" Mer asked.

" Circuit City. Toys "R" Us." He sighed, rubbing his eyes. "And a *Big K* off of 501."

"Do they think they're connected?" Mer asked.

Braff exhaled sharply, shaking his head. His jaw tensed, lips pressing into a tight fold. Winter steam billowed from his nostrils as his face darkened to a furious shade of red. He pointed his cigar at his two children, biting his lip hard.

"I'm gonna kill 'em," he whispered. Then, louder: "*What did you two numbskulls do?*"

STAGE 15

"WHAT DID YOU say your major was?" the girl asked.

She sat beside a young Black man wearing a red hoodie with gold Greek letters—Sigma Gamma Alpha—on the chest. They were squeezed together on a blue suede couch beside four-foot speakers. The bass thudded so hard it rattled their eardrums. The living room in front of them had become a makeshift dance floor, packed with bodies. "Yeah!" by Usher featuring Lil Jon and Ludacris had just come on. The crowd roared, chanting, "The roof's on fire!"

Between the pounding bass and the stomping crowd, conversation was almost impossible.

The young man leaned in, shouting in her ear, "Biology!"

"Sorry," he added, noticing her flinch. "Didn't mean to yell."

He gently rubbed the lobe of her ear between his thumb and index finger. She giggled, her freckled face blooming red. Uncrossing and recrossing her legs, her long floral dress fanned a soft lavender perfume that drifted up to his nose.

"Not at all," she said, leaning in. "It's loud in here, right?"

He nodded.

"You're a biology major, huh? Then why are you in my writing classes?"

He looked down at his red cup and shrugged. "Might mess around and write a book someday."

"That's awesome!" she said, tucking a strand of red hair behind her ear. "What genre?"

"Romance," he said with a grin.

Her face lit up. "Awwww! I *love* romance."

"But I want to give it an edge, you know?" he added. "Like a *Sex and the City* vibe. Know what I'm sayin'?"

"Shut up!" she said, sitting up. "Don't tell me you're a *Sex and the City* fan."

He nodded.

She leaned in, grinning. "Okay. Which character are you most attracted to?"

"To be honest," he said, casually draping his arm around her, "I think each character represents a part of someone's personality. Carrie's the dreamer, creative and free. Miranda? She's intellect. Tough but caring. Charlotte's loyal and a little demure. And Samantha—well, she's sexuality, pure and simple."

He took another sip from his drink. Her green eyes locked onto his like he'd hypnotized her.

"I'm sorry," she said, a little breathless. "I didn't catch your name."

"Theo," he said with a smile.

"Well, Theo… " she glanced at his hoodie. "So you're Greek?"

"Sho' nuff," he said. "Matter fact, we got a little something going on at my frat house just down the street. You wanna check it out?"

"Fer sure," she said, standing.

Theo rose, grabbed her hand, and led her out of the house.

They walked down West Cameron Avenue, making small talk. At the end of the block stood a two-story, whitewashed brick house. Floodlights illuminated a large banner: SIGMA GAMMA ALPHA.

"This is it," Theo said.

She wrinkled her nose and wrapped the lapels of her black leather jacket closer to her neck. "Kinda quiet over here."

"We do things differently on Friday nights," he said.

As if on cue, the house erupted with cheering and profanity. She whipped her head toward the noise.

She laughed. "What was that?"

Theo grinned. "Let's find out."

He took her hand again and led her up the porch and through the open front door. The hallway was lined with posters—*Sonic the Hedgehog, Double Dragon, Dead or Alive.*

"Are these…" she frowned, "video games?"

Theo nodded.

"What kind of fraternity are you guys?"

Down the hall, a group crowded around a room, eyes locked on something. Theo led her toward them.

"This is crazy," she said with a smile.

The room was packed. In the center, five sixty-five-inch projector TVs were arranged in a circle. Five frat members sat in foldout chairs wearing headsets and gripping Xbox controllers. The crowd watched in tense silence, occasionally cheering.

"What game is this?" she asked.

"*Halo 2*," Theo replied. "Just dropped a few weeks ago."

She watched as the players chugged Red Bulls and smashed buttons with wild precision.

"Are they playing each other?"

"Nah. They're online—battling our brothers over at UCLA."

"Seriously?"

"Colleges have the fastest internet connections," Theo said.

A cheer went up as the announcer called, *"You win!"*

She turned toward the corner of the room. A small group gathered around a retro *Pac-Man* arcade cabinet.

"Is that *Pac-Man*?"

Theo nodded.

The player gulped a shot of vodka, and another frat brother quickly poured him another.

"What are they doing?"

"That's Pac-Man Pong. Every time you eat a ghost, you take a shot."

She burst out laughing. "That's cray cray."

Theo led her into the galley kitchen and grabbed two Red Bulls from the fridge. He tossed her one.

"Thanks," she said, cracking it open. "What's the story here? I didn't even know you could have a video game fraternity."

"It's not that hard," Theo said, mixing vodka and Red Bull into a red cup. He hopped up on the counter. "In eighty-three, a group of computer programmers tried to pledge. The frats weren't having it; said they were too dorky and would bring the whole image down. One of them never forgot. He graduated from Chapel Hill, made a fortune in software, and came back to start Sigma Gamma Alpha. A fraternity where people could just be themselves, game, and chill."

"You guys ever get bullied?"

Theo shook his head. "Nah. No one really cares anymore. Actually, a lot of the other frats come game with us now."

"That's cool. So, what do your letters stand for?"

"What do you mean?"

"Well, most frats and sororities have history. Like, real history. What do your letters *mean*?"

Theo sipped his drink. "You ever heard of Sega?"

"The Sega Genesis?"

He nodded. "Sigma Gamma Alpha."

She laughed. "Shut up. That's hilarious."

She tilted her head. "Who was this software tycoon who started all this? Wait—let me guess!"

Theo gave a mock bow. "You have the floor, m'lady."

"Bill Gates?"

"Nope. Dropped out of Harvard."

"Michael Dell?"

He shook his head.

"Ugh! I give up."

"Jo Gabe."

"No way!"

"All our frat houses are incorporated through his company. We get a nice little endowment. Actually," he said, hopping off the counter, "I live upstairs."

"Oh, do you?" she asked, batting her lashes.

"I got a Sega Genesis up there. You up for a game?"

She smiled. "Sure."

♨

Knock! Knock!

"Theo!" a voice shouted.

Theo stumbled out of his room, eyes half open, wearing a black tank top and a pair of *X-Men* boxers. His socks slipped along the wooden floor as he rubbed the sleep from his eyes and made his way downstairs, holding onto the railing.

"Somebody open the damn door!" the voice yelled again.

Theo grumbled, unlocked the deadbolt, and opened the door. Jason rushed past him into the house.

Theo yawned. "Good morning to you too."

"Where your line at?" Jason called out, walking down the hallway.

"What?"

"Your line, Theo," Jason said. "Do they know?"

"Know what?" Theo frowned.

Jason turned and scrunched his face. "The fuck you mean you don't know? You better recognize and get with the 4-1-1, playboy."

Theo stared at him, shaking his head. He cleared his throat and walked past Jason.

"It's too early for the hood persona, dude."

Theo stepped into the kitchen and grabbed a bag of instant coffee from the cabinet, mumbling to himself, "Some ol' bullshit."

"What you mean 'persona'? Bro, this is who I am."

"No, it isn't," Theo said, filling the coffee pot.

"I was raised in the Chocolate City!"

"Yet you're not chocolate."

"So? This is still my hood, playboy."

Theo laughed and turned on the pot. "Jason, your high school was Durham School of Science and Math. The only hood you know is Cameron Street! May I help you!?"

At that moment, Theo's friend came down the stairs, adjusting her dress and slipping on one of his vintage T-shirts: *Batman 1989.*

"Morning," she said with a smile. She walked over and kissed him. "Sorry about the morning breath. Didn't bring a Mentos."

"You taste like strawberries to me." Theo grinned, and they kissed again.

"Look, I uh… don't have your number, but I'll see you in class, okay?"

"Bet."

As she walked toward the kitchen door, Jason gave her a smirk. "I see someone got into a little punani."

She cut her eyes at him.

Flash!

That's all Jason saw before her open-handed haymaker landed flush across his cheek. It looked like she was winding up for a pitch. Jason staggered back, grabbing the door to steady himself. She walked out a moment later, the door slamming behind her.

Jason clutched his face and let out a guttural cry. "Who the fuck was that?!"

"I dunno," Theo said.

"You don't *know*?" Jason glared, his face red. "Didn't you just have relations with her?"

Theo snapped his fingers and pointed at him. "There's the Jason I grew up with."

Jason winced, feeling his cheek swell.

"You want some ice?"

"I can't right now," Jason said. "Just follow me."

They walked into the living room. Jason grabbed one of the five remotes and turned on a TV, flipping it to G4. *Icons* was on—a show about pioneers of the gaming industry. Under the interview with Miyamoto Shigeru was a ticker that read: *Jo Gabe's new console, the Link, drops this Black Friday.*

"You see that?" Jason asked.

"Oh, snap," Theo smiled. "The Link drops this November."

Jason shook his head. "No, Theo. *No* 'oh, snap.'"

He pulled out an open envelope and tossed it like a frisbee at Theo's feet. Theo picked it up and pulled out a letter.

"What is this?" Theo asked.

"It's an eviction notice," Jason said, still nursing his cheek. "On all the frat houses owned by Sigma Gamma Alpha."

Theo's breath caught. "H-how? Gabe bought all the properties outright."

"No, he didn't." Jason was now squatting, face in his hands. "He financed all the houses. His company was still making payments."

"Then why are we getting evicted if payments were being made?"

"Think, Theo!" Jason stood, wiping a bit of blood from his nose. "He *sold* all the properties!" Theo staggered back like he'd been punched in the gut. "He bought those houses in the nineties. With their locations, they've gotta be worth triple."

"What's that got to do with the Link's launch?" Theo's eyes widened. "Shit."

"I see homegirl didn't fuck *all* your brains out."

"He's gonna lose, on average, a hundred dollars per console for the first two, maybe three years. He's liquidating the frat houses to free up cash."

Theo folded his arms and began to pace.

"Where's your line?" Jason asked.

"Doing their community service in Boone. Can't we go to the police?"

"And say what? Jo Gabe sold off some frat houses and evicted us? There's a whole war going on in Afghanistan. No one's gonna care."

Theo snapped his fingers and said, "We need to assemble the Three Kings."

Jason threw up his hands. "Aw, fuck *that!* It's hard enough I gotta come to Franklin Street to deal with your Tar Heel ass! And now you want to bring Brentwood into this?"

"Jason," Theo said firmly, "listen to me carefully. This goes beyond college rivalry bullshit. Call Dustin in Brentwood and your second-in-command. Put the Duke and NC State pledges on standby. It's all hands on deck."

Jason rolled his eyes and pulled out his Nokia phone. Theo did the same.

"Who are you about to call?"

"You remember my parents' neighbors?"

Jason nodded.

"I still have their son's number. He told me to call if I ever needed anything."

"Wait." Jason walked over and leaned in close. "You're calling *Merlin Braff?*"

Theo nodded.

"Merlin? Are you out of your fucking mind? That's *Jewish Mafia!*"

"What choice do we have?"

"Many!" Jason said, holding his head. "We have *many* choices. Like *breathing!*"

"Shut up, it's ringing!" Theo said. "Mer? Hey, how's it going, neighbor? This is Theo Cooper… Yeah, your next-door neighbor. I'm well, how are you?"

He paused.

"Picking up Gwen from rehab? Wasn't she just *out* of rehab? That bites. Look, I hate to be that guy, but remember when you said to hit you up if I ever needed something?"

Theo let out a nervous chuckle.

"Welp, Thundercat's, ho."

&

"Thanks for seeing us," Theo said.

He, Jason, Dustin, and Brad sat in a half-circle of black plastic chairs in the back kitchen of a closed restaurant. The place was empty, quiet. A single flickering fluorescent bulb buzzed overhead, casting shadows across Merlin's face as he clipped his nails with a small silver clipper.

"Don't mention it," Merlin replied. "Least I can do."

He glanced at Brad, then Dustin, and smiled. "When I was a kid and got locked out the house, Theo was the only one on the block who'd let me in."

The smile faded when his eyes landed on Jason. "Jason. How are ya?"

Jason squirmed. "I—I'm straight."

"You look like someone used your face for a punching bag," Merlin said. "Who won?"

"She did," Theo said.

Merlin's eyes lit up. "Oh, a *she*, was it?"

"Hold up," Jason said quickly. "I don't hit girls, you know what I'm sayin'?"

Merlin chuckled, shaking his head. "Still talkin' like a knockoff member of N.W.A. Cute."

"This your dad's restaurant?" Theo asked, steering things back.

Merlin nodded. He leaned back, brushing invisible lint off his navy pinstriped suit.

"Tough break about your frat," he said.

"We were hoping—maybe—you could help us buy the houses," Theo said. "If we can buy the three frat houses—Franklin Street, Cameron Street, and Brentwood—we might be able to salvage the chapters at UNC, Duke, and State."

Merlin raised an eyebrow. "You want to borrow money?"

Theo nodded. "Yeah."

"How much we talking?"

"Each house is around two hundred grand," Theo said. "But the bank's willing to sell them to us at the original price. All cash. No financing."

"How much per house?"

"Eighty thousand," Jason said.

Merlin laughed, leaned forward, elbows on his knees, silk tie hanging between his legs.

"Guys—even if I had that kinda money, I wouldn't loan it to you."

"Why not?" Theo asked.

Merlin clasped his hands. "Because if you don't pay me back, I can't hurt you."

Theo and Jason exchanged a look, jaws slack.

"You still playin' those video games?" Merlin asked.

"Yeah," Theo nodded.

Merlin scratched his cheek. "Thought you'd have grown outta that."

"You know," Theo smiled nervously, "old habits and all."

"Old habits?" Merlin frowned. "Theo, smoking is a habit. Gambling's a habit. Video games? That's like an eight-year-old pissin' the bed. Why's this so important to you?"

Theo looked at the floor, closed his eyes, then looked back up.

"All I know is that it brings me comfort. Everyone here started at third base. I'm expected to be successful; it's not a hope, it's a pressure. Sigma Gamma Alpha is the only place I can just… be myself. Kick back. Video games are no different than my old man golfing with his buddies."

Merlin studied him, then cracked a grin. He turned to Jason.

"Your parents still assholes?"

Jason nodded. "Sho' nuff."

Merlin looked up at the ceiling, exhaled. "I can't give you the money. But I do think we can help each other."

Theo narrowed his eyes. "How so?"

"You remember my sister, right?"

Both Jason and Theo nodded.

"Me and Gwen—we're breaking away from Pop. Starting our own thing."

"You?" Theo asked.

Merlin nodded.

"With your sister?" Jason added.

Merlin nodded again.

Theo frowned. "Didn't she… isn't she a dope fiend?"

"Recovering," Merlin said, visibly annoyed. "But brilliant. She was a surgeon."

"Didn't she get kicked out of her residency?" Jason asked.

"Fine," Merlin snapped. "She's a junkie doctor. But still brilliant. And very dangerous."

"She still breaking cement blocks?" Theo asked.

"Cement blocks?" Merlin scoffed. "The girl can snap a glass

bottle neck clean with a chop. Her sense of planning is… let's say, faulty."

The four boys exchanged baffled looks.

"We're not following," Theo said.

"When we decided to go independent, we knew we needed something big. A con. Something that lets the underworld know we've arrived."

"Okay…" Jason said.

"But Gwen's idea is trash."

"What is it?" Theo asked.

"She wants to rob Perkins Library."

All four frowned.

"Perkins?" Jason asked. "There's nothing of value there."

"She wants to stick up the students."

"Even worse," Jason muttered. "What's that get you—canceled credit cards and pepper spray?"

"It gets better," Merlin said, shaking his head. "She wants to do it next week."

Silence.

"Next week is Thanksgiving," Theo said.

"Exactly," Merlin said. "No one'll even be there."

"She's serious?" Jason asked.

"Oh, one hundred percent. Dope-fiend logic. And somehow, she's got it in her head the idea was mine to begin with. Again, dope-fiend logic. But once we clean her up, she'll make a great soldier. Just not a general."

Theo exhaled. "So how can we help you?"

"I want you to help us rob Perkins Library."

Theo blinked. "I don't get it. You just said it's a bad idea."

"It is," Merlin said. "It's not the con. It's just the setup."

The boys leaned in.

"My father, Braff, owns malls, corner stores, all that. He keeps a master key to every property. Janitor-style. Keeps it on the fireplace, hung up by a single nail. Real shrine-type shit. I need that key. But I can't get near the house right now. My uncle just passed, my dad's sitting shiva, and me and Gwen are persona non grata."

"So where do we come in?" Theo asked.

"I got word the new video game console drops Black Friday. We all know this. What you *don't* know is that the stores will already have them the night before. If I can get that key, we hit those stores, trash the place, loot the consoles, and my old man gets a fat insurance payout."

The four stared at him, trying to process.

"What does robbing a library have to do with that?" Jason asked.

"Well," Merlin said, "a robbery needs guns, a getaway car, and hired muscle, right?"

He pointed at Theo and Jason.

"You two are helping me and Gwen hit the library. Halfway through, you bail. Run out screaming."

"Wait," Jason said, sitting up straight. "No one said anything about armed robbery."

"The guns'll be empty," Merlin said. "Props. You think I'd trust you with live ammo?" He grinned. "But my old man won't know that. When he finds out I used his chop shop for the car and his gunsmith for the hardware, he'll summon us. Still a risk though. Might be putting myself in an early grave, but when his goons beat the living shit out of me and Gwen, *that's* when I grab the key."

STAGE 16

Gwen stood looking at her brother in awe. Mer, shrugging his shoulders, looked back at her. She stood with her arms folded, shoulders tensed, and a calm rage behind her eyes. She held up one finger and said, "A soldier? Not a general?"

"Gwen, I—"

Gwen held up her hand and said, "We will talk about this later."

Braff tossed his cigar onto the pavement and barked, "Guy! Give me a piece. They're *my* kids—I'll do it myself."

"Pop, will you *hold on*?" Mer said, throwing up his hands.

Braff's nostrils flared. "Why?"

"Because," Mer said, nodding toward the parking lot, "we got company."

Braff looked up to see the U-Haul vans pull into the lot. The trucks jerked to a stop, tires skidding slightly in the dirt before parking on the grass beside Braff and his children.

Theo and Jason hopped out of the driver's seat. The second they saw Braff's crew—a cluster of suited men gripping black handguns—they both took a step back, Theo's eyes flicking to the speedboat humming softly at the dock.

"Woah," they both murmured.

"The *fuck*?" Braff muttered, narrowing his eyes.

"Pop," Mer said, pointing casually, "You remember our neighbors, Theo and Jason? Jason and Theo—Pop."

Braff's men remained still as statues, their squinting eyes locked onto the newcomers, teeth clenched. Jason and Theo hesitated, then offered an awkward wave. No one waved back.

Braff slowly turned to his son. His voice was low, controlled, but laced with venom. "Merlin, you wanna tell me why these *kinderlach* are standing in the middle of a *crime scene*?"

Jason's eyes widened. "Crime scene?"

"Mer. Dude. I thought you said we were good," Theo hissed, his eyes darting between the siblings, Braff, and the army of mobsters standing at the dock. He elbowed Jason's side and whispered, "Should we run?"

Jason shot him a look of pure disdain, shaking his head. "Are you *stupid*?"

Braff smiled—a polite, practiced expression that didn't reach his cold blue eyes. "Boys?" He tilted his head slightly. "Stay the *fuck* where you are."

"Yeah," Gwen muttered, narrowing her eyes at them. "I wouldn't do that."

"J," Mer said, holding his hands up. "Chill out. He's not gonna kill you. Show him the take."

Braff turned to Mer, his gaze sharpening. "Hey."

Mer met his father's cold stare and swallowed. He turned back to the boys and shrugged. "*Probably* not gonna kill you. Show him the take."

Jason and Theo hesitated. Then, moving slowly, hands half-raised, they backed toward the U-Haul. Jason crouched, fumbling with the rusted latch. When he finally yanked it open, the latch creaked in protest, flakes of rust raining down as Theo shoved the door upward. He winced, ducking his head. Braff walked toward the back of the U-Haul. Inside, the stacked boxes gleamed under the pale morning light. Glossy black packaging, accented with neon-green and electric-blue trim, stretched from the floor to the ceiling. Each one had *The Link* emblazoned in a sharp, retro-futuristic font across the front. The air inside the truck was thick with that crisp, new-electronics smell: fresh plastic, factory-sealed cardboard, and the faint metallic tang of circuits waiting to be powered on.

Braff sighed. He rubbed his clean-shaven chin, eyes shifting to his children as he walked toward them. Both of them stood slouched, hands in their pockets, exhaustion weighing heavy under their eyes.

Braff walked over to Mer, his eyes locked onto the box. "Is that what I think it is?"

"Yup," Mer said, wiping sweat from his brow.

Braff's gaze darkened. "How many?"

"We got twenty in this truck," Mer replied, rubbing his damp palms against his face. "Dustin and Brad are bringing the next twenty."

Braff blinked, his voice rising. "Forty units?" His expression darkened further. "All stolen from stores in *my* strip malls?"

Mer stole a glance at his father's face, red with rage, nostrils flaring. He raised his eyebrows and nodded.

Braff's voice dropped to a near growl. "Are you *fucking* mental? How did you even pull this off?"

Mer smirked. "Why do you think we stopped by after Uncle's funeral? You thought we came to *sit shiva*?"

Braff's jaw clenched. "He was your uncle!"

"He was a piece of shit!" Mer shot back.

"How can you say that?" Braff snapped.

Mer let out a dry chuckle. "You *do* know he was stealing from you, right?"

Braff's eyes narrowed. "He *what?*" He shook his head. "That's not important right now. *How* did you pull off the job?"

Mer pulled the set of janitor keys from his pocket and tossed them at Braff's feet.

Braff stared down at them, his black loafers barely shifting. He let out a slow breath, closed his eyes, and massaged his temples. "You lifted my skeleton keys."

Mer and Gwen grinned.

Braff scoffed, his voice dripping with sarcasm. "Oh, you *think* you're smart, huh? *Geniuses!* The cops will see *no forced entry*! You don't think that's gonna lead straight back to me?"

Silence.

Then, slowly, Theo raised a trembling hand like a nervous student in a classroom.

Braff exhaled sharply, rubbing his temples. "Son, this *isn't* biology class. *Speak.*"

Theo gulped. "W-we, uh… we trashed the places we hit."

Braff's eyes flickered to him, voice light and mocking. "Oh, *did* you now?"

"Y-yeah," Jason jumped in quickly, nodding. "As per Mer's instructions, of course."

"I told the boys they can have the console money," Mer said with a smirk. "With the insurance payout, you're about to get a half million on each property."

Braff took another step toward his son, folding his arms. His jaw worked as he inhaled slowly, scratching the back of his ear, eyes locked on Mer.

Another long silence.

"How much do these things go for, Mer?" Braff asked.

"They're hitting six grand a pop on eBay. If you move them for four or five, you can dump 'em fast before anyone's the wiser."

Braff looked at the van, then at Theo and Jason, their hands stiff behind their backs. His expression stayed unreadable as Mer continued.

"I know you're trying to be more legit these days, Pop. But we ain't *there* yet."

Braff exhaled through his nose. "So your solution is to *rob me?*"

Braff rubbed the bridge of his nose. Then, after a beat, he stretched his arms open.

Mer and Gwen exchanged a quick glance before stepping forward. Braff gave them each a light slap on the face—just hard enough to make a point—before pulling them into a firm embrace.

He stepped back and shook his head. "You two…" His lips twitched, still holding onto his frustration. "I *am* very upset with you. But we can discuss punishment over breakfast."

He turned to Guy. "Get some sanitation trucks here, get these toys off the street, and have our tech guys control the online chatter."

Guy nodded, already pulling out his phone.

As Mer climbed into the SUV, he grinned at his father. "You weren't *really* gonna kill us, were you, Pop?"

Braff scoffed, waving a dismissive hand. "What? No. This was a *mock* execution. What are you, crazy? I'm not some savage."

"Shit," Gwen muttered, rolling her eyes.

Mer shot her a triumphant smirk. "Told you! Pay up."

"I'm not paying you *shit*," Gwen grumbled as the SUV rolled out of the parking lot.

❧

Rick pulled up to Zelda's mansion, easing onto the circular brick driveway. His breath fogged in the cold air seeping through the busted rear windows. He undid his seatbelt and shivered, then glanced at the trunk.

The shit I had to do to get you.

A voice cut through the silence.

"Rick!"

Lloyd's frantic shout jolted him. His entire body jerked. Pain shot through his neck. He groaned, rubbing the spot while staring through the windshield.

Lloyd stood in front of Zelda's grand entrance, pacing like a caged animal, checking his Rolex every few seconds. His wild gestures beckoned Rick forward with urgency.

Rick brought the Toyota to a stop, quickly turning off the ignition and unclipping his seatbelt. He pushed open the door, stepping into the freezing air.

Lloyd looked like hell.

His dark-blue suit was still sharp, but everything else was unraveling. His burgundy tie hung loose, matching the half-untucked dress shirt clinging to his sweat-drenched torso. Wet stains darkened his armpits, trailing down his sides.

His scalp dripped with sweat, streaking through his frosted tips, revealing a patchwork of hair plugs and graying roots.

Rick's frown deepened. "Mr. Lloyd… what happened to

your—" His eyes dropped to Lloyd's hands, where flakes of skin peeled from his knuckles. "Why is your skin *falling off?*"

Lloyd's expression was ice-cold, unreadable. Then, with a slow, deliberate movement, he reached into his pocket, pulled out a pair of dentures, and stuffed them back into his mouth.

Rick's stomach churned.

"I don't know, Rick," Lloyd said, unnervingly calm. "Went to get a tan before the Sight Beyond Sight Summit, scheduled for…" He checked his watch. "Less than *twenty* minutes from now. And guess what?" His left eye twitched.

"I fell asleep in the tanning bed. *Five*, maybe *six spots;* second-degree burns." His voice flattened, his fists clenching at his sides. "It is *excruciating.*" Then his voice snapped like a whip. "But that's *not* what I'm worried about." He stabbed a finger at Rick, eyes burning with rage. "Where the *fuck* have you been?!"

Rick squinted. "Sir, you *know* where I've—"

"Shut up!" Lloyd wiped the cocaine residue from his nose, slicked back his thinning, sweat-drenched hair, and let out a slow, shaky breath.

"All that matters right now," he seethed, slamming his fist into his palm, "is *one* thing." His nostrils flared. "If we don't have that *little Satan spawn's* console, she won't give me the outcomes of her *fucking experiments* out back!"

He wiped his forehead with a trembling hand, his pupils blown wide.

"Without that data, I don't know if the oranges are gonna survive the winter, *or* if I should invest in coffee stocks, *or* if fucking *pigs* are worth buying this year! Do you understand?!"

Rick swallowed, his lips parting to speak, but Lloyd wasn't done.

"The Sight Beyond Sight Summit…" Lloyd's voice

dropped, but the rage in his eyes burned hotter. "The *only* thing keeping this company remotely relevant will be a *joke* without that data!" His entire body was trembling as he wiped his face again, his neck damp with perspiration. "So, do you have a Link?"

Rick nodded. "Yes." His voice was calm. Controlled.

Lloyd's bloodshot eyes flickered quickly.

Rick's lips curled ever so slightly into a smile. *Here we go,* he thought. *A slap on the back. A "you son of a bitch," but in a nice way. Probably not partner—yet—but second-in-command? I'd take it. A king crab among the crabs. At the very least, dinner and drinks with the boss.*

"You *stupid* motherfucker."

Rick's smile vanished. Lloyd *shoved* him, sending him stumbling back.

"I've been standing out here with my *dick in my hand* while you *pussyfoot* around with my *future*? My *family's* future?! You son of a bitch. You'd better start thinking about *your* future." Lloyd's whole body tensed, shoulders rising, veins bulging against his sweat-slicked skin.

Rick rolled his shoulders and slipped his hands into his pockets. His body loosened. His head shook. He raised an eyebrow. "It's in the trunk."

Lloyd *grabbed* him by the collar, yanking him close. His breath reeked of tobacco and stale coffee. His bloodshot eyes bore into Rick's like an animal ready to maul. "Go. Get. It." He *shoved* Rick away and turned toward the door, jamming the doorbell with a trembling finger.

Rick patted down his sweater as he strolled toward his car. Behind him, Lloyd banged on the front door, his voice frantic. "Zelda! Zelda! Open up! We found a Link!"

Rick reached his trunk and popped it open. His eyes flicked down at the pristine console box, then shifted his weary eyes toward the spectacle unfolding on the steps. Zelda stood in the doorway, shouting back at her father, her face flushed with rage.

Think about the future. Rick thought to himself.

A smirk tugged at his lips. Without hesitation, he ripped open the box, pulling out the sleek console—a shimmering gold-and-green parallelogram. He placed it carefully on the hood of his car, making sure both Zelda and Lloyd had a clear view.

Hands behind his back, he watched them argue, his grin widening. "Hey, guys!" Rick called out.

Their shouting ceased. Slowly, they turned to face him.

Zelda squinted, confused. "Adam, whath he doing?"

Lloyd's face drained of color. His body stiffened. "Rick, no!"

Rick twirled a metal baseball bat once in his fingers, gripping the white-taped handle, winding back like a batter waiting for the perfect pitch.

Lloyd threw his hands up. "No. No. No. No. No—"

Rick planted his feet firmly onto the pavement, grounding himself.

Zelda's eyes widened, glistening. Her lips parted.

"Rick," Lloyd whispered, voice trembling. His hands shook, his breath hitching. "Please don't—"

Rick swung.

The crack of metal meeting plastic split the crisp morning air. Shards of the Link console flew in every direction, glittering like broken glass as they landed at Zelda's feet.

For a moment, there was nothing. No words. No sound.

Just Zelda's small, trembling frame, her eyes fixated on the shattered remains of the one thing she had been obsessing about. Her brilliant mind, capable of solving complex equations and outmaneuvering corporate titans, simply *could not compute.*

Zelda collapsed to her knees. Her hands hovered over the wreckage, fingers twitching uselessly.

"It's not fair!" she wailed, her voice cracking.

Lloyd's fists curled at his sides, his entire body trembling with barely restrained fury.

Rick chuckled, shaking his head. "You can have the bat," he said, tossing it at their feet. "You're gonna need it if you ever come near me or Candace again."

Lloyd's rage-filled stare faltered, his expression flickering into something vacant, almost hollow. Like he was staring past Rick, beyond him, into nothing.

Rick turned without another word. He slid into the driver's seat and turned the key in the ignition.

Click.

The car sputtered.

"Damn alternator," he muttered, twisting the key again. The engine roared to life on the second try. Without hesitation, Rick peeled out of the driveway, tires screeching as he sped onto the highway.

SEVEN MONTHS LATER

"No, Mom," Rick said. His voice echoed in the empty office space. He held his cellphone between his shoulder and ear while sweeping soot from the bare cement floor.

He looked around. Aside from two filing cabinets, a white table, and a pair of matching chairs, the space was nearly empty, except for a string of arcade cabinets and faded anime posters lining the back wall.

"The previous owners didn't need a carpet. It was an arcade, I think. I don't know what they were doing, Ma. What?" Rick stopped sweeping and stood straight up. "Were they selling drugs? Money laundering? This is Research Triangle Park, Mom, it's not downtown Durham."

He kneeled down and picked up the dustpan. "Yeah," Rick nodded. "I think I got a good deal. I think. I mean, I have to have something professional, Mom. If I ran this from my apartment, clients would just think I was some kind of poser."

"No, I can't make it for lunch, Mom. I got an interview at noon. Dinner? The Cheesecake Factory? Fancy! I'll meet you at Southpoint. Better call for reservations now, I hear the wait is like three hours. OK. Love you, Mom."

Rick put the cellphone in his pocket and bent to scoop

the debris into the pan. He walked over to the single plastic trash can in the middle of the room. Just as he dumped the dirt and broken glass inside, he felt his chest tighten. It was hard to breathe.

What am I doing here? he thought. *It's not too late. I can probably get out of this lease and go job hunt...*

He shook his head. Took a breath. Then he began chanting quietly to himself, "Up, up, down, down, left, right, up, up, down, down, left, right..."

Knock-knock.

Rick looked up and saw a woman with striking features. She pulled her bangs back and smiled through the window. He dusted off his black dress shirt and straightened his fat pink tie, then walked over to the glass door and unlocked it.

"Ms. Malinowski?"

"Please," she smiled. "Christine."

"OK," Rick said, holding the door.

Christine gave a demure smile and walked past him. Her black high heels echoed on the cement floor. She looked around.

"You weren't kidding about an opportunity at the ground up," Christine said.

Rick let out a nervous chuckle and asked, "You hear about us in the want ads?"

"Monster.com."

He nodded. Christine walked over to the white table with two chairs. Rick moved quickly and gestured for her to sit. She took off her long leather jacket and straightened the bottom of her pinstriped gray business suit. She sat down, placing her black leather briefcase beside her. She pulled out her resume. Rick slid into the chair across from her.

"I would offer you coffee but…" He looked around. "As you can see…"

"I can see," Christine said, handing him her resume. "It's fine." She crossed her legs and clasped her hands together on her knee as he read. "Can I ask you a question?"

"Sure."

"I heard you worked for Branson and Lloyd."

"I did."

"You were there for the end?"

"I was."

"If you don't mind me asking, what happened? I heard the company imploded."

Rick raised his head from the resume and looked at her. "Shattered is more like it," he said. He clicked his teeth. "It was almost as if someone took a baseball bat and smashed the company into a billion pieces."

Christine's eyes widened. "Wow," she said. "It's cool you landed on your feet."

"Graduated from North Carolina Central School of Business. Impressive. Interned at Enron. Scary." Christine let out a demure chuckle. "Had a desk at Morgan Stanley…"

Rick set the resume down and stared at her. "Christine, I…"

"Something wrong?" Christine sat up. She leaned forward, as if a knot had formed in her stomach. "It's the resume, isn't it?" She hissed her teeth. "I knew I shouldn't put all of that on there."

"What?" Rick frowned.

"Look, I know I'm overqualified to be a secretary and all, but I type like really fast and…"

"Whoa," Rick said, holding up his hands. "What are you talking about?"

"That's what everyone's saying. I'm too qualified. I'm not right for a secretarial job." She laughed. "One lady told me if she hired me, I'd have her job in less than a week."

"Christine," Rick said, placing his hands on the table. "I'm not looking for a secretary. I mean, look around. Does it look like I can afford a secretary?" Christine's eyes glanced at the string of arcade machines along the back wall.

"I'm looking for a partner."

Christine swallowed. She cleared her throat and grabbed her briefcase.

"It's been great talking to you, Rick," she said, standing. "I appreciate the opportunity—"

"Ms. Malinowski—"

"Thank you so much, but I must—"

"Christine," Rick said, pointing to the chair. "Please."

She let out a forced sigh and sat back down. Rick leaned forward, his elbows on the table.

"I get it. I'm scared shitless too."

"What?" Christine eyebrows narrowed.

"I've drunk my weight in Maalox. I even thought about applying for a job at the mall!"

"Was your intention for me to stay or…"

"My point is that you've been there. As have I. Working for some asshole who you know you're more qualified than, just to have him send you on a manhunt for some toy that almost gets you killed!"

Christine nodded slowly. "I'm not following you."

"The point is you're looking for a job that is beneath you just to make ends meet, and the sick joke here is that the ends never do meet. Whether it be financially, physically, or emotionally."

Christine shook her head and closed her eyes. "You are not going to make a dime anytime soon."

"Broke," Rick said. "Kinda used to that."

"How far out from business school are you?"

"Fresh out."

"How old are you?"

"Young enough that if I told you, you would probably walk out of that door."

"The market is a mess! Who's going to take a chance on us with their money?"

"An old friend once taught me: Where there's chaos, there's opportunity."

"OK," Christine said, holding up her hands. "Save me the sound bite, Warren Buffett."

Rick smiled.

"This is crazy!" Christine laughed. She looked around at the empty storefront. "We can't bring anyone here."

"I got you saying 'we' now?" Rick smiled.

"Don't get cocky." She leaned back and shook her head. "I have two boys at home that need tending to. My son and injured husband. I have to be home by seven every evening."

"Oh," Rick said with concern. "I'm sorry to hear that. What happened to him?"

Christine giggled. "Trampled during a Black Friday stampede. Cracked two vertebrae in his neck trying to get one of those new Link video game things."

Rick raised an eyebrow. "You seem really concerned."

Christine's chuckle turned into a full-blown laugh, complete with snorting and tears.

"I'm sorry," she said, wiping her eyes. "You have no idea."

"Your marriage is giving me a *War of the Roses* vibe."

"Well," Christine said, settling in, "I'm not a Kathleen Turner and he is definitely no Michael Douglas, but let's just say now that he's in a wheelchair, he's less of a liability."

"Yikes," Rick sighed. "Listen. You need a job. But maybe, just maybe, if we stick together, we can build a future."

Christine folded her arms and leaned back. She shook her head.

"How long did you rehearse that?"

"Past two days. How did it sound?"

Christine smiled, rolling her eyes. "Shit. Good enough, I guess, since I'm still here."

Rick smiled back.

She looked past him again at the arcade cabinets along the wall. "I see you got a *Marvel vs. Capcom* back there."

"You game?" Rick asked, his face lighting up.

"Tell you what," Christine stood from her chair and said, "You can tell me all about the leads you have while I kick your ass with Chun-Li and Iron Man. Partner."